UNEASY LIES THE CROWN

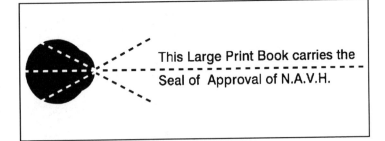

This Large Print Book carries the
Seal of Approval of N.A.V.H.

UNEASY LIES
THE CROWN

TASHA ALEXANDER

WHEELER PUBLISHING
A part of Gale, a Cengage Company

Farmington Hills, Mich • San Francisco • New York • Waterville, Maine
Meriden, Conn • Mason, Ohio • Chicago

**LIBRARY OF CONGRESS CIP DATA ON FILE.
CATALOGUING IN PUBLICATION FOR THIS BOOK
IS AVAILABLE FROM THE LIBRARY OF CONGRESS**

ISBN-13: 978-1-4328-6178-0 (hardcover)

Published in 2019 by arrangement with Macmillan Publishing Group, LLC/St. Martin's Press

Printed in Mexico
1 2 3 4 5 6 7 23 22 21 20 19

ACKNOWLEDGMENTS

Myriad thanks to . . .

Charles Spicer, a top-notch editor with a talent for making every book he touches better.

My spectacular team at Minotaur: Andy Martin, Paul Hochman, Sarah Melnyk, April Osborn, Danielle Prielipp, and David Rostein.

Anne Hawkins, Tom Robinson, and Annie Kronenberg: best secret weapons ever.

Anne Easter Smith, an uber-talented writer who was generous enough to share her title with me. When her *Uneasy Lies the Crown* comes out, you won't want to miss it!

Friends I could not do without: Brett Battles, Rob Browne, Bill Cameron, Christina Chen, Jon Clinch, Jamie Freveletti, Chris Gortner, Jane Grant, Nick Hawkins, Robert Hicks, Elizabeth Letts, Carrie Medders, Missy Rightley, Renee Rosen, and Lauren Willig.

Xander, Katie, and Jess.

My parents, stalwart supporters of all my creative schemes.

Andrew: everything, always.

For my son, Alexander,
full of grace and fair regard

No matter where —
of comfort no man speak:
Let's talk of graves, of worms,
and epitaphs;
Make dust our paper,
and with rainy eyes
Write sorrow on the
bosom of the earth;
Let's choose executors and talk of wills.
And yet not so —
for what can we bequeath
Save our deposed bodies to the ground?
Our lands, our lives,
and all are Bolingbroke's,
And nothing can we call our own
but death;
And that small model
of the barren earth
Which serves as paste
and cover to our bones.
For God's sake, let us

sit upon the ground
And tell sad stories of
the death of kings:
How some have been depos'd,
some slain in war,
Some haunted by the ghosts
they have depos'd,
Some poison'd by their wives,
some sleeping kill'd;
All murder'd: for within
the hollow crown
That rounds the mortal temples
of a king
Keeps Death his court,
and there the antick sits,
Scoffing his state and
grinning at his pomp;
Allowing him a breath, a little scene,
To monarchize, be fear'd,
and kill with looks,
Infusing him with self and vain conceit
As if this flesh which
walls about our life
Were brass impregnable;
and humour'd thus
Comes at the last, and with a little pin
Bores through his castle wall,
and farewell king!
— RICHARD II, ACT 3, SCENE 2,
WILLIAM SHAKESPEARE

17 January 1901
Osborne House,
Isle of Wight

The stench of death already clung to the salmon pink walls of Queen Victoria's bedroom; it assaulted Colin Hargreaves the moment the footman opened the massive oak doors. Not death, he corrected himself, but dying, when musty decay had not quite given way to the cloying foul rot soon to come. He hesitated for a moment, not because of shock at seeing how small Her Majesty looked, as if a child had been placed in a formidable marriage bed, but because the odor sent him reeling as he remembered the first time he had smelled it, on a snowy afternoon at Anglemore Park. He was home for Christmas during his first year at Eton and had found his grandfather in the library. The old man, sitting in his favorite high-backed leather chair, read aloud from Malory's *Le Morte d'Arthur* until Nanny came to fetch him for supper. Colin had noticed the odd scent, but didn't think

11

anything of it until the next morning, when his father delivered the news that Grandfather had died overnight. He smelled it again when he was summoned home from Cambridge to his father's sickbed. Then, too, for just an instant, he had felt like a schoolboy stunned by his first loss.

He shook off the feeling and approached the queen. Her enormous bed faced windows with a sweeping view of the countryside, a stark contrast to the paintings on the walls, nearly all of which depicted religious subjects. She was sitting, propped up by pillows, beneath a favorite portrait of her long-dead husband and a memorial wreath. Her eyes, dull, stared ahead, and he wondered if she knew he had entered the room.

"Your Majesty," he said, his voice low as he bowed. "You asked to see me."

She managed a half smile and nodded. "There are things I would like to settle, but I fear I shall not be given enough time to accomplish them all." She coughed, cleared her throat, and motioned for him to give her the glass of water sitting on her bedside table. He held it to her lips as she drank, swallowing with difficulty. "One never knows, does one, what shall happen in the end? My dear Albert . . ."

Sir James Reid, her physician, standing on

the other side of the canopied bed, met Colin's eyes and shook his head, exhaustion and worry writ on his face.

"How can I assist, ma'am?" Colin asked.

"So much, so much to be done," she said. "And the dogs . . . I do not see them. Are they here?"

"No, ma'am, they are not," Sir James said. "Shall I have them brought to you?"

"Why are you here?" Her voice, though weak, grated with a tone of scathing disapproval. "We are not in need of your services. I must speak to Mr. Hargreaves privately. Disperse." Sir James shot Colin a pointed look and left the room. When she heard the doors close, the queen pushed herself up on the mountain of pillows. "It is too much to be borne. The loss of Lady Churchill . . ." Her voice faded and she stared out the windows. A lady of the bedchamber for nearly fifty years, Lady Jane had long been one of the queen's closest confidantes. Keenly aware that learning of her death, on Christmas Day less than a month ago, would come as a tragic blow to the already ailing monarch, Sir James had done his best to deliver the news gradually, trying to shield Her Majesty from suffering the shock all at once.

"It was devastating to lose her," Colin

said. "I know she was a dear friend —"

"That is of no significance now," she said. "No death matters but that of Albert." Her eyes clouded. She raised a hand, its skin yellowing and dry. "Nothing has been right since then, and now I am left to summon you and demand a service that only you can provide."

"Of course, ma'am, whatever you need." He shifted on his feet, wishing he had been able to speak to the doctor before seeing the queen so that he might better understand her condition.

"Take this and do as it says." She pulled an envelope from under her pillow and handed it to him. "All will be clear in time. We need you for this. There can be no one else. I had five others during my reign, but he will need no one save you. He's never been so strong as I." She dropped back onto the pillows, the effort of holding up her head too much. "I shall not see you again, Mr. Hargreaves, but I have always valued your service above all others and thank you for your devotion to the Crown." She lifted her hand again, holding it up as if to be kissed, but lowered it almost at once. "Tell no one of this meeting, of what we have discussed. Discretion is of the upmost importance, as you shall know when you read my note. Albert would concur, and will, I am sure. Have you seen him of late? He is such a fine gentleman."

"The finest, ma'am," Colin said, seeing no reason to acknowledge her confusion.

"That is all," she said, her voice so low he could hardly make out her words. "Disperse, Mr. Hargreaves, with our thanks."

He did as ordered and found Sir James waiting in the corridor outside. "She has been struggling since December and is growing more muddled by the day," the doctor said. "I fear she does not have long. No one but the family and the household here knows of her illness yet. I trust I can rely on you to keep what you have seen to yourself?"

"Of course."

"Soon enough we shall have to notify the press," he continued, "but I should like to delay that while I can."

"Understood," Colin said. "If I can be of any further service, you need only ask." He took his leave from the physician and retired to an empty sitting room, where he opened the queen's envelope, ready to follow her instructions, but the words scrawled on heavy linen paper inside did nothing to illuminate her desires:

Une sanz pluis.
Sapere aude.

One and no more.
Dare to know.

1
1901

The death of Queen Victoria stunned the nation, myself included, although I cannot claim to have suffered a personal blow from the loss. My mother, who had served Her Majesty as a lady-in-waiting, mourned and keened (more than strictly necessary, I suspect, but she wanted no one in doubt of her close relationship with the monarch), while I sat shocked as my husband, Colin Hargreaves, delivered the news. He had seen her at Osborne House only five days before her demise, and although I had surmised her to be ill, it had never occurred to me that she might be near death. Colin, always the soul of discretion, had revealed nothing about the meeting. The truth is, because she had been queen for so long, was such a formidable personality, and had survived eight assassination attempts, part of me believed she would never quit the mortal world.

But she did, as we all must, and I sat with my parents on a special train from London to Windsor, en route to the funeral service. Colin, who would be walking in the procession to St. George's Chapel, was on another train altogether. My mother, her eyes red behind her crêpe veil, would accept no words of consolation, so my father, long immune to the glares of his spouse, dedicated himself to rereading Mr. Dickens's *A Tale of Two Cities* until we were ushered off the train into flower-filled waiting rooms at Windsor Station to await the carriages that would carry us to the castle. The crush of people in the small town was like nothing I had ever seen. Boys climbed fences and lampposts to get a glimpse of the gun carriage pulling the royal coffin, draped in a white pall, with the Imperial Crown, Orb, Sceptre, and the Collar of the Order of the Garter on top of it. Crowds, ominously silent, lined the streets, every person dressed in black, all the men wearing wide crêpe armbands. The only sounds were those of the horses' hooves clattering and their harnesses jingling.

We reached the grounds of the castle, and hence the chapel, long before the procession, which wound slowly through town. Inside, we mourners sat, not speaking, all but afraid to move and disturb the sanctity of the place. For a while, at least. There was so little heat that before long we were all too focused on keeping our teeth from chattering to think about anything else. By the time Colin slipped into the seat next to me, I was half-frozen. It seemed that an eternity passed before the pallbearers carried the coffin to the choir and the Archbishop of Canterbury and the Bishop of Winchester presided over a thankfully short service. After the final notes of Beethoven's Funeral March rang from the organ, we joined no fewer than six hundred other guests for lunch in St. George's Hall. The somber occasion had left everyone preternaturally quiet, but we were not dining with the royal family or those closest to the queen, and by the time the second course arrived, conversation had returned to normal. Only a handful of people in the room could remember a monarch other than Queen Victoria; all of us would have trouble getting used to King Edward VII.

I had just leaned over to my husband to ask him what he thought of the profligate Bertie now having such a grand title, when a member of the Household Cavalry approached, bent down, and whispered something to him. Colin's face grew serious, his dark eyes flashed.

"There's been a murder in the Tower," he said, folding his napkin neatly and placing it next to his plate. "I must return to London at once."

A murder in the Tower of London! I must confess the idea sent a thrilling little shiver down my spine. The Tower loomed large in the imaginations of every child growing up in England, and as the young (my own three boys included) are inexplicably drawn to hideous and ghastly tales of ghosts and violence, there was no place that could better satisfy their cravings for such things. I thought of the poor little princes, sons of Edward IV, who went into the Tower never to return. Had their uncle Richard III murdered them? Personally, I suspect not, but that is a topic for another day. When we took our boys to the Tower for the first time, Henry insisted that he could hear the ghost of Margaret de la Pole shrieking as we approached the site of the scaffold where she had been executed. And who has not heard it said that a hooded figure, missing her head, is often seen wandering in the chapel where Anne Boleyn is buried? I could not help but succumb to a touch of juvenile titillation at the thought of a new murder at the

Tower. Would this incident enter into the lexicon of legend?

My husband and I are no strangers to violent crime. He, as an agent of the Crown (and a particular favorite of the late queen's), was called upon to serve in countless investigations that, as he often said, required more than a modicum of discretion. I had proven myself a capable detective on numerous occasions, and whenever possible, we worked together. When he was acting in his official capacity, it was more difficult for me to contribute, but I am never deterred by an arduous path. And an arduous path was precisely what I faced that afternoon.

To start, Colin murmured that there was no need for me to accompany him to London, but as I knew he would never be so gauche as to argue at a funeral luncheon, I insisted on boarding the train with him. A lively discussion ensued until we reached Paddington Station, by which point he admitted defeat and abandoned all attempts to dissuade me from going to the Tower. I cannot credit my powers of persuasion for his decision; more likely it resulted from exhaustion. He hadn't slept more than ten hours total since the queen's death and was nodding off for much of our journey, becoming fully alert only as we alighted at the medieval fortress.

Like all the flags in the country, those at the Tower flew at half-mast. We approached the sturdy outer wall and met a yeoman warder who ushered us in through Lion Gate, devoid of its usual swarms of tourists as the site was closed due to the queen's funeral. Once inside, he led us past the Bell Tower, with its oddly placed small white turret at the top, containing, appropriately, a bell. My attention then turned to the stark face of Traitors' Gate and I felt the skin on my neck prickle, the sensation disappearing only as we approached Wakefield Tower. Built by Henry III in the thirteenth century, its thick stone walls — the second tallest in the fortress — were designed to safely house the king and his family. No longer a royal residence, it now held the Crown Jewels. Had the murderer's victim been slain in an attempt to steal them?

Yes, once again, the romance of the Tower was getting the best of me. But who could resist? The timing was almost perfect for such an audacious heist; the royal funeral had distracted all of Britain. Yet an ambitious thief would be unwilling to miss the prizes of the collection, particularly the Imperial Crown, currently sitting atop the queen's coffin. I was about to voice this to Colin when I realized we were going not to the room that held the jewels, but instead to the modest chantry chapel originally intended as a private place of worship for medieval kings.

There, on the ancient brown tiles covering the floor, knelt a man dressed in black tights, a black tunic with white trim, and a matching hat. His hands were folded as if in prayer, his legs neatly together behind him, but his position was at odds with the expression on his face. His gray eyes were open wide and his mouth gaped in what looked like a silent, terror-filled scream.

He was dead, of that there could be no question. A sword stuck in his chest, penetrating all the way through his back, but no blood pooled around his body. That he remained upright rather than sprawled on the ground seemed inconceivable until my husband revealed thin wooden posts constructed to form a sort of frame and hidden by the tunic and tights. Fishing line held his arms and hands in place.

Colin crouched to examine the sword. "It's in the style of late fifteenth century. The sort we're led to believe would have been used to kill Henry VI —"

"Who was stabbed to death in this very

room," I finished for him. "And our victim is dressed in an outfit nearly identical to that the king is depicted wearing in the painting at the National Portrait Gallery."

"Yes." He rose and paced the perimeter of the chapel. "I recall the hat in particular."

"Do we have any idea who he is?"

"Not as yet," Colin said. "The police are checking missing person reports."

I nodded. How awful that his family had no idea that their loved one was kneeling here, dead. "There's too little blood for the crime to have been committed here," I said.

"And we've found none elsewhere," the yeoman warder said. "Madam, I must warn you that when Scotland Yard arrive they'll insist you leave. I shouldn't have allowed you to enter in the first place. The inspector is rather touchy."

"I am all too aware of the limitations of Scotland Yard," I said, "but thank you for the warning." I smiled at him. One never knows when an individual may prove help- ful in an investigation, particularly in those from which one is — theoretically — banned from participating. Colin glanced at me, raised an eyebrow, and then turned back to the guard, inquiring as to whether he or his colleagues had noticed anything unusual during the course of the day. The yeoman warder admitted that they had all been affected by the queen's death, but was adamant that no one had been derelict in his duties. The warden had increased surveillance of Wakefield Tower as a precaution against anyone viewing the occasion of the funeral as an opportunity to make off with the Crown Jewels.

We combed every inch of the structure but unearthed nothing we could consider a clue. I was about to suggest interviewing the wives and children of the guards who lived in the Tower — they might have noticed something out of the ordinary their husbands had not considered significant, like an unfamiliar tradesman delivering goods — but was stopped by the arrival of a humorless man from Scotland Yard. He introduced himself as Inspector Gale and ordered me from the room with little ceremony, explaining in cursory fashion that the interference of a lady would not be welcomed by His Majesty.

Rather than engage in a fruitless argument, I retreated with uncharacteristic silence; I saw no sense in antagonizing Inspector Gale. At least not yet. Outside of the fortress, I marched to the banks of the Thames. Obviously, the crime had not taken place in the chapel, and I suspected the murderer had brought his victim's body from outside the Tower. Unless he was one of the guards — a possibility I could not eliminate — but as I could not investigate inside, I was forced to explore other options. I followed the river until I found a man, rather scruffy, with a rowboat and offered him a not quite princely sum to take me for a little excursion on the river. He hesitated at first when I told him my destination, but, as I had hoped, the money was too good to ignore.

The boat bobbed as I stepped off the dingy pier to which he had tied it, but I managed to steady myself and avoid falling into the filthy-looking water. Our journey was a short one, to the most notorious of all entrances to the Tower, Traitors' Gate, through which had passed countless prisoners on their way to execution at Tower Green. I thought of Thomas More and Anne Boleyn coming this way, beneath London Bridge with its severed heads on pikes serving as reminders of what lay in store for them. I considered the tragic story of Lady Jane Grey, the sixteen-year-old queen, whose reign lasted a mere nine days, and whose execution led many to consider her a martyr.

But once again, the Tower was leading me

astray. I could not allow myself to become mired in history, however tempting it might be. Today another man had died, and I suspected that he, too, had entered the Tower through Traitors' Gate. The boat churned in the water, fighting the rising tide. I asked the man to row closer, until I realized my mistake. Although the words "Entry to the Traitors' Gate" were painted clearly above the arch marking the space, the gate itself had been bricked up, probably in the middle of the previous century during the construction of the Thames Embankment. It was a blow. I had never noticed the alteration during previous visits to the Tower, where Beefeater tour guides always pointed out the notorious place. From the inside, it was not so easy to tell there was no access to the river.

A voice cut through the cold air and I looked up to see Inspector Gale standing on the rampart above. "Lady Emily, I must insist that you stop meddling. This investigation will be treated with the utmost sensitivity and I shall not tolerate any interference. Return home at once or the king will have words with your husband."

Frowning, I ignored him, continuing my study of the brickwork near the top of the arch. Traitors' Gate might no longer be an easy way into the Tower, but the fortress held many secrets, not to mention many entrances. Some might now be sealed, but were there any, long forgotten, that might provide a vicious criminal with a path into this place that once protected kings?

2
1415

Cecily Bristow — or Hargrave, as she now was — could not recall a single detail of her wedding. The ceremony had passed in a blur of incense and candles. Yet she could not deny it had occurred, for here she was, sitting at the high table next to her husband, William, a splendid feast before them. The gold and silver plate on the cup board gleamed, and Lord Burgeys's magnificent saltcellar, made from French porcelain and depicting scenes from the life of Hercules, was barely five feet from her. She and William spoke very little during the meal, but he took her hand three times and squeezed it, which she found reassuring.

"You play the part of anxious bride well," Adeline, Lord Burgeys's granddaughter said, leaning close as she spoke. "I wonder if your groom believes the act."

"You ought not speak in such a manner,"

Cecily said. "He won't know you're teasing."

"He knows you're as good and as boring as you seem." Adeline scowled. "Yet he agreed to the marriage nonetheless. I'm only trying to make things more interesting for you."

Cecily had no need for interesting. Was she anxious? Yes, but not because of what lay in store for her that night. Adeline, whose own marriage had taken place only six months ago, had done her best to instill terror in her, but Cecily knew better than to listen to her harsh words. She did not fear William; she feared France. France, where he would be off to in less than a fortnight, to fight with the king to secure his rightful place on the throne of that country. Henry V, King of the Britons, was brave and good and would lead his men well. Yet battle was full of uncertainty, and although William had won tournament after tournament, this would be his first time at war. He might not return.

Could she bear the loss with equanimity? Perhaps. He wrote her pretty poems and sang to her, but she had not spent enough time with him to come to rely upon his presence. And as his wife, she ought not expect to. A knight was gone from home more often than not, and her role would be to manage their estate. Except that for now, there was no estate to manage.

William served under the king's youngest brother, Humphrey, Duke of Gloucester, and lived on the duke's estate rather than in the manor house he had inherited upon his father's death. That house, William had given to his own brother, who had married before him. Cecily was to stay with Adeline while her husband was in France, and upon William's return, the couple would set up housekeeping together. Everyone agreed it was an excellent plan, particularly Lord Burgeys, who hoped Cecily would prove a tempering influence on his granddaughter, assuming, as did the rest of his household, that the girls were great friends and would be delighted to continue living together.

Except that he was wrong. Cecily and Adeline had never been friends. Tenuous rivals for Lord Burgeys's attention, perhaps, when they were children, but from the moment they reached adulthood, the differences between them could not have grown more pronounced.

On the surface, one could be excused for thinking they had more in common than they did, but only because they were unaware of Cecily's true feelings about her mother, whom, at the age of two years, Lord Burgeys had found wandering alone on the road more than thirty miles from his estate. He brought her to the nearest village, thinking to reunite her with her family, but found it shuttered and silent. The child seemed to recognize the place, and rushed into a house near the green. Burgeys followed, pulling her out the instant he saw the bodies inside. The most terrible of the plagues that devastated England had ended the decade before, but the disease still recurred from time to time, and now it had wreaked havoc on the girl's home. She was the only one in the village who had not fallen victim to it.

Burgeys arranged for the burial of the dead and then had the buildings burned, lest any bit of the pestilence remained. But the girl who had so miraculously escaped death he adopted as his own, calling her Beatrix, explaining to her when she was old enough to understand that it came from the Latin word that meant traveler and that, later, Christians changed the spelling to reflect the word for blessed. Beatrix certainly was a blessed traveler.

As the solitary survivor of such a deadly outbreak of the plague, Beatrix was revered in the household. God had chosen her to live, and everyone viewed her with respectful awe. But the girl cared only for the spiritual side of life, eschewing all worldly pleasures and spending her free time in prayer. She blossomed under the direction of Lady Burgeys's confessor and soon gained a reputation as a lady of impeccable holiness. Visitors came with sick children, asking her to heal them, and before long, she was known in three shires as someone who could perform miracles.

Beatrix might have lived out her days lost in contemplative prayer and meditation had Geoffrey Bristow never come to the estate. He fell in love with the quiet girl the moment he set eyes on her, and begged Lord Burgeys to let him marry her. Bristow's fortune and position at court both recommended him, but neither mattered to Beatrix, who resisted her adopted father's decision, pleading with him to allow her to enter the convent instead. She wanted nothing more than to dedicate her life to God. Lord Burgeys refused, and the wedding took place a few weeks later. By the end of the year, Beatrix, who took no pleasure in her new life, was heavy with child. She fasted and prayed and begged God to remove her from the chains that bound her to the earth. She wanted only to serve Him.

God must have listened, because Beatrix

died the moment her daughter was born. Geoffrey shunned the child, whose thick hair and dark eyes were the image of her mother's. He believed her to be cursed, and sent her back to Lord Burgeys, who named her Cecily and once more raised a child who was not his own. He insisted that Beatrix be buried on his estate, and her tomb soon became a place of pilgrimage, the desperate and unfortunate coming to pray to this woman who had miraculously escaped the plague.

Most pilgrims viewed Cecily with dubious caution. Was not she the result of a forced marriage, the daughter of a woman denied her true religious calling? But Cecily rejected the image of her mother as some sort of saint. To her, Beatrix was a flawed mortal who, not caring to bring up her child, died instead. Cecily hated being paraded in front of the pilgrims, hated tending to her mother's tomb, and of all the instruction she received in Lord Burgeys's household, she liked religious teaching the least. Not because she doubted the truth of her faith or because she was not devout, but because she always felt as if she were being judged as the instrument of her mother's death. How did one atone for such a sin? She heard mass every day and prayed with a fervor unusual in one so young, leading everyone to consider her a fine example of piety. But that, Cecily knew, was only because they were ignorant of the depth of her sin. She had killed her mother.

Adeline, so far as everyone on the estate was concerned, was equally pious. Admittedly, she had mastered the art of appearing so at an early age, a skill she practiced because she found it exceedingly useful. She pretended to go to chapel when in fact she was sneaking to the barns to visit the horses. When she got older, she discovered she preferred the company of the stableboys to their charges. She was careful to avoid any truly licentious behavior, but relished what she considered her safe rebellion, all the while maintaining a reputation for sincere religious devotion.

The two girls did nearly everything together, but not by choice. Neither could tolerate the other's true nature. Adeline loved toying with Cecily and did all she could to heap trouble upon her. Cecily, always feeling like a guest in the Burgeys household, never dared speak a word against Adeline. Cecily had rejoiced when Adeline married and left home, never suspecting that her own marriage would lead her to become a companion to the nemesis of her youth.

The scent of resin from the flickering torches hanging on the walls of Lord Burgeys's great hall brought Cecily back to the present. She had hardly noticed the spectacular subtlety, a swan fashioned from sugar, when it was paraded in front of her. Mummers had started to perform now that the feast had ended, but Cecily did not give much attention to their act. She chewed on her lower lip and watched Adeline flirt with the gentleman seated next to her. A gentleman who was not her husband. She flashed Cecily a knowing look when William pulled his wife to her feet when the mummers had finished, but Cecily felt nothing but relief when he led her upstairs to the bridal chamber Lady Burgeys had organized for the couple. The guests cheered and her husband smiled at her.

"I knew the moment you gave me your favor that you would be my bride," he said. They had met at a tournament — one of the many he had won — and he had paid court to her ever after, until Lord Burgeys agreed to their betrothal. Cecily fingered the gold and emerald ring on her hand, the one William had placed there to mark the occasion. "I know you will desire your ladies to help prepare you for bed, but I asked that we be left alone, just for a moment, as I have a gift for you. Come."

He opened the door to their room. Once inside, he handed her a small package carefully wrapped in soft linen and tied with a red silk ribbon. She tugged at the bow and it fell away with ease, revealing a small wooden diptych. Covering the surface facing her was William's coat of arms. On the other, his badge, a griffin rampant. She unfolded the hinge to reveal the interior panels, both gloriously painted. On the right, Mary held the infant Jesus, a chorus of angels surrounding them, their gilded halos glowing. On the left, a scene of the crucifixion.

"I had two made," William said, "so that when we are apart we can both pray in front of the same images. And when I return, victorious, from France, I will commission a third, large enough for the chapel I will build for us." She looked up at him as he spoke, her dark eyes scared. "Do not worry that I won't come back. I shall never abandon you." He took the diptych from her, laid it on a table, and raised his hand to her cheek. "There is no silk so soft as your skin." He kissed her, gently, first on the cheek and then on her lips.

She could hear Alys, her old nurse, shushing the laughter of ladies outside the door. William took his leave, promising to return when she was ready. Hours later, when she lay in his arms, afraid to move lest she disturb his sleep, she prayed that she would be able to recall every detail of him when he left and prayed that he would be returned safely to her. Finally, she prayed that life in Adeline's household would not be so dreadful as she feared. Guilt consumed her over this last, selfish request. One more sin to plague her.

3
1901

After my lackluster adventure on the
Thames, I returned to our house in Park
Lane and retreated to the library, where,
comfortably ensconced in my favorite chair
near the large fire roaring in the hearth, I
opened *The Infidel: A Story of the Great Re-
vival,* the latest novel from sensationalist
author Mary Elizabeth Braddon. Her work
never failed to distract me, and I laughed
aloud when she referred to Madame de
Pompadour — *The existence of such women
is, of course, a disgrace to civilization, but
while their wicked reign lasts persons of quality must dress like them* — who would not
adore a writer capable of such wit and
insight when describing society? Delight-
fully buried in my reading, I was aware of
nothing around me until I felt Colin's hand
on my shoulder. I had not even heard him
open the door.

"Bent on pleasure again, my dear?" he

asked, a wicked smile on his handsome face as he looked at the book and leaned over to kiss me. I'd known him for more than a decade, and the man only grew handsomer as he aged.

"I have grave concerns about the fate of Antonia Thornton, our intrepid heroine, a devotee of Voltaire," I said, closing the novel and placing it in my lap. "I fear she will come to a tragic end."

"I'm confident Mrs. Braddon would have it no other way," Colin said, dropping into the chair across from mine. "You'll be glad to know you've succeeded in traumatizing poor Inspector Gale. I had to all but physically restrain him to keep him from running off to the king to report your appearance at Traitors' Gate."

"However did you manage that?"

"I reminded him that His Majesty was most likely at that very moment kneeling before his mother's coffin and wouldn't like to be disturbed." He pulled a cigar from his pocket and clipped the end before lighting it.

"Why would he think Bertie — I should say the king, but I shall never get used to someone other than his mother being the monarch — would be interested in any of my activities?"

"It's down to the nature of the murder at hand, manufactured to look like the death of Henry VI. The timing of the crime has raised a great deal of concern in the palace."

I nodded. The queen is dead, long live the king! For someone to choose the day of Victoria's funeral to stage a death to look like the heinous murder of an earlier sovereign was bound to raise the alarm with the new monarch's protection detail, but I did not see how that pertained to me.

"Have you any clue as to where the murder took place?" I asked. "And, have you identified the victim?"

"We believe him to be Edmund Grummidge, a shopkeeper in the East End. His wife reported him missing and is going to confirm his identity after viewing the body today."

"His wife? Not on her own, I hope. Perhaps she would appreciate the comfort of having another woman present at such a difficult moment." Do not think, Dear Reader, that my motives were altogether selfish, for although I did want my part in investigating the crime, more important at this moment was to offer whatever assistance I could to the widow left behind.

"Gale will not let you near the morgue," Colin said. "As for location, we've nothing as of yet. The body was posed before rigor mortis set in. We believe he was killed this morning."

He appeared more tired than usual, but as I have already explained, he had not had much sleep since the queen's death. There was something else, though. Something that had etched worry onto his noble brow. I leaned forward and brushed a tumbled curl from his forehead. "What's troubling you?"

He sighed. "This murder, obviously. The manner in which the corpse was displayed."

"I know you well enough to realize that is not all."

"When I met with the queen at Osborne, she gave me a note." He reached for his cigar, took a drag, held the smoke in his mouth, and slowly exhaled. "I was to tell no one of this, you understand."

I said nothing, respecting his reluctance to break a confidence. This is not to suggest that I waited patiently for him to decide what — and how much — to tell me. Anyone who knows me is all too aware that I cannot claim a close acquaintance with the virtue of patience, despite numerous attempts to woo it. I could hear the clock on the wall and the traffic in Park Lane. I chewed on my bottom lip. I avoided making eye contact. In short, I did everything possible not to pressure my husband to speak. And then, when I could stand it no longer, I crossed to his chair, sat on its arm, and dropped my head onto his shoulder, hoping the intimacy of the gesture would remind him that sharing a confidence with his wife was hardly a betrayal. Were we not, after all, joined by God, one soul in two bodies? I may mix my religious metaphors, but have never objected to a touch of the pagan at appropriate times.

At long last he spoke. "The queen was not herself. Our conversation was muddled and she was confused. But she gave me this" — he removed an envelope from the inside pocket of his jacket and handed it to me — "and led me to believe it was a set of instructions I should follow."

"*Une sanz pluis,*" I read aloud. "One and no more. One and no more. Why is this familiar?"

"It was a French motto used by Henry V at the time of Agincourt. You may have seen it on one of the tombs in the chapel at Anglemore Park."

"Of course," I said. "I remember it now. The alabaster with the knight standing on a dog."

"It's a lion, my dear, and it is beneath his

feet as he reclines. He is not standing on it."

I frowned and vowed to take a closer look at the tomb the next time we went to the country. "*Sapere aude . . .* dare to know? My Latin is not what it ought to be. Margaret would be scandalized." One of my closest friends, Margaret was a devoted Latinist, currently living in Oxford with her husband. I had met her more than a decade ago, soon after having embarked on my study of all things ancient Greek. Although firm in her belief that my time would be better spent focusing on the Romans, she had nonetheless encouraged my intellectual pursuits, the first of my friends to do so.

"She is well aware of the gaping holes in your education," Colin said. "Too much Greek, too little Latin. She reminds me of it whenever I see her. *Sapere aude* was a phrase common during the Enlightenment, championed by Kant, although I believe Horace was the first to use it, centuries earlier."

"You can always rely on the ancients," I said. "Even the Romans. But what could the queen have meant by giving you this?"

"I have not the slightest idea. I had hoped that your rampageous imagination might provide some insight."

"And it is intended as an instruction?"

"Yes, so she said. I was inclined to dismiss it as a product of her illness until I found this when I arrived home today." He handed me a second envelope. It and the three sheets of paper inside matched that given to him by the queen. The first page was covered in a sketch of a medieval-looking lance. The second, a map of the Tower of London. The writing — bold and confident — that covered the third had come from the same hand as that on the note he received at Osborne House.

"The queen is sending you notes from beyond the grave?"

"Don't get so excited," he said. "Neither is in the queen's hand."

Again, I read aloud. *"Lead me, thus wounded, to the front line so that I may, as a prince should, kindle our fighting men with deeds not words."* I read it to myself, silently, a second and a third time. "I do not recognize this at all."

"It is a translation of a life of Henry V written by Tito Livio Frulovisi, commissioned by the king's brother, Humphrey, Duke of Gloucester. *Vita Henrici Quinti* it was called."

"More Latin." I wrinkled my nose. "How is it that you know so much about all this?

45

I've never known you to have a particular interest in Henry V."

"You know perfectly well the land on which we live at Anglemore Park was given by Henry to an ancestor of mine who distinguished himself at Agincourt. Can you imagine there is any English boy who would not be obsessed by such a thing? I was quite taken with it when I was young."

"I'm picturing you getting into a great deal of trouble with a longbow."

"No, the ancestor in question was not an archer, but a man-at-arms, so I played with swords."

"Promise me you will not breathe a word of any of this to the boys until they are at least twelve years old," I said. The three of them would soon turn five. Tom, our adopted ward, had a saintly disposition, and I thought it unlikely he would ever get into an awkward scrape. Richard and Henry, our twins, were altogether different. While Richard would likely be more interested in studying the method of manufacturing swords — he had already begun to show great proficiency for building, analyzing, and all things mechanical — I did not doubt for a moment that Henry could cause a great deal of chaos in a shockingly short span of time the instant he learned of any family connection to Agincourt.

"You cannot stop little boys from reenacting battles," my husband said, in a tone that signaled no room for debate. "The passage in the note refers to the Battle of Shrewsbury, where Henry, then Prince of Wales, took an arrow to the cheek. Despite the severity of the wound, he made a full recovery, although he was left with a not insignificant scar."

"I've never pictured him with a scar," I said. "More like a shining example of English goodness. Golden hair, bright eyes, polished armor, rallying his troops to follow him once more unto the breach. Who would not do the bidding of such a man?"

"He had brown hair, my dear, and you're getting carried away. What do you think it can all mean? Particularly in the context of the queen's death followed by a murder staged — in the Tower, no less — to mimic the violent demise of another king."

"Another king who just happened to be Henry V's son." I studied the map of the Tower, but no location was marked on it. "It would be less confusing if the murderer had reenacted Henry V's death."

"Dysentery would not make for such a visually effective scene." Colin crossed his arms over his chest. "As I said, Henry was

Prince of Wales when he fought at Shrewsbury. Bertie, er, King Edward, was Prince of Wales when the queen gave me the first note."

"Do you think it is a warning of some sort?" I asked. "The queen's mind was failing when you saw her. Perhaps she received the note, recognized it as a threat to her son, and passed it on to you, not realizing that she failed to give you the necessary context to understand. Although why the drawing of a lance instead of a sword?"

"That I cannot explain. Regardless, your notion that it's a threat to the king is the same conclusion I reached. If we're correct, Bertie could be in a great deal of danger."

4
1415

Cecily did not weep when William departed for France. She stood motionless in front of Lord Burgeys's manor, the only home she had ever known, as her husband mounted his chestnut-colored horse, his plate armor, perfectly fitted to his lean body, gleaming in the sun. He left the visor of his bascinet raised so she could see him grinning as he set off, eager for the challenge of battle. She watched until she could no longer see his standard, carried by his squire, who followed behind. And then, when he was out of sight, she let her tears flow free and readied herself for her own journey, to Adeline's new home.

Alys, her old nurse, prepared the chests of clothing and jewelry and other essentials, but Cecily packed her most prized belonging herself: a beautifully illuminated copy of Christine de Pizan's *The Treasure of the City of Ladies,* given to her by Lady Burgeys. It offered what Cecily considered excellent advice for ladies, the authoress providing instruction on how to behave in nearly every situation. She stressed the importance of a wife being able to competently run her estate, going so far as to suggest she must even know how to use any weapons necessary for defense. Cecily pored over the vellum pages, tracing the letters some anonymous monk had copied so carefully, and vowed she would follow the French woman's advice.

Adeline had never shown a glimmer of interest in de Pizan's work. Her marriage to the Baron Esterby had elevated her social status, bringing with it a retinue of ladies and followers eager to do her bidding, and she saw no need to exert herself for anything but pleasure. The baron's estate in Sussex encompassed tens of thousands of acres and countless tenants, ensuring the family fortune did not suffer, even during the agricultural depression that followed the great plagues of the previous century. This meant Adeline could surround herself with every luxury. The day Cecily arrived, she found her friend — for she had decided she would view this chapter of her life as a new start, and make every effort to befriend Adeline — choosing fabric for new gowns.

Bolts of the finest silk and the softest furs surrounded her, and her laughter, which Cecily had always considered one of Adeline's best charms, echoed through the castle.

"Cecily, dear, you must have a new gown, too," Adeline said, greeting her with a distracted kiss. "Pick anything you like. Lord Esterby is rich enough to pay for both of us. But I don't think silk for you; it would be a waste on someone of your curious intellectual leanings. Whatever you desire, though, make it known quickly. I want to go for a ride this afternoon and you must come with me."

Cecily did not mind eschewing the silk, asking instead for a soft, midnight blue wool and not commenting when her hostess all but dragged her to the stable. Given past experience, Cecily half expected to be introduced to a handsome groom, but instead, a middle-aged man, stocky and competent, took them to their waiting horses and helped them mount. Adeline treated him with perfect courtesy; Cecily hardly recognized her.

"The baron is most generous," Adeline said as they set off across a green meadow to explore the estate. "I knew not how fortunate I was in my marriage until I came here and saw what my life will now be. My husband is kind and gives me anything I desire. It's what I've always wanted, and what I always knew I deserved."

Cecily murmured a reply, knowing all too well that Adeline had no interest in anything she might have to say. They rode along in silence until they reached a stream. Adeline stopped her horse and slid off of her saddle, urging Cecily to follow suit. A charming picnic awaited them. Servants had set up a low table covered with a fine damask tablecloth. Pewter dishes held cold pies, fruits, and an astonishing assortment of sweets. A servant handed Cecily a glass of wine cut with just the right amount of water.

"I brought you here so that we might speak privately," Adeline said. "Understand that I am the mistress of this house and you are here, at great inconvenience and expense, only because my husband wanted it so. He thought I should have a companion from home and erroneously identified you as the best choice. I seek neither your counsel nor your friendship. You will wait on me as I require, but your pert opinions and that look of judgment that creeps onto your face are not welcome here. Pray that your husband returns safely, because you will not remain here if you are widowed."

The wine no longer tasted sweet, and Cecily bit back nervous laughter at Adeline's final statement. How could anyone think that she would want to stay here, widowed or not?

William's trip to Southampton passed quickly. The roads were good, the weather fair, and the Duke of Gloucester made sure his men were well-supplied with every comfort one could hope for on such a journey. William's squire could not contain his excitement as they reached the town and could see the king's standard flying above Portchester Castle. Not that he expected to see the king — William had counseled him against unreasonable hopes — but just to be part of the invading force thrilled the young man.

The summer was hot, and they were all eager to embark for France. But their mission would not start quite yet. William had been in a pub thinking about his pretty wife when the chatter began. Something had happened — something that threatened the king. He assumed the danger came from the French — perhaps there were spies among them? — but instead, it was traitorous Englishmen behind a nefarious plot to kill their sovereign and his three brothers, the Dukes of Clarence, Bedford, and Gloucester, as they boarded their ship for France. Edmund Mortimer, the Earl of March, the man they planned to put on the throne once Henry was dead, learned of the plan and informed the king straightaway. Henry did not hesitate to act.

First, he invited the conspirators to Portchester Castle. Then, he had them tried and executed. Their lofty titles and high positions could not protect them from such grievous villainy. And so, on the warm August day when the army at last set off for France, the heads of the Earl of Cambridge, the Baron Scrope, and Sir Thomas Grey remained in England, stuck on spikes for all to see. A gory scene, but nothing so bad as what awaited them abroad. They were soldiers, though, and none among them balked at the horrors of battle. If anything, they looked forward to heaping violent misery on their opponents. They knew too well of the ghastly horrors inflicted by the French on the defeated English archers at the siege of Soissons the year before; mercy was something the French no longer deserved.

5
1901

While my husband stuffed himself with kedgeree that morning before setting off for Marlborough House, I retreated to my desk in the library, the room I had always considered the most comfortable in the house. There is no greater pleasure than being surrounded by books. At the moment, however, frustration tainted that pleasure, as I considered the body found at the Tower. Colin and the wretched Inspector Gale had both agreed that a stab wound — even if made by something other than the sword found in the body — had ended Mr. Grummidge's life. But as I would have access neither to the coroner's report nor Scotland Yard's file on the case, I had only my wits to rely upon. I rang for the carriage — lamenting that we did not have a motorcar — and set off for the East End. Once there, I convinced my driver that he did not need to escort me from shop to shop (he, despite all evidence to the contrary, remained convinced Jack the Ripper might resurface at any moment) and began my search for Mr. Grummidge's widow. Jonathan Swift rightly observed that *falsehood flies, and the truth comes limping after it,* but I have found that if anything is capable of traveling more quickly than a lie, it is bad news. Particularly bad news that contains any hint of gore or violence. Truly, people are a dreadful lot.

I had only to inquire in three shops before I found someone who was eager to discuss Mr. Grummidge's demise. Ironically, it was a woman in a butcher shop who offered assistance. The glee with which she reported what she knew, coupled with the wild state of her hair and a terrifying look in her eyes, reminded me of the awful Mrs. Lovett, who baked Sweeney Todd's victims into meat pies. She was purchasing soupbones, not something suitable for pies of any sort, and I found this filled me with an inexplicable sense of relief. Rumor had it, she said, that Mr. Grummidge (who owned a grocery in Whitechapel) had not returned home the previous evening. Something, she confided, leaning uncomfortably close to me and exposing a shockingly long set of yellowing teeth, that most likely had not surprised his wife, who would be used to his philandering ways. I asked her if she knew where I might find Mrs. Grummidge. She offered to take me there herself.

Not wanting to burden myself with a companion who seemed likely to terrify the new widow, I thanked her and said I only required the address. Disappointment clouded her face, but she complied with my request, and before long I was knocking on the door of a snug terrace house in a section of Whitechapel that was very nearly respectable. I introduced myself to the young girl who answered, dressed in a worn but well-cared-for maid's uniform, and asked to see her mistress. She hesitated and I leapt on her uncertainty, explaining that I had come to assist Mrs. Grummidge after her heartbreaking loss.

This convinced the girl to let me in. She led me to a small parlor and went off to fetch the lady of the house. The furniture was solid and well made, the tables covered with gorgeous lace doilies. The work was finer than I had seen anywhere, impossibly delicate and perfectly executed, the sort of thing that would inspire even the famed lacemakers of Burano to envy. Two photographs stood on the mantel, one showing a couple dressed in wedding clothes — I recognized the unfortunate Mr. Grummidge

— and the other of his bride, this time dressed in a mourning gown, holding an infant, presumably deceased. The image unsettled me. I turned away from it and took a seat near the piano situated between the two front windows.

The door opened, and Mrs. Grummidge entered, her face pale and drawn. I rose, introduced myself, and expressed my condolences for her loss. She looked more flustered than bereaved, and this endeared her to me. She offered tea, which I accepted, hoping the genial beverage would help her open up to me, and as soon as she had sent the maid off to fetch it, she met my eyes directly and spoke.

"While I am most grateful for your kind attention, Lady Emily, I am confused as to why you have come to me. Surely a lady of your status has better things to do than to pay social calls in the East End?"

"My husband, who works for the palace, was called to the scene of your husband's demise," I said, deciding it was not necessary to explain that his body had been moved. "I happened to be with him, and as a result feel a personal connection. I wanted to seek you out, first, to offer any assistance that might be of use to you in this difficult time, and, second, in the hope that you might be able to tell me something — anything — about Mr. Grummidge that could assist in bringing him justice."

"Justice?" she asked, her eyebrows shooting almost to her hairline. "I don't think Edmund will ever get that."

"I can assure you, Mrs. Grummidge, that with my husband on the case, justice will be achieved. No doubt Scotland Yard have already called on you and asked loads of tedious questions, and I am more sorry than I can say if you feel I am piling on. I help Mr. Hargreaves with challenging cases when I can, and more often than not find that we ladies know more than detectives give us credit for. Men don't always realize what details are important. Can you tell me when you last saw your husband?"

"The day before yesterday," she said and then pressed her lips together. "The shop was to be closed yesterday, on account of the queen's funeral, and Edmund went to the pub with his mates the night before. I wanted to see the procession, but he had no interest in it and stayed out all night. I set off quite early in the morning to get a good place near Paddington so that I might pay my respects to Her Majesty. Edmund hadn't returned home by the time I left."

"Was it unusual for him to stay out all night?"

"Yes," she said. "This was only the third night since our wedding that he wasn't home. The other two were after we lost our little girl." Her eyes went to the photograph on the mantel and filled with tears. "I couldn't blame him for not wanting to come home then, not to a wife who let his daughter die."

"I'm so very sorry, Mrs. Grummidge." I hated to press her when she had suffered such dreadful losses and paused, giving her time to regain her composure. "Do you know where he went after the pub closed?"

"Most likely he stayed with Jimmy Weston," she said. "They've been friends for ages and stay up half the night talking whenever they're together. He knew I was planning to rise early and wouldn't have wanted to disturb me by coming in late. He's always considerate that way, Edmund, more considerate than any wife could deserve." She tugged at the black lace edging on the sleeve of her dress as she spoke, pulling it down over her wrist and covering a dark bruise.

"How very thoughtful," I said, watching her. She was perfectly put together, not a hair out of place. Her complexion was like alabaster, smooth and pale, except for one small spot on her left cheek, where I could see she had applied pearl powder that did not successfully disguise the fading bruise beneath it.

"The most thoughtful of men." She gave a wan smile and met my eyes. I recognized something in her, akin to the relief I had felt when I heard the news of my first husband's death, more than a decade ago. I had not mourned him because I had not known him. Perhaps I was misjudging Mrs. Grummidge; the shock of the news she had received might not have yet sunk in. Perhaps she did not feel comfortable expressing tender emotions in front of a stranger. But my intuition told me otherwise. My intuition along with the way she kept pulling her sleeves over her wrists.

I thanked her for the tea and complimented her on the excellent lemon biscuits she served with it. When I rose to take my leave, Mrs. Grummidge herself escorted me to the door. Just as I stepped onto the stoop, she reached for my arm and grabbed it tightly.

"Find the person did this to him, please, Lady Emily. I must look into the eyes of whoever took his life."

■ ■ ■ ■

I could not call on Jimmy Weston after I left Mrs. Grummidge, as she did not know where he lived, so instead I went home, where I found Colin in his study, bent over one of his many chessboards.

"Mate in two, my dear. Can you see any way forward?"

I picked up the white queen, moved it, then countered with the black rook, leaving an unsuspecting white pawn in the unusual position of being the ultimate threat to his opponent's king. Colin's dark eyes danced and he pulled me close, giving me a kiss.

"Most impressive," he said.

I kissed him back and flopped into a chair. "Have you discovered any leads in our case?"

"No. I spent half the day going through threats against the king. None stood out, just the usual sort of ranting." He ran a hand through his curls. "The palace is most concerned. We've put extra men on Bertie's — His Majesty's — protection detail."

"What have you learned about Edmund Grummidge?" I asked.

"He was a respectable greengrocer with a handful of close friends. Much beloved by his neighbors, lauded by his vicar. The usual sort of thing. Spent the night before he died at the home of his best mate, Jimmy Weston, who had nothing of use to offer. Insists that when he woke up, Grummidge had already gone home."

I knew all of this information would have come from the police conducting interviews. I also knew better than to take any of it at face value. People are loath to speak ill of the dead. "Did no one mention that he beat his wife?"

"What exactly have you been up to today, my dear?"

"I called on Mrs. Grummidge, who is the perfect picture of the wife of your respectable grocer. Except that the pearl powder she used to cover a fading bruise on her cheek wasn't quite effective, nor were her efforts to hide the fresher marks on her wrists. The manner in which she praised her husband while criticizing herself confirmed my suspicions. Not that any of it was blatant, mind you, but —"

"Your intuition convinced you," he finished for me, smiling. There was a time, years ago, when we had frequent disagreements about my faith in intuition, but Colin had come to respect — grudgingly at first — my skills in this department. "Do you think she killed him?"

"She might have." I could picture the scene: Mr. Grummidge home late from the pub, having had too much to drink, berates his wife for some perceived slight. He drags her out of bed, flings her against the wall, and beats her savagely. She, desperate to escape, picks up the only instrument of defense she can find: her grandfather's sword, which hangs conveniently above the mantel. He laughs, goading her, and she lunges forward, not realizing just how sharp the blade is until it slices through his chest, piercing his heart. "Imagine, if you will —"

"No, stop there, Emily. I know exactly what you're thinking. This is the time for facts, my dear, not fancy."

I sighed. "It is not inconceivable that she killed him in an attempt to defend herself. It is impossible, however, that she could have moved the body and staged it at the Tower without assistance. Perhaps she has a lover or a devoted brother — yes, I prefer the latter — who —"

"No." Colin's voice was stern, but his dancing eyes betrayed his amusement. "I don't need fiction, but I do need you to find out what you can about the Grummidges, will you? I don't believe Scotland Yard and the palace are approaching this in the correct manner."

My eyes widened. "I've never heard you so openly critical of your colleagues."

"I may be wrong, but my own intuition tells me that they are too focused on the theoretical threat against the king," he said. "Not, mind you, that I am suggesting we ought not consider it a most serious situation. We must protect his majesty, but to find the person behind the threats, we have to figure out why the murderer chose Grummidge as his victim. The connection could prove critical to unraveling the larger problem."

"Colin Hargreaves, trusted agent of the Crown, relying on his intuition. Truly, I am shocked. So shocked that I may be incapable of coherent thought, let alone useful action."

"Your mind is agile enough," he said, a smile creeping onto his face. "And it is unlikely in the extreme that anyone or anything could keep you from useful action, particularly when there is a murder to be solved. There's one more thing. The coroner found what appears to be river water in Grummidge's lungs and the guard who first discovered the body said that the hair was damp."

"Traitors' Gate may be bricked up, but

perhaps there is another way into the Tower via the river," I said. "Our murderer might have an ally inside, someone who —"

"Facts, my dear, facts." He tilted his head. "You might help me with one more thing, though. I've been considering the message slipped into the letterbox — the one that included the map of the Tower. I had initially assumed this was meant to refer to the spot where the murderer left Grummidge's body, but I'm wondering if it's something else altogether. What if the map is a clue directing me to the lance drawn on the note? Her Majesty thought I would view the message she gave me as an instruction, which didn't appear to make sense. But if the second letter is meant to be similar in nature, the map, combined with the drawing, could be viewed as a sort of direction. There is a large collection of weapons and armor on display at the Tower, including a not insignificant number of lances. Your comments about river access make me suspect you plan to make another trip there?"

"You know me too well," I said. "It would be a disgrace not to investigate the possibility of the murderer bringing the body in via an entrance we have overlooked."

"I shan't try to persuade you otherwise.

My feelings on futile endeavors are well-known. While you are there, will you look for any sort of hidden clue among the lances on display? I would go myself if I could get away from Marlborough House for long enough, but I don't see that happening in the immediate future."

"It would be my pleasure," I said.

"I am most grateful." He pulled me to my feet and held my gaze as he kissed my hands. "And while you are seeking out your mysterious water entrance to the Tower, please resist the urge to leap to conclusions. And do be careful about accusing the guards of treason. They don't react well to such things. I shouldn't enjoy seeing you fed to the ravens."

6
1415

Those first weeks in Sussex were all but intolerable. Adeline had given Cecily one of the pokiest rooms in the castle, with a fireplace too small to provide adequate heat, but she considered it a refuge rather than an insult. It was the only place she knew she would never see Adeline. Lord Esterby was a generous husband, indulging his wife's every whim, and their household rang with laughter, singing, and much dancing. Minstrels performed every evening, and a troubadour from Milan was expected before the end of the month, but Cecily did not find their merriment contagious. She preferred the privacy of her cold and barren chamber.

Every morning, she heard mass in the chapel. The baron's priest was a severe, humorless man whose sermons rained with fire and brimstone. A part of her craved chastisement, for she felt it cleansed some of the sin of her role in her mother's death. She felt lighter after mass and wondered if someday, far in the future, she would be altogether free of that burden of guilt.

The rolling hills in the countryside surrounding the castle provided endless hours of amusement, whether on horseback, when picnicking, or if one craved a meandering stroll. Cecily, who had never before liked needlework, found herself newly inspired by the flowers that filled the meadows: violet knapweed, deeper purple round-headed rampion, bright yellow wort, crisp white saxifrage, and flashing scarlet pimpernels. Her embroidery improved, and soon she found herself taking on more and more difficult projects, designing complicated patterns of entwined flowers and vines.

In the evening, she retired to her room, where she would open the wooden diptych, William's wedding gift to her, and fall to her knees to pray. Only when she could no longer stand the hardness of the stone floor — the room boasted no carpet — would she cross herself and rise. The pain felt more cleansing even than mass. Then she would open her book and read rather than cavort with the rest of the household. She did not feel right dancing when William was away, and even though there had been as yet no news from France, she could not help but worry. The words of Christine de Pizan always brought her comfort.

Adeline hardly spoke to her, except to chide her for being too serious, but this did not trouble Cecily. She liked solitude. It was only when the much-anticipated troubadour arrived that she began to spend her evenings downstairs with the others. Dario Gabrieli, born into a noble Milanese family, came with minstrels of his own, and when he sang, the purity of his voice intoxicated all who heard him, Cecily included. His soulful good looks — dark hair and melting brown eyes — enhanced his work. His rendition of the tragic story of Tristan and Iseult brought all the ladies to tears.

Lord Esterby enjoyed the songs as much as anyone, and invited Gabrieli to stay at the castle through the winter. Cecily wondered if she would still be here, or if William would have returned from France by then. No one knew how long the invasion would take.

William's first view of the French coast underwhelmed him. Perhaps it was anticlimactic, following the army's glorious departure from England, when the soldiers spotted an eagle flying above the king's ship. An omen of good fortune; no one could doubt that. Nothing so spectacular occurred as their ships dropped anchor beyond the salt marshes on the shore. The city of Harfleur awaited them, behind a moat and miles of thick stone wall that surrounded both town and harbor. The enemy expected them and had spared no expense preparing. Huge Dutch guns as well as ammunition, food, and other supplies had poured into Harfleur. The city was ready for a siege.

The Duke of Clarence and a large force of men approached Harfleur in the dark, cutting off French reinforcements and setting themselves up in a position of strength on a hill across from the rest of the English army. King Henry's navy blockaded the port, separating the citizens of Harfleur from the support of their countrymen.

Soon they would hear the deafening sound of the guns, for the French were not the only ones with artillery. The pounding would begin, relentless and brutal, its deadly rain destroying everything upon which it fell.

And when the guns went silent, William would be ready to fight.

First, though, King Henry sent a final message offering peace.

7
1901

It was categorically essential to determine why the murderer had chosen Mr. Grummidge as his victim. Although I wished to speak with his widow again, it would not serve my purpose to call on her too soon, so the following day I went in search of other leads, starting at her late husband's shop. The two men employed at the green-grocery, Bob Hayner and Gareth Jones, had agreed to stay on at Mrs. Grummidge's request. She needed the income her husband could no longer provide himself.

Mr. Jones explained, in a (naturally) heavy Welsh accent, that he had been at the store for more than five years and insisted there could be no better employer than Mr. Grummidge. Mr. Hayner concurred, although with somewhat less enthusiasm. When pressed, he admitted to resenting being paid less than Mr. Jones, whom he believed did not have a thorough understanding of produce. This started a bitter argument, much of which I did not try to follow. Regardless of the veracity of the accusations against Mr. Jones, there could be no question that I, at least, lacked a thorough understanding of produce.

I left the shop frustrated. After managing to calm the clerks down enough that I could question them, neither told me anything of use. They knew of no one who would wish to harm their employer, they sang the praises of Mrs. Grummidge, who brought dinner to her husband most afternoons, and could offer no insight into the character of the slain man beyond that he was a fair and successful businessman.

After equally fruitless conversations with nearby shopkeepers, I decided there was nothing more to be done in the East End, where the victim's acquaintances had taken to heart the adage *de mortuis nil nisi bonum.* Feeling deflated only for a moment, I set off for the second of my planned destinations, the Tower. Sleet started to fall as my carriage crossed the steel gray river, and I insisted that my driver wait for me in a nearby pub so that he would stay warm. He objected at first and was obviously distressed that a lady would make such a suggestion, but I pressed some coins into his hand and told him not to disobey me.

I tightened my scarf around my neck and then buried my hands in my muff as I joined the short queue for tickets at Lion Gate. Sadly, there were not many tourists willing to brave the weather for a glimpse of our nation's glorious history. Once inside the grounds, I proceeded to Traitors' Gate, where a Beefeater was regaling a small tour group with tales of the Tower's famous prisoners. I stopped, pretending to listen, and inspected the area. Given the coroner found river water in Mr. Grummidge's lungs and given that he had not been killed where his body was found, I considered that he might have been stabbed in a boat, and perhaps fallen out as he struggled for his life, inhaling water before succumbing to his wounds. Once he had stopped flailing, his murderer could have brought him here, somehow gaining entrance to the ancient fortress. But how?

I hadn't noticed the yeoman warder had finished his story, nor that the paltry collection of tourists was continuing on to the next stop on their tour. The guard, however, noticed me.

"Have you a special interest in Traitors' Gate, madam?" he asked. "Remembering Queen Anne Boleyn, perhaps?"

"It's such a shame it's bricked up now," I said. "Quite ruins the romance of the place, don't you think?"

"Well, I suppose so, if you're inclined to find traitors romantic. Of course, you wouldn't be the first lady to succumb to the charms of Sir Walter Raleigh. Queen Bess herself was quite taken with the man. Do you know the story?"

"I do. He was too good for her if you ask me." I bestowed on him my most charming smile. "Is there no longer any way into the Tower from the river?"

"No, madam. The water you see on this side of the gate comes either from rain or when we flood the moat, but one can no longer pass through from the river."

I thanked him and continued on my way, climbing the stairs to the battlements that joined the fortress's medieval towers, hoping to gain a vantage point suitable for discovering how Mr. Grummidge's body might have been brought into Wakefield Tower. The sleet was falling harder now, and my coat was nearly soaked through. St. Thomas's Tower, directly above Traitors' Gate, loomed in front of me, its thick walls menacing. This was a place that held on to its secrets. I turned away from the river and looked back beyond Wakefield Tower toward

William the Conqueror's White Tower. It was time to look for Colin's lance.

The Council Chamber in the White Tower, the very room in which Richard II had abdicated his throne, now served to display armor and weapons. I climbed down from the walls and marched across slick cobbles to the ancient structure, where, once inside, I began examining every lance I could find. The long, sleek weapons did not hide another clue, so I turned my attention to the walls and cases around them. There, tucked into a space in the mortar behind a rack holding fifteenth-century examples, I saw an envelope. The map — albeit in vague terms — had, in fact, led to a clue. The smooth paper bore no name or address, only a coat of arms: that of the Hargreaves family. I debated opening it. Was I not, after all, a Hargreaves? In the end, however, I knew I should take it to Colin. With a little sigh of resignation, I slid it into my reticule and set off to find my driver.

I had not told him to meet me for another half an hour, so I walked along the embankment until I reached the pub. The poor man was a picture of shock and distress when he saw me, and did his best to bundle me back to the carriage, but I was half frozen and insisted on having a cup of tea before I went back outside. The landlord brought me a sad little cup, but I cannot say it offered much satisfaction. Next time I would ask for ale. Just a half pint, my driver insists. Anything more and I'd have a scandal on my hands.

We left the warmth of the pub and were immediately pelted with more sleet. The wind had started to howl, but not louder than the voice of a newsboy who was shouting with a mixture of horror and glee.

"Special edition! Another king's dead! Special edition! Another king's dead!"

My heart nearly stopped and I froze in my tracks. Surely Bertie had not been cut down in, well, not quite the prime of his life, but so soon after inheriting the throne for which he had so long waited! I approached the boy and started to quiz him for more information, but he insisted on my buying the paper if I wanted to know more. I fumbled for a coin and took the damp tabloid from him, noticing his bare hands. I took more coins from my purse and gave them to him, crouching down so that I could look in his eyes and make him promise to use the money to buy gloves. He nodded enthusiastically and then ran down the pavement, continuing to shout about the king's death.

I shook as much of the sleet from the newsprint as I could. The ink had started to run, but it was obvious at a glance that Bertie was not the subject of the headline story. Rather, a man called Clive Casby had been brought to an inglorious end by the same heinous method inflicted upon King Edward II. Should the reader be unfamiliar with the indelicate manner in which this fourteenth-century sovereign was killed, I recommend the excellent play by Sir Christopher Marlowe. Short of that, I will say only that red hot pokers ought never meet any part of the human anatomy.

8
1415

The baron's household had fallen under the spell of Dario Gabrieli, the noble troubadour from Milan. There was nothing about the man that did not fascinate, from his accent to his clothes, his manner of carrying himself to his raucous sense of humor. At least three of Adeline's ladies declared themselves to be in love with him, but none of them had the courage to admit it to the man himself. They parsed his every word, imitated his mode of speech, and argued over who would bring him spiced wine and sweets in the evening after his performances. Adeline alone held herself apart from Gabrieli. She listened attentively when he sang and praised him without reserve, but she never sought him out during the day, nor did she ask him to go riding in the afternoon with her ladies.

Cecily enjoyed the troubadour's company more than she expected. She adored his songs, but was more taken with his stories of life in Milan. Everything there sounded exotic, from the art to the music, and she wished she could travel to see it herself. It was only when Gabrieli began to praise her nobility and told her that in his heart he was never away from her that she realized he was attempting a flirtation, following the manner of Andreas Capellanus, whose treatise *The Art of Courtly Love* had for centuries guided those in search of romance. She reacted so strongly against his advances — heeding none of the advice given by Capellanus, preferring instead to rely on Christine de Pizan, who insisted in no uncertain terms that a lady must never allow herself to be seduced in such a way — that she feared Gabrieli would flee Sussex altogether. If he did, she might have to explain to Adeline what had happened.

Her fears were unjustified, born from youth and lack of experience. Dario Gabrieli would not be so easily discouraged. He recognized that he had chosen the wrong object for his affections, but there were other ladies in the castle. Two days after she had rebuffed his advances, Lord Esterby called Cecily to his parlor. Frightened that he believed she had encouraged the Italian, she silently recited a simple prayer as she stood before him. His broad face, normally bright and quick to smile, bore a grave expression, and Cecily feared the worst.

"Word has come from France," he said. "The fighting has begun."

It surprised no one that the French rejected King Henry's offer of peace.

The English cleared the land around the city, making way for their guns and trebuchets. They built defensive screens and dug deep trenches. The sound of the cannons and the acrid smell of the thick smoke they spewed as they shot their enormous stones made the earth seem like hell itself. Miners from Wales excavated beneath Harfleur's walls at an inhuman pace, their goal to cause the collapse of the city's defenses. Many soldiers died in those mines, when the French, digging as well, broke through and attacked their attackers.

This hand-to-hand fighting in the mines, a part of every siege, was always the most dangerous combat — claustrophobic spaces, men relying on their poleaxes and battle hammers, swords and knives. It was dark and dirty, the air close and hot, the ground slick with blood. Those who succeeded in besting their opponents earned reputations for being the bravest and most skilled of all knights. Even those who were vanquished were lauded for their feats.

Though he was no miner, William dug every day, listening for any sound that might suggest the French were nearby, just on the other side of the dirt, digging a tunnel of their own. When it came, first the soft scratching of axes, then shouts as the enemies knew they were about to clash, William pushed his way toward the front, ordering archers to prepare a line of defense. They might stop the first men through the break in the tunnel, but eventually they would be overwhelmed. And when they were, William and the other men-at-arms were ready.

The bite of arrows striking armor and blades clanging against each other echoed, sounding more like the death blows of mythical beasts than the work of mortal men, and the scant light provided by flickering torches made it difficult to distinguish friend from enemy. William raised his sword, brought it crashing down hard on the helmet of a man running toward him, and then used his ballock to stab through the man's visor as he fell. He took a glancing blow to his arm, but hardly felt it and charged ahead, cutting down anyone who stood in his way. He tasted blood and felt it

running warm down his face, but he continued moving forward until there was no one
left to fight.

Both sides retreated. There was no real
victory to be had, but every man who fought
in the mines had made himself worthier
than he had been the day before. William
had proved his mettle. And now, all he
wanted was to fight more.

9
1901

Grateful though I was for my closed carriage after we'd left the pub, I was nonetheless half frozen and desperate for a warm bath when I reached home, but this did not make me regret finding myself unable to take advantage of these comforts. No sooner had I started for my chamber, than my butler called to me from the bottom of the stairs. When I had first met Davis, more than a dozen years ago, he was a model of propriety, a butler among butlers. I like to think that I had corrupted him, just a bit, during our time together. He still objected to my smoking cigars, but he had accepted my habit of taking port after dinner with such equanimity — and at such an early stage of our association — that I could forgive him nearly anything. He ran a tight ship, and my households, both here and at Anglemore Park, were the envy of my neighbors.

"Mr. Hargreaves on the telephone for you, madam."

Colin had installed the contraption the moment it became possible, and although I understood — and, at least intellectually, appreciated — the benefits and convenience of it, I still could not count myself among its admirers. I went into the library, where the odious object sat on his desk. My husband's voice sounded odd and faraway, not like himself at all. But on this occasion, I had to admit I was grateful for the invention. He had called to summon me to Berkeley Square, the scene of our murderer's latest tableau.

My husband must have told Davis as much, because my butler was waiting for me in the front hall with a dry coat, my warmest scarf, gloves, and an umbrella. I thanked him profusely and set off on foot, as the location to which I headed was both nearby and as familiar to me as my own home. I had, in fact, once called it home, as the house I had briefly shared with my late first husband was situated in Berkeley Square. As I rushed along Mount Street, I struggled to remember what I could about Edward II. Beyond the poker and his death having occurred at Berkeley Castle in Gloucestershire, I knew very little.

The sleet was starting to turn to snow, a change I welcomed, and by the time I reached my destination, thick white flakes coated the pavement. The police had cordoned off the area, but there was very little activity to be seen. There was no sign of the wretched Inspector Gale, who must have already left. Obviously, the crime had occurred long enough ago for the papers not only to have learned of it, but to have printed and distributed their special editions on the subject.

Colin ushered me past the police barrier. "I would have called for you earlier," he said, "but you understand that, officially, you are not allowed to be here. The coroner is going to remove the body soon, so we'll have to be quick. I've delayed him as long as possible."

I had never seen anything quite like it. In the center of the square rested a large wooden tabletop. Next to it, lying facedown, was the body of a man wearing a medieval-looking crown. I could not recall having seen a portrait of Edward II, but I assumed the dead man's attire — his feet were shod in pointed leather boots — was meant to evoke the proper era. A sheet of canvas covered him from the torso to the knees, but did not entirely hide what I could only assume was a poker, no longer red-hot.

"Edward II," I said.

"Yes," Colin replied. "He was under the tabletop when discovered."

"And the cause of death was . . ." My voice trailed.

"Yes. The poker. Unless the postmortem reveals something else." He cleared his throat. "I apologize for bringing you to such an unorthodox scene."

"You know perfectly well I would never have forgiven you if you hadn't. What do we know about him, other than his name?"

"Not much, I'm afraid," Colin said.

I approached the body and reached into the back of the tunic worn by the dead man. "The label says Carson's Theatrical Supply and I shouldn't be surprised if the costume worn by our Henry VI came from the same source. How does one place a body in such . . . such . . ." I took a deep breath. "In such a fashion with no one taking notice? It's dark now, but it couldn't have been when it was brought here."

"The man who reported it saw it out his window around noon. We called at every house in the square and several people said they saw a large tarpaulin covering the spot earlier in the day and assumed there was some sort of work going on. We suspect the scene was staged before the sun rose."

"No one saw the tarpaulin being re-moved?" I asked.

"No." Colin shook his head. I looked around. This was hardly the most trafficked part of town, but neither could it be called out of the way. Surely someone had seen something. I said as much to Colin.

"We've asked all the papers to publish an appeal for information," he replied, "but it is perhaps too much to hope that anyone reliable will come forward. Even if someone does, we're unlikely to get more than a description of an unremarkable-looking person in a coat and hat with a scarf hiding his face."

I raised my eyebrows. "It sounds almost as if you witnessed the crime."

"More like I have enough experience to know that whoever is responsible for this would have been careful not to leave himself vulnerable to identification."

I crouched next to the body. The crown, fashioned from metal painted gold, had been secured with hairpins. I did not remove the sheet altogether, content — rather, grateful — to rely on Colin's description of the manner of death. If, like our other victim, this one was killed in another loca-tion, why choose such a difficult method?

Far easier to stab, shoot, or poison the man first and then choreograph the scene. I tugged at the man's tunic so that I could see his back, but found no signs of injury and rolled him onto his side. No wounds on his chest either.

Colin cleared his throat. "Marks on his wrist suggest that he was bound before the, er . . ."

"Quite." The victim's pained expression was haunting. Eyes wide open, his face frozen in a horrific grimace. A large port-wine birthmark covered nearly half of his left cheek. Colin rolled him back over and pulled me to my feet.

"Home?" he asked. "Carson's Theatrical Supply is unlikely to still be open by the time we could get there, wherever it is."

"No doubt the wretched Inspector Gale has already called there."

"I don't believe he looked inside the tunic."

"A shocking oversight," I said. "Home sounds lovely, but I think you should look at this first." I recounted for him my visit to the Tower and handed him the envelope I had found there. He opened it and read aloud:

The mercy that was quick in us but late,
By your own counsel is suppress'd and
    kill'd:
You must not dare, for shame, to talk of
    mercy;
For your own reasons turn into your
    bosoms,
As dogs upon their masters, worrying you.
See you, my princes, and my noble peers,
These English monsters!

"Henry V again," I said. "But this time, Shakespeare's version. Surely his choice of passage — Henry about to dole out punishment to the nobles who planned to usurp his throne — is significant."

"Quite," Colin said. "It makes me all the more concerned about the king. What do you make of the drawing?"

At the bottom of the page, beneath the quote, was an odd sketch. "I haven't the slightest idea. Is it a rock?"

"It looks that way. At least now we know that it's meant as a clue to be followed. A scavenger hunt, if you will, and now I'm to find a rock of some sort." He frowned and returned the note to the envelope. "I must go to Scotland Yard. In the meantime, I'd like you to ring Nanny at Anglemore. It looks as if we shall be in London for some time and it's been too long since we've seen the boys. Have her bring the little chaps as soon as she can."

He gave me a quick kiss and hailed a hansom cab to take him to the Yard, knowing I would prefer to walk back to Park Lane. I watched as he drove away and then turned back to the unfortunate Mr. Casby. What sort of a person would do such a thing to anyone? Surely this was not meant solely as a warning to our current King Edward. It felt too personal for that. To choose such a brutal method of attack . . . I cringed thinking about it. In my estimation, that required a burning anger that would not be sated by anything less violent. If Bertie were the cause of the murderer's ire, would he squander it on someone else? Unless he had something even more awful planned for the king. I crouched next to the body again and closed the dead man's eyes, vowing that I would seek justice for him.

Back home, I indulged in a long — and extremely hot — bath. No matter how much I scrubbed, I could not cleanse the horror of Mr. Casby's death from my skin. It had permeated every pore of my body. After pulling on a dressing gown, I retired to the library, where I gathered all the books I could find on the English monarchs. I sat close to the fire so that my hair would dry more quickly and read everything I could about Edward II.

In short order, I reached the conclusion that Edward had been treated very badly by historians. Some might criticize me for once again relying on my intuition, but it was shouting for me to reject the commonly accepted narration of his reign. His wife, Isabella of France, famously had a long affair with Roger Mortimer, and we are meant to consider this as a natural result of her husband's . . . shall we say, lack of interest in her. I am no naïve girl, and understand perfectly well what our writers of history mean when they refer to the king's close friendship with Piers Gaveston. We have crossed the threshold of the twentieth century and ought to be more enlightened than we were in the past. Has the torment of Oscar Wilde taught us nothing?

Isabella, only twelve years old when she married Edward, could hardly have complained that the marriage went unconsummated for some time. She did eventually bear the king four children, so could not argue that she was cast aside. It seems to me wrong to condemn the man when we can know nothing about the intimate details of his personal life.

By the time Colin came home, I was so wound up that I subjected him to a half-hour rant on the injustice of historians' views of Edward. He listened patiently and without comment until I finished.

"I agree that we know very little about him as a person," he said. "But it cannot be denied that he was not the best sovereign England has ever had."

"There are plenty of others no better," I started. "He is tarred because of speculation about his . . . his most private moments, and that is unjust. And for him to have been killed in such a manner —"

"You will get no argument from me. For the moment, however, I think it best that we focus on someone else killed in such a manner: Mr. Casby. You may find your outrage at his treatment somewhat lessened when you hear what I have to say. He was a notorious procurer in the East End, known for his brutal treatment of the women who worked for him. The police could never get enough evidence to convict him of anything, primarily because the women were too afraid to speak against him."

"Hideous," I said, "but even so, no one, not even the most awful amongst us, deserves to die in such a manner. This does, however, confirm my belief that this crime was personal and vindictive. Surely you can no longer suspect that our murderer is acting only to give notice that he intends to kill the king?"

"I don't think that is his only motive, no, but he is certainly sending a message that no one — not even a king — is safe. Why else would he go to such trouble to stage his victims? If his motive stems only from a belief that these men should die, he would kill them and be done with it. There is something more to his crimes."

"Perhaps he is a vigilante, righting wrongs. He has saved Casby's women from abuse, and stopped Mrs. Grummidge from being beaten."

"We do not have any solid proof that Mr. Grummidge beat his wife. I have great faith in your intuition, my dear, but even if you saw bruises — and I do not doubt you did — that does not necessarily mean her husband was the cause of them."

"It was not only the bruises," I said. "It was everything about her. Her manner, the obsequious way she talked about her husband, how she didn't blame him for staying away from her after their child died. We cannot dismiss the possibility that we are dealing with a murderer who believes he is stopping gross injustices."

"Why, then, is he making his victims look like dead kings?" he asked.

"Perhaps to warn those who would take advantage of a position of power?"

"And who in Britain is better situated to take advantage of a position of power than the king himself?"

"The messages you have received — particularly the one the queen gave to you — it is almost as if someone else in a position of power is behind all this. *Une sanz pluis.* One and no more. *Sapere aude.* Dare to know. Two murders staged to look like the deaths of medieval kings. Is there someone in Britain who believes he has a better claim to the throne than Bertie?"

"We're not on the verge of a crisis of succession, if that's what you mean," Colin said. "There is no question that King Edward is his mother's son."

"Yes, but Victoria was not William IV's daughter, she was his niece. And he had plenty of illegitimate children who might have thought they deserved the throne more than she."

"Illegitimate children — even those of kings — do not expect to inherit the throne. Not in this day and age."

"Of course, the sensible ones don't, but

we are dealing with an individual who is an unhinged murderer. He could have any number of unreasonable expectations. What was the surname of William's illegitimate children? FitzClarence? Their mother was an actress, I believe?"

"I have not the slightest idea. Furthermore, it is unlikely any of them are still living —"

"Their children could want the throne," I interrupted.

"I do not think it would be a good use of your time to investigate the descendants of William IV's bastard children. Your crazed vigilante theory has more merit."

"Then that is what I shall pursue," I said. I agreed it was a more likely solution to our case, but was not altogether prepared to abandon the notion of a war of succession. What better motivation for murder could a person have than a desire to usurp the throne of Britain?

10
1415

The baron had no news about William, but the knowledge that the fighting had begun, in a town called Harfleur on the western coast of France, haunted Cecily. She started hearing mass twice daily, spent hours praying before her diptych, and said the rosary every night before she went to sleep, often while the others were captivated by Dario Gabrieli's songs. She could not entirely comprehend her feelings. They seemed to her deeper than perhaps they ought to be, but she could not bear the thought of losing her husband.

She took to going for long walks in the afternoon, desperate for solitude. Adeline mocked her for being such poor company, but the baron gave her a small Book of Hours and told her he hoped she would find comfort in the words that filled it. Cecily did just that, poring over the prayers and psalms and the gleaming illuminated images that accompanied them. Her faith had always been strong, even if dominated by the complicated emotions she felt for her mother. Now, though Beatrix Bristow loomed in her daughter's mind, Cecily began to have a greater sense of clarity. She had been taught — and believed — that God could forgive any sin. Jesus Christ had died on the cross to make this possible, yet this alone did not relieve humans of the burden of their sins. Forgiveness went hand in hand with penance, but no penance she'd been given had ever freed her from the weight of her mother's death.

One bright September day, Cecily had wandered far from the baron's castle, beyond the walls, and toward the forest. England was at its most beautiful that afternoon, the sun shining, the autumnal air crisp, and the rolling green hills a picture of pastoral perfection. Here she stood, surrounded by beauty, while William fought in Harfleur. She fell to her knees, suddenly terrified, fearing for his safety. A clap of thunder sounded above her, and the weather changed in an instant. The sun disappeared and rain pounded from the sky. Cecily scrunched her eyes closed and begged God to forgive her for her part in her mother's death.

Punish me in whatever way you see fit. I will accept it with grace and welcome the penance. Then, please, dear Lord, bring my husband home from France alive.

Death might be preferable to this.

William surveyed the camp, the stench of death heavy in the air. Not just the stench of death, but the stench of the bloody flux, the disease that was ravaging the English army. The king and his brothers, following the advice of the royal physician, had moved their camp high on a hill, where the air was fresh, but even that could not guarantee immunity. The Bishop of Norwich, trusted advisor to the king — a man, it was said, who was *the most loving and dearest* of his friends — succumbed to the sickness with Henry at his side.

Despite the hideous atmosphere of the siege, the illness and the horror, the king was never a stranger to his men. He fought beside them. He praised their bravery. He spoke to them, anonymously sometimes — at least that's what many soldiers claimed. He would come in the night, when they were on watch, and present himself as an ordinary man. A soldier, like them. But his words, inspiring, pious, and strong, revealed something of his nature, and eventually, they guessed his identity. Not that they ever confronted him about it. If their sovereign wanted to travel amongst them unknown, they would not disrupt his plans.

An oppressive heat beat down on the army, the air thick with humidity, trapping the vile smell of death and disease in the soldiers' lungs. Nothing shook the king's confidence, however. He promised them Harfleur would fall soon.

But then, hours after the Bishop of Norwich died, the French attacked, overpowering the English near the Leure gate and forcing them to fall back. The army began to fear the siege would fail. The French were shouting from the walls, hurling insults with their arrows. William saw the king, his noble face serious. He would do whatever was necessary to rally his men. God was on their side; Henry was the rightful king of France. With divine help, he would lead them to victory.

11
1901

The following day, while Colin was in his study preparing for a meeting with the king, I found myself more concerned with Carson's Theatrical Supply than with the FitzClarences. The establishment was near Leicester Square, barely a mile and a half from the house. The weather was no longer so foul as it had been yesterday — the sun had even made a rare winter appearance — and I quite fancied a walk. I was just pulling on my gloves when the blaring of a motorcar's horn sounded in front of the house. The noise was repeated over and over until Davis marched past me to the door and opened it, ready to express his displeasure to the driver of the vehicle. He was standing on the threshold when I heard a familiar voice from outside.

"Now, now, Davis, you mustn't scold me. I'm looking for Lady Emily. Is she at home?" I would recognize that bored drawl anywhere. It belonged to Jeremy Sheffield, Duke of Bainbridge, my dear friend since almost before I could walk, and the bane of Davis's existence.

"Allow me to check, your grace."

I believe there is a common expression about people in whose mouths butter would not melt. Davis might well have been the inspiration for it. He stepped back inside, closing the door behind him.

"I'll go to him, Davis," I said, pushing past. If Jeremy had bought a motorcar, it was news to me, and I was desperate to see it. He was there in the street, dressed in a long coat and a pair of motoring goggles, leaning against the machine, a Daimler which was painted the same bright blue that appeared in the arms of the dukedom of Bainbridge. The engine was still running. "When did you get this?"

He grinned. "Yesterday. I came into town specially to collect it. If you're a good girl I'll teach you to drive. In the meantime, hop in. We'll go for a ride."

"I've work to do. Can you take me to Leicester Square?" I asked, accepting his outstretched hand and climbing onto the leather seat. I had been desperate for a motorcar for years, but Colin was utterly against the idea.

"The murders, I assume," he said, sitting next to me, handing me a spare set of goggles, and taking the steering wheel in hand. "I knew the instant I read the papers this morning that you'd be on the case, so to speak. Leicester Square it is."

Once I'd fastened the goggles around my head and secured my hat firmly, I leaned across him and blew the horn. Jeremy moved a long lever and the Daimler lurched forward. We were on our way! Between the noise from the engine and the wind lashing our faces, conversation was difficult, if not impossible, during the trip. We were not able to reach a very great speed, as the glut of carriages on the roads impeded our progress, but I was delighted nonetheless. So taken was I with his vehicle that, after we had parked, I almost delayed going into the shop in order to inspect it and pepper my friend with questions about it, but I am nothing if not dedicated to my work. Pleasure could wait.

Another person might have wanted to know something about my mission before entering Carson's Theatrical Supply, but Jeremy had spent years cultivating a lack of interest in virtually everything. He valued little more than ignorant bliss. I introduced myself to the clerk at the counter and then introduced my companion — having a duke on hand would make it simpler to accomplish what I hoped to — and asked to see the owner. Before the clerk could even turn to fetch the man, he had appeared of his own volition.

"George Carson, at your service," he said, a little bow, a broad smile on his face. "How can I help, your grace?"

"What I'd like, Mr. Carson, is for you to personally see to it that my friend here, Lady Emily Hargreaves, gets whatever she needs."

"Of course, your grace. Lady Emily, are you looking for something in particular? For a masquerade, perhaps?"

"Nothing quite so diverting, I'm afraid," I said. "I was hoping you might be able to tell us the identity of one of your customers. Someone who has recently purchased two costumes, both medieval, both meant to be kings."

Mr. Carson, momentarily nonplussed, steadied himself and stepped behind the counter. "Kings, you say? Let me see . . ." He pulled a large ledger from a shelf and began to flip through it. "Was this for a Shakespeare production, do you know?" Not surprisingly, he directed the question to Jeremy, not me.

"Was it, Lady Emily?" My friend flashed me a wicked grin. "You know how I can't keep track of these things. Shakespeare, Marlowe, who could say? I never could tell the difference."

I debated how to respond. Did I let Mr. Carson know immediately about the connection to the murders? What if he himself was the villain behind the horrific deaths? The shop had only just opened for the day, so it was unlikely the police had been here before me. I might have the opportunity to catch him unawares. Who was I to squander such a thing?

"It's an awkward situation, Mr. Carson," I explained. "I saw two gentlemen wearing costumes supplied by you and was much struck by their quality. The first was portraying Henry VI, and he looked as if he had stepped out of the picture of that king in the National Portrait Gallery. Black tunic with white trim, black tights —"

"And a smallish black hat," Mr. Carson finished for me. "Yes, I remember the outfit well. It was a custom order for a high-class masquerade. I don't get many of those — most of you lot use your tailors, even for fancy dress, don't you?"

"My tailor, Mr. Carson, would flail me to within an inch of my life if I went to someone else," Jeremy said, leaning forward conspiratorially. "It's as if I am his prisoner. You can't imagine the horror." I glared at him.

"Could you tell me who placed the order?" I asked.

"Oh, now, Lady Emily, my customers do like their privacy."

"I know all too well of the need for discretion," Jeremy said, pulling a pound note from his jacket and placing it on the counter. "It's a delicate situation, you see. My friend here would very much like to learn the gentleman's name, but it would have been awkward for her to have inquired when she saw him." He dropped his voice to a ridiculous whisper that he must have thought sounded dramatic. "Her husband can be a bit . . . well . . . I should say nothing more."

My eyes bulged and my hand ached to slap him, but instead I bit my bottom lip and looked at the floor, hoping Mr. Carson would take this as a sign of my reluctance.

"I understand," he said. He flipped through the ledger, running down the pages with his index finger. "Yes, here he is. Mr. John Smith. No address, I'm afraid."

"John Smith?" Jeremy sighed with inappropriate dramatic flourish. "Are you quite sure?"

"Unfortunately, I am. No doubt it is an alias. He paid in full — in cash — when he placed the order."

"Did he purchase anything else?" I asked. "There was a second costume, meant to be Edward II. The crown in particular was lovely work."

"Yes, in fact he did order that and two other costumes as well," Mr. Carson said, studying the page open before him. "They were for a series of masquerades."

I blanched. Our killer was not finished with his evil work.

Armed with detailed descriptions of the other costumes Mr. Carson had supplied to this so-called John Smith, I asked Jeremy to take me to Marlborough House, where Colin was meeting with the king. I had no intention of trying to see him myself. Bertie and I had a difficult relationship. Our mothers had been close, which meant that, on occasion, we were thrown together, but not in a romantic fashion; I was much too young for him, at least to my mind. I will admit to having been subjected to at least three awkward flirtations when he was Prince of Wales. Once I even slapped him, but he forgave me with the charismatic good nature for which he was known and never mentioned the incident again. Nonetheless, I was never much fond of him and didn't like the Marlborough Set. They were too fast, too reckless, and too vapid for my taste. Yet I did feel some sense of responsibility to inform him of what I had discovered. I wrote a quick note giving him all the details and gave it to the king's butler, who promised to deliver it posthaste. That done, I directed Jeremy to take me to a place so scandalous that he nearly lost control of the motorcar when I mentioned it.

"I am not taking you to a brothel, Em. No. Absolutely not. Shan't consider it. Don't ask again."

"It's not a brothel, it's a pub."

"It's essentially a brothel."

I saw no use in arguing technicalities and decided not to mention that this would not be my first brothel. I had visited one in Venice during another murder investigation. "It would be much safer for me to go with you than alone, and I promise you that go I will, one way or another. Would you like to tell Colin you preferred to leave me on my own?"

"You're an absolute menace, Em, and I don't know why I tolerate you." I explained to him about Mr. Casby and what I hoped to learn from the women subjected to his disgraceful treatment. He offered to go in my stead, trying to convince me that his title would make it the simplest thing ever to get the girls to talk, but I was having none of it. While I would never deny there was much a handsome duke could accomplish — even if he was not nearly so handsome as Colin — I knew I was in a better position to understand the plight of these women than he. I didn't only seek information from them; I wanted to see if there was something I could do to improve their situation.

Our former prime minister, William Gladstone, had devoted a not insignificant amount of time and energy to giving a new life to the prostitutes in our fair capital. Few of his colleagues looked kindly on his actions and there was much nasty gossip on the subject. When I learned about his efforts, years later (I had not even been born when he started), I was touched by the thought of the great man trying to help those so much less fortunate than himself. Now I hoped I could emulate his example. Jeremy did not react well when I endeavored to explain this to him.

"No, no, Em," he said. "That makes it all the worse. What will Hargreaves do to me when he finds out I'm an accessory to this madness? The man never could stand me. Probably because I'm more dashing than he."

"You are not nearly so dashing as he. If you don't take me, I shall leap out of the motorcar the next time we stop and hail a hansom cab. You will be freed from all responsibility."

"Not in Hargreaves's mind. If he were here, he'd tie you up rather than let you go, and he'll judge me fiercely for not having the courage to stop you."

"Colin knows better than anyone that I cannot be stopped when I set my mind to something."

And that was the end of that. Before long, Jeremy was easing the Daimler along the curb outside a nondescript pub called the Black Swan on the infamous Ratcliffe Highway.

"It could be much worse," I said, climbing down from the motorcar and inspecting the building's façade. It wasn't on the verge of falling down, and the windows looked to be in decent shape. Still, I knew that this part of London was notorious, even if conditions had improved in the past decades. A group of filthy children had already gathered around the vehicle, the tallest of the boys calling out questions. None of them looked adequately fed or had on a warm enough coat. Two of them were wearing boots with holes large enough to reveal tattered socks and one, leaning on a rough wooden crutch, was missing his right leg below the knee. Jeremy explained the workings of the motor to the curious lad and then offered him a handful of coins to stand guard over it while we went inside.

"What? You're taking her in there?" The boy pointed to the Black Swan. "I don't think she'll like it, sir. And I don't think they'll like her. You aren't a religious reformer, are you, madam?"

"No, I'm not," I said. "I'm here to offer assistance to the women who work there."

"Sounds religious to me," he said. "They won't like it. Not at all." The other boys laughed. I ignored them and headed straight for the pub's door.

Jeremy took me by the arm. "Are you sure about this, Em?"

"Absolutely. But do please leave the talking to me. I've already suffered enough mortification this morning." He sighed but pulled open the door and gave what could only be described as a sarcastic bow as he motioned for me to enter ahead of him.

The interior did not look all that different

from the pub in which I had met my driver near the Tower. It featured a long, wooden bar, with stools in front of it and gleaming taps behind it. There were tables like one would find in any tavern. It was the people who signaled that this was no ordinary pub. To begin, there was a group of women in the room, dressed in what I can only describe as a style meant to entice the basest of instincts. This in itself did not shock me; I know what goes on in brothels. But at this time of the day? Before luncheon?

A burly man in a well-tailored suit approached us. "Madam, sir, may I be of assistance?" He looked me up and down in a most off-putting fashion, seeming to gloat at my discomfort.

"Have you stepped up to take Mr. Casby's place?" I asked. "What is your name, sir?"

"Mr. George Brown, at your service. Presuming it's a service I'm willing to supply."

The look he gave me — something between a leer and a threatening glare — frightened me just a bit, but I ignored his impertinent comment. "I'm here to speak with your women about Mr. Casby. I'm sure you can have no objection."

"I have plenty of objections," he said.

"First, who the bleeding —"

Jeremy raised his hand. "Please, watch your language in front of the lady. I am the Duke of Bainbridge and can assure you that I am more than capable of making your life immensely difficult should you prove uncooperative." Mr. Brown studied Jeremy, as if sizing him up as a potential customer.

"That's quite enough, sir," I said. "If you'd prefer not to give us what we need, we can leave these interviews to the uniformed police, although I imagine your business would suffer as a result."

"There's nothing illegal going on here," he said.

I pulled myself up to my full height. "Really, Mr. Brown, you cannot think me naïve enough to believe that. I'm here to do a job and I shan't leave until it is done."

"You're with the police?" he asked.

"Not officially, but I assist them on occasion. I shall need to speak to each of the ladies individually. Would you prefer I do that here or somewhere more private?"

"If you want time with the girls, you'll have to pay. Conversation is a service, you know."

"Not one for which legal establishments charge," I said and marched to a table in the corner near a window. "Jeremy, would

you please fetch me the first young woman."
He looked remarkably uncomfortable, but
did as I asked.

I had no precise expectations about the
outcomes of my talks with them, but did
my best to earn their trust and convince
them to tell me what they could about Mr.
Casby. It was clear they were all terrified of
him. Two of them actually questioned his
death, as if they could not believe any force
could remove him from the world. One,
called Mary Skypton, who seemed much
younger than the rest — although I could
not judge whether this was due to her age
or to having only come to the Black Swan
recently; she had not been ill-used for as
long as the others — had tears in her eyes
when I confirmed his demise.

"He's gone? Really gone?" She wiped her
eyes with the back of her hand. "Do you
think I'll owe my debt to him to whoever
takes over? George there isn't as cruel as
Casby, but I'd rather not work for him. He's
brutal, too, in his way. Might go out on my
own instead."

"No matter what debt you owe anyone,
you cannot be forced to do this sort of work,
Mary. It's illegal."

"I don't see that the law matters much
here," she said. "The coppers don't care

what goes on in places like this."

"I care," I said, "and if you want a different kind of life I will do everything in my power to help you get it."

She looked at Jeremy, who was standing next to the table, his arms crossed tightly over his chest, bouncing nervously on his toes, and blew him a kiss. "He's quite attractive. Do you think he might have a use for me?"

"That is not what I meant, Mary. You should be considering other, more respectable options. You have your whole life ahead of you."

"That's what Lizzie always thought, and look what happened to her."

"Lizzie?" I asked. "Tell me about her."

"Lizzie Hopman. Her own mother brought her here and gave her to Casby. She knew how bad the life is — she'd done it herself for years. And when she wasn't bringing in enough customers, Casby asked for Lizzie, said it was the only way her mother could pay off her debt."

"What exactly did she owe him? What do you owe him?"

"Well, you see, he's not an entirely bad gent," she said. "He can be — could be, I suppose, now that he's kicked it — real sweet when he wanted. It's not easy to make your way on your own, is it? Sometimes you need a little money for rent or food, and when you got desperate, he'd help out. Give you food or a place to stay. That's why we all live here, you know. We can't afford anywhere else."

"And he forces you to earn the rent?" I asked.

The girl shrugged. "Well, you've got to pay somehow, don't you? And the rooms here are better than an alley."

"Where's Lizzie? Does she still work here?"

"Oh, no. She died the same day as the queen. A bit of rough handling that went a little too far."

This was too much for Jeremy. He slapped his hand on the table. "Who was the cause of it? I want a name." He started for Mr. Brown. "Were you here when this girl was killed? Lizzie?"

"Sir, you have the wrong idea entirely," the man said, holding his hands up and stepping back. "It weren't like that."

"What was it like?" Jeremy's hands were balled in fists.

"Lizzie liked it that way and asked Casby to do it," Mr. Brown said. "Preferred working off her debt straight to him, if you understand my meaning. Had no one to blame but herself."

Jeremy looked as if he might explode. I went to his side, took him by the arm, and spoke in a whisper. "Fighting will not change anything. Consider what he might do to Mary after we're gone."

"Then we can't leave her here."

"Whatcha going to do?" Mary asked. "Take all of us to your house? You live in Mayfair, I bet, don't you? I like it there. Went once with a fancy gent. You remind me a bit of him."

"Where is Lizzie's mother?" I asked.

"She died last year," Mr. Brown said. "Consumption. Not here, mind you, we've no disease here. She had a room somewhere between St. Clement Danes and Holy Trinity in Lincoln's Inn Fields. Now, look, you've talked to the girls and I'm going to have to ask you to leave. I can't have a commotion. This is a legitimate place of business, a licensed public house."

"There is very little going on here that is legitimate," Jeremy said. "I shall personally see to it that you lose your license."

"See here, sir, those things are none of my business. Clive — er, Mr. Casby — he might have made a bit on the side with the girls, but I'm not going to do that. I'm an honest businessman. Ask anyone. Nobody's done a thing since Clive died."

"He only died yesterday," Jeremy said. "And I have no faith in the veracity of any of your statements. This establishment will not continue to operate." Now he took me firmly by the arm and marched me outside and back to the motorcar. The boy he'd paid to watch it was rubbing it with a dirty rag.

"Polishing it for you, sir."

Jeremy gave him another coin and went to turn the engine crank. His face had gone a sickly shade of gray. I'd never seen him so consumed with fury.

12
1415

Cecily expected her penance would prove difficult, but she had not imagined it would come as it did. Not that she'd had much time to imagine it. The rain had stopped the moment she rose to her knees. She was soaked, but did not care, so full of God's love did she feel. Instead of walking back to the castle, she went into the woods, some unknown — and, she was certain, divine — force guiding her. She went to the stream and followed its banks until she reached the clearing where Adeline liked to picnic. That was where she saw them.

Dario Gabrieli was standing close to Adeline, and there was no one else with them. Not a single lady accompanied the baroness. The couple, too, were drenched from the rain, but showed no sign of so much as noticing this. The troubadour had his lute, and was strumming it, singing softly, something about Lancelot and Guinevere. Adeline's face glowed with rapturous joy.

Cecily stood, frozen. They had not seen her. Unsure of what to do, what to say, she started to back away, turning and running once they were out of sight. She ran until she reached the castle, then raced to her room and fell again on her knees, praying for guidance. Was this to be her cross?

She composed herself, changed into a dry gown, and sat at her table, Christine de Pizan's *The Treasure of the City of Ladies* in front of her. She opened the book and her eyes rested on a passage at the end of the first part:

As people are not all the same, there are some men and women so perverse that whatever good correction and instruction they are given, they will always follow their own wicked inclinations. It is fruitless to show them the error of their ways, and nothing is gained but their resentment. We will now describe the instruction of the good lady who has in her charge and control some young princess or lady and the attitude that she ought to adopt in the event that she should see her mistress go astray in a foolish love affair and refuse her wise and good advice.

She knew then what God wanted from her. She must save Adeline from committing a grave sin.

Would this be the final assault? The king had commanded his archers to prepare flaming arrows. He had ordered the army forward, across their defensive ditches to the gates of the city. What followed passed in a blur of blood and screams and pain and death. The French proved themselves formidable opponents, but the English pressed on. William raised his sword again and again, slashing and stabbing, ignoring all cries for mercy.

Then, everything changed. He felt a sharp, searing sensation erupt in his cheek, more like heat than pain. He tasted blood. And he fell to the ground. The sounds of the battle faded to a dull din. He could hardly see. With great effort, he tried to stand, but could not get to his feet. So he crawled through the dirt, dragging himself with his arms, pushing with his legs, away from the walls of Harfleur.

A blow landed across his back, dampened by his armor. He rolled over, managed to raise himself to his knees, and lifted his sword, striking his attacker with an upward jab. He could feel rage coursing through his body, and suddenly the pain from his wound no longer troubled him. He saw the king, fighting with his men, and with a ragged cry, "For Harry!" William ran back to the front line, prepared to go on as long as necessary, not stopping until his king had achieved victory.

13
1901

After we left the Black Swan, I expected Jeremy to drop me in front of the house and refuse to come inside, having no desire to see Colin, but on this count, he surprised me. When Davis opened the door for us, Jeremy immediately inquired as to whether his master was home, and when the butler answered in the affirmative, demanded to see him at once. Davis's face remained as impassive as ever. He murmured, "Of course, your grace," and went to fetch him. I all but dragged my friend into the library, pressed a glass of whisky into his hand, and insisted that he take a seat, half-afraid of what he was planning to say to my husband. Colin appeared in short order, looking rather bemused. I wondered what Davis had told him.

"Forced you to let her drive, did she?" he asked, pouring some whisky for himself. "I could have warned you it would be a bad idea."

"Look, Hargreaves, I didn't let her drive," Jeremy said, "but when you hear what I did do, you'll be furious, so you might as well throttle me and get it over with."

My husband looked at me, raised his eyebrows, and sat across from Jeremy. "Now I'm curious."

"It was nothing, really," I said. "I wanted to interview the women at the Black Swan and Jeremy was kind enough to take me there in his motorcar. Naturally, he exhibited a great deal of reluctance when I proposed the excursion, but I assured him you would prefer that I undertake the errand in the presence of a gentleman rather than on my own. And as you were not available to escort me . . ."

Colin rose to his feet without a word, crossed to the table on which the whisky stood, picked up the decanter, carried it back toward his chair, and refilled Jeremy's glass. "Bainbridge, I am all too familiar with the futility of trying to dissuade my wife from any of her outrageous schemes. I shouldn't dream of holding you accountable."

"The place is a scandal, Hargreaves, worse than I could have imagined. The women are all but slaves. Something must be done."

"I couldn't agree more," Colin said. "And I give you my word that when the rest of this business is sorted, I shall personally see to it that it is taken care of."

"I'm much obliged. And I suppose I should be off."

"No, stay," my husband said. "You've proven yourself useful in the past and I may need to call on you again. You may as well know what we're dealing with." He gave a brief summary of the events of the previous days, including the contents of the messages that made up what we now considered some sort of diabolical scavenger hunt. The potential threat to the king made it no longer possible to keep this a secret from anyone who might help. Jeremy looked more alert than I'd seen him in years as he listened, nodding occasionally.

"What can it mean, other than to suggest that someone wants to do the same to Bertie?" Jeremy said. "Or King Edward, I should say. I'll never get used to that."

"I don't agree with your hypothesis," I said. "I did initially, but upon further reflection am convinced the last clue flies in the face of our theory. The writer, through Shakespeare's words, shows us the king stopping his enemies, not being broken by them. And remember that the late queen said the first note was meant as an instruction."

"Yes," Colin said, "but she did not write it herself and may only have been passing on what someone else had given to her. She trusted that I would be able to understand the message and act upon it."

"Hargreaves is right," Jeremy said. "This is a strongly worded threat. How else could we interpret it?"

"I'd say it's more like a message of hope," I said. "The king is safe and strong, even when threatened by traitors."

"And what about that awful sketch on the one you found in the Tower?" Jeremy asked. "What's it meant to be? A lump of some sort?"

"A rock, I believe. I thought it might be the Stone of Scone, but an embarrassingly thorough search of Westminster Abbey proved me wrong on that count. I found no envelope there. I've several other possibilities to investigate." He pressed his lips together. "When I spoke to His Majesty this morning, he expressed the gravest concerns about the entire situation. Scotland Yard are on full alert and shall do their best to prevent any further murders."

Scotland Yard on alert! Well, if I were a

murderer, I'd hardly be quaking in my boots. I doubted very much that the wretched Inspector Gale could prevent much of anything. Prudence, however, cautioned me to keep this opinion to myself. "Richard II and Harold Godwinson are the two other costumes ordered by Mr. Smith," I said. "Richard's was far more lavish, fitting for a king who was so obsessed by fashion. Harold died in battle, so Mr. Carson suggested a suit of armor."

"No one was wearing plate armor at Hastings," Colin said. "A mail hauberk would be more appropriate."

"I don't think our killer is concerned with strict historical accuracy," I said. "He merely wants a visual that will convey the correct information. Any English person, faced with what looks like a slain king with an arrow stuck in his eye would immediately think of poor Harold at Hastings, regardless of his armor."

"Even I know that much," Jeremy said, "although I'm certain I slept through all of history at school."

"At any rate," I continued, "Mr. Carson's customer did not buy plate armor. It would have cost a fortune. Instead, you'll be pleased to know, he got a long shirt that looked something like mail, a surcoat with the cross of St. George on it —"

"The English did not use that in battle until —"

"Now is not the time for a history lesson," I said, wondering how I had never before noticed how well-versed in medieval warfare my husband was. "He also had a helmet with a crown attached. Now, who do we think our killer will go after first? Richard or Harold?"

"Harold would be first chronologically, but given that he staged Henry VI before Edward II, we've no reason to expect he's following a linear timeline," Colin said.

"Harold's death is much more dramatic," Jeremy said. "Didn't poor Richard starve to death in prison at some far-flung castle? How would one even stage that? Completely devoid of visual impact."

"He wouldn't be able to actually starve his victim," I said. "Unless . . . Colin, can you ask Scotland Yard to check missing person reports? It's possible that we could intervene before the unfortunate individual is dead."

"It's unlikely, but worth a look," Colin said.

"Thinking on it, I'd do Richard last," Jeremy said. "Yes, the death itself might not look dramatic, but imagine that portrait of

Richard in Westminster Abbey — the one where he's sitting on the Coronation Chair. If someone managed to bring a dead man, dressed like a king, ermine robes and all, into the Abbey, and left him on that chair . . . that, my friends, would be a scene worth seeing."

"And a clear threat to King Edward," Colin said.

I sighed. "Yes, I see the wisdom in your thinking. So, what do we do?"

"You, Emily, should continue to look for something that connects our two victims," Colin said. "If our murderer is selecting his targets at random, it will make things far more difficult for us."

"I don't believe he is," I said. No, I was convinced that his victims were carefully chosen, and although I could see how one might interpret Colin's messages as threats against the king, I wasn't wholly convinced. Blame my intuition, perhaps, but I felt certain we were missing something of critical importance.

"Find me something that proves a connection," Colin said, his face grim. Then he turned to Jeremy. "And you, Bainbridge, help her however you can. I'm afraid I'll be at Marlborough House most of the time, but you can reach me there should the need arise. Let me make myself very clear about one thing: whatever you do, under no circumstances are you to teach her to drive that motorcar."

I made no comment on Colin's directive to Jeremy. My poor husband felt harassed enough between the murders and trying to keep the king safe, and the irony of the situation was not lost on me. Colin and Bertie had never got along. It would be near impossible to find two men more different. Where Colin was honorable and dignified, the perfect English gentleman, Bertie had been profligate and reckless. I had heard story after story of his scandalous behavior. His stable of mistresses included some of England's most noble women as well as some far more notorious. Rumor said he had forced his wife to attend the performance of one of his lovers in Paris. I believe she was a singer of some sort. But his crimes — if I may call them that — were not limited to the ladies. Bertie's friends were not safe from his excesses. Once, he had poured a bottle of brandy over the head of one of his closest mates while the man chanted, "As Your Royal Highness pleases." His own mother railed against his bad character, even going so far as to keep him from participating in matters of state when he was Prince of Wales.

I could not help but wonder, though, how much of this resulted from a chicken and egg sort of situation. There was no doubt that his mother had blamed him — at least initially — for his father's death. There was some dalliance with a girl in Oxford, and the Prince Consort had marched off to the scene to lecture his wayward son. His stern words, delivered outside in a cold rain, led Albert to catch a chill that brought on the fever that took his life. My mother insisted that the queen never forgave Bertie.

For a man whose sole purpose in life was to be king, it had to be difficult having spent decade after decade after decade doing next to nothing. Cut out of most official business, what was the Prince of Wales to do? A stronger man might have focused on his education, charitable works, or something of equal merit and value, but that was not Bertie's way. Edward the Caresser, as one of our always-creative papers referred to him, had other interests.

Yet, one could not claim him to be all bad. By all accounts, he was kind to his mistresses, even after he had left them, and his loyalty was lauded by all who knew him. Betray him, though, and his wrath could be brutal. It was almost as if he were two different people — one affable and charismatic, the other vindictive and unforgiving.

Not the sort of man my husband would befriend. His role as agent of the Crown put him in a difficult position, working for and protecting a man he did not respect. He would never reveal to the king even a hint of his private feelings, but that would take a toll. He would defend crown and country at any cost. I could only hope the cost would not be too high. And one never knew; after the case at hand was put to bed, the king might no longer require Colin's services. Would he, after all, want to keep on one of his mother's favorites?

After Colin left us to return to Marlborough House, I asked Jeremy to take me back to the East End. Not to the Black Swan, but to the place between St. Clement Danes and Holy Trinity in Lincoln's Inn Fields so that we might inquire about Lizzie Hopman and her mother.

St. Clement's was a gorgeous confection of Sir Christopher Wren's, and Lincoln's Inn had once been a fashionable place, home to the wealthy and powerful. The latter is now the site of the offices of many respectable solicitors and barristers, but the broader area between Holy Trinity and St.

Clement's housed some of London's most destitute citizens. I had thought that I might find something out about Lizzie's mother in either of the churches — she might, after all, have been a parishioner — but neither vicar knew her, nor had any record of her death.

Jeremy, who had once again paid a motley-looking boy to keep an eye on his motorcar, kept a tight grip on my arm as we knocked on door after door, looking for anyone who knew the Hopmans. The slum, depressing and dank, was as awful a place as I'd ever been. Ramshackle buildings in a state of appalling disrepair housed scores more people than they could comfortably hold. Most families could only afford a single room, and even that rent was often too steep for them to afford. It took hours before we came across an elderly woman, Mrs. Bagstock, living in a ground-floor room in a dark and dingy building on Clare Street, who identified herself — her tone rife with irony — as Lizzie's governess.

"The girl needed some education, you see," she said. "Her mother did her best, God rest her soul, but she had nothing, did she? What was she to do? Couldn't find honest work, so did what the desperate among us must. Took in whatever piecework she could — putting together matchboxes, making flowers to decorate the grand gowns and hats your sort of lady wears — but it was never enough even to pay the rent. So she turned to the only other job she could. She left Lizzie with me whenever she was out. Bright little thing, that one. I taught her how to read and thought she might be able to make a go at finding a place in service. But fancy folks like you don't hire girls who can't provide a character, do you?"

"I cannot argue with your tone of judgment," I said. "It is a scandal what happens to the young people of these neighborhoods. Something must be done to give them better opportunities."

"Lizzie tried, you know. She had grand friends. Well, not grand perhaps, but the little Atherton girl, whose parents owned a shop . . . oh, I can't remember where it was exactly . . . she was a clever one, quiet and studious. She and Lizzie were thick as thieves. You couldn't keep them apart."

"Did they remain friends?" I asked.

"What do you think, madam? A shopkeeper's daughter and a common whore?"

The coarseness of her language shocked me, as I suspect she intended. I felt Jeremy tense next to me. "My understanding is that Lizzie had no choice in her profession. I've been told her mother forced her into it," I said.

A look of profound sadness clouded Mrs. Bagstock's wrinkled face. "Her mother had many debts and no way to pay them but one. When she got sick . . . what else could Lizzie do? See her mother thrown out of her home?"

"Where did she live?" Jeremy asked.

"Right upstairs. Most of her colleagues, if you can call them that, lived at the Black Swan, but she had Lizzie, so she had to have a place of her own, didn't she? She died on the settee the two of you are sitting on now. Couldn't take care of herself anymore, so I took her in. Horrible, her last days was. Horrible."

I looked around the squalid little room, despairing at the thought of the poor woman having so little comfort in her final days, and tried not to shudder at finding myself sitting on the very spot where she had died. "Did you see Lizzie after that?" I asked.

"No. She never came back here again. Hated the place, I think, and hated me, because I reminded her of the time when she thought she could have a better life." The old woman crossed to a battered cupboard that hung from the wall and opened the door. She pulled out a book and handed

135

it to me. "This was my Lizzie's. Her favorite book. Don't know where she got it, but I can't help thinking it poisoned her a bit, making her believe things could be better than they were. Still, I wouldn't have wanted to take any bit of hope away from her. Most of the time that's all we have here."

I recognized the volume, John Law's *In Darkest London* (rumors said John Law was the pseudonym for a lady writer of radical background; I wish I could confirm this). It told the story of a captain in the Salvation Army and his work in London's East End. I opened the cover and saw written in a girlish hand *This book belongs to Elizabeth Anne Hopman, who someday won't live in the East End.* Tears smarted in my eyes.

Jeremy cleared his throat. "Mrs. Bagstock, I am dreadfully sorry to have to ask this question, as I fear it may bring you pain, but have you had any recent news of Lizzie?"

"No, sir, I have not. Why, have you heard something?"

He crossed to her, and crouched down next to the rocking chair in which she sat. "I'm afraid she has passed away, Mrs. Bagstock."

"Oh, dear, how very sad. Are you quite sure? I don't believe she was ill?"

"She wasn't. The man she was working for . . ." His voice cracked and trailed.

"Say no more, your grace," Mrs. Bagstock said. "I always knew that Casby fellow was trouble. Have the police got him at least?"

"He was found murdered yesterday."

"He deserved no better," she said. "So why have you two really come here? Not only to bring me this sad news."

"We are seeking justice," I said. "Justice for Lizzie. The more we know about her, the more likely we can achieve it."

Mrs. Bagstock shook her head. "I'll tell you anything you'd like, but you should know that in these parts, there's no such thing as justice."

14
1415

Cecily spent the better part of the next day in the chapel, praying for guidance. She feared for Adeline and the dangerous path the lady was on, but she had no idea how to dissuade her from it. By the time the bells chimed six o'clock, her knees were aching and she had no more clarity than when she'd entered its arched doorway that morning for mass. She struggled to her feet and turned to leave, surprised to see that she wasn't alone.

A young priest she did not recognize was standing against the back wall, near the entrance. Cecily felt suddenly self-conscious and wished she could exit without passing him, but the warm smile on his face eased her concerns.

"Your husband told me of your piety, but I assumed he exaggerated, as new bridegrooms have a tendency to do," the man said. "I am Father Simon Dunsford. William's father and mine were best friends, so he and I all but grew up together."

"Yet chose very different courses in life." Cecily regretted the words the instant she had spoken them, but Father Simon only laughed.

"Indeed, we did. I'm the younger son and was always destined for the church, but that doesn't mean I wouldn't be twice the man-at-arms he is if I'd gone a different way. When he returns from France, ask him how many times I bettered him with a sword."

"I'm not sure such a query would endear me to him."

Cecily's sweet smile charmed Father Simon. Truly, his friend was lucky in his choice of wife. "William has always enjoyed good-natured teasing. You will discover that soon enough."

"I shall give your advice serious consideration," she said. The bottom of his black cassock showed evidence of dust from the road; he must have only just arrived at the estate. "What brings you to Sussex?"

"You," he replied. "William asked me to call in during his absence and see if you were in need of anything, be it spiritual consolation or something more mundane."

"Baron Esterby and Adeline have been most kind to take me into their household.

I am fortunate to have such generous friends." She was not about to air her problems to a stranger.

Father Simon looked into her eyes and stood quiet for some time. "Yet you look troubled."

"It is only that I did not sleep well last night and am worried about William. They are fighting at Harfleur."

"Yes, I know." He was still staring directly at her. His eyes, a soft cornflower blue, could have coaxed a confidence from nearly anyone if he let them, but coaxing was not his goal. "The baroness tells me you have been at prayer since morning."

"Is it unnatural to fear for one's husband when he is at war?" Cecily asked.

"Not at all," Father Simon replied, his clear tenor soothing. "Nor is it unnatural to have concerns, fears, and anxiety separate from those fears, even in times of war. I am here at William's request to be your friend, Cecily, and your confessor, should you wish."

"You don't assume the baron's priest has already filled the role?" Cecily asked, laughter creeping into her voice as she considered the baron's stern priest.

"You're a better person than I if he doesn't terrify you," Father Simon said, smiling. "I look forward to seeing you at supper tonight."

How long he kept fighting, William did not know. He pressed forward, on and on, ignoring the arrow still in his cheek. He had broken the shaft as close to the skin as he could so that it would not deter him. The bodkins dipped in pitch and set aflame, which the English archers had fired at the start of the day's fighting, had done their work, and thick smoke still hung over the enemy's defenses. As more and more men-at-arms attacked, the French fell back, until King Henry's army had forced them once again inside the city walls. As darkness fell and the fighting stopped, the driving energy that had kept William upright slowed, and it felt as if his blood had grown thick. He staggered back to camp, where he collapsed, unconscious, not six feet in front of the king, who, still in armor covered with blood and dirt, was walking with his brothers.

"Someone attend to this man," Henry shouted, kneeling beside the soldier. The arrow in the man's cheek had struck in nearly the same place that Henry had been wounded years ago at Shrewsbury, when he was Prince of Wales.

The Duke of Gloucester, who had been

standing behind his brother the king, stepped forward. "He is Sir William Hargrave, one of my bravest and most skilled men-at-arms. I saw him take that arrow in the morning. He never stopped fighting, despite the wound."

"I know the pain — and danger — that comes with such an injury," Henry said. "Call for my physician. He shall perform the necessary surgery."

15
1901

Jeremy and I were both subdued on the drive back to Park Lane, Mrs. Bagstock's story of Lizzie's life sitting heavy with both of us. He refused my invitation to come inside for a cup of tea and drove off with a profound look of sadness about him. I went up the steps to the house craving the quiet comfort of my library and a pot of Earl Grey, but the moment Davis opened the door I knew it was not to be.

Henry's voice accosted me from above the instant I crossed the threshold. He was whooping in the manner of a Red Indian and had flung his leg over the bannister, ready to slide down, despite Nanny's admonitions that he stop. Richard and Tom were hanging back, as if waiting to see what their brother would do next. Ailouros, our cat, whom I had adopted after finding him in Nice while catching a particularly vile murderess and named for his ancient Greek ancestors, was seated at the top of the steps, a look of disdain on his face.

"Mama!" Henry shoved back and careened down the bannister. Davis, without blinking, caught him at the bottom and placed him gently on the floor. The little boy flung his arms around my knees. I bent over and kissed his head, mussing his golden hair.

Nanny took the other boys by the hands and led them down the stairs, where they each greeted me with a bow and a kiss.

"That, Henry, is how little gentlemen behave." I had a hard time being stern in the face of his unbridled enthusiasm.

"I'm not a little gentleman," my wayward son replied. "I'm a Red Indian here to kidnap you and take you to my fort. Where's Papa? He'll help me, I'm sure." This explained the smudges of paint on his cheeks and the deplorable state of his clothes. Henry seemed to attract dirt the way a magnet pulls in shavings of iron.

"You're not to trouble your mother," Nanny said. She looked even older than when I'd left Anglemore Park for the queen's funeral less than a week ago, and I had no doubt Henry was the cause. Nonetheless, I knew her to be more than capable of managing the boys. She would have lectured me if I suggested she might require even the slightest assistance, and as she had raised Colin and his brother, William, with spectacular results, I saw no reason to doubt her on any count.

"It's perfectly fine, Nanny," I said. "Why don't I take them into the library for tea and jam sandwiches while you have a rest? You must be tired from the journey."

"I am never tired, Lady Emily," she said. "But I could use the time to get the boys' things in order in the nursery." She turned to Henry. "Do not think, young man, I will forget that you disobeyed me. We shall discuss it after you have your tea."

Henry squirmed, but his face was expressionless. I did not envy him the conversation he would have with Nanny; she could be very fierce. That said, he deserved whatever scolding he got. I knew how naughty he was.

Davis disappeared downstairs to direct Cook to prepare our tea and I took the boys to the library. Richard immediately went to his father's desk, sat down (looking very small in the chair), and opened the book Colin had left on top. All the boys had started to read at a shockingly early age, but Richard took the most pleasure in it. The tome he perused was a history of medieval

England I knew to be written in a dry, academic style. I did not expect he would find much to recommend it. Tom came over to me quietly and took my hand.

"I've missed you very much, Mama."

I pulled him close and embraced him. "And I, you."

"You'll wish you were missing me after I've taken you prisoner!" Henry shouted as he leapt on top of my desk. He was brandishing a stick that he had tried to fashion into a bow with a piece of dingy string. I wondered where he had hidden it, as I hadn't spotted any sign of it when Nanny was present.

"I shouldn't draw that bow and point it at your mother," Colin said, entering the room. "Her fighting skills are not to be sneered at and I doubt you'd want so formidable an enemy."

"Papa!" the boys shouted almost in unison and raced toward him. He grinned at me and gathered them in his arms.

"Can she really fight, Papa?" Henry asked. "Really?"

"You'd have no better soldier at your side," Colin said, lifting him down from my desk.

I rolled my eyes. "You shouldn't encourage him."

"I'm a Red Indian and require no encouragement," Henry said. "I cannot be stopped."

"You've been at Montagu Manor again, haven't you?" Colin asked. It was the house nearest to ours in Derbyshire, occupied by dear friends. The fact that Lord Montagu employed a Red Indian as his valet had solidified Henry's unshakable admiration for the man, although it was clear the boy held the valet in higher esteem than he did the marquess.

"I want a tent like his, Papa, please."

"You'd be too cold in the winter, but we can discuss it again in the summer, when the weather is better."

Davis arrived with the tea trolley and soon we were happily nestled in a scene of domestic bliss. Richard peppered Colin with questions about the medieval kings — apparently, he had not been put off by the academic nature of the history on his father's desk — and Tom, who always behaved like a perfect gentleman, inquired after our health and engaged us in delightful conversation about the pleasures of country life. Henry, who I'd had to stop from stabbing his tea sandwiches — he was wielding a butter knife as if it were a spear — was sitting quietly now, having eaten enough to feed seven boys of good appetite.

Tea finished, Colin rang for Davis. "I hate to send you upstairs, but Nanny will have my hide if I make you late for your baths," he said.

"Baths?" Henry balked. "We never bathe until at least —"

"It's the perfect time for a bath," I said. "Go upstairs, all of you. We'll see you again before bed." It was not like Colin to ever send the boys to the nursery, and even more unlikely for him to suggest they would take baths in the middle of the afternoon. Delighted as he had been to see them when he arrived home, I had not missed the look of strain in his eyes.

"Have Scotland Yard uncovered any new information?" I asked him, handing him a glass of whisky.

"No," he said. "They've no leads pertaining to either murder. You?"

I updated him on my discoveries. "Revenge is the obvious motive for Casby's murder. He was the worst sort of man and Lizzie the kind of girl who would have inspired any honorable man to defend — or avenge — her."

"Have we any reason to believe she had an acquaintance with any honorable men?"

"No," I admitted.

"I feel so bloody useless — forgive me, my dear." He had risen from his seat and started to pace. "We have every reason to expect two more murders, and I've no way to stop them."

"Let's consider the scene of the first. I am still at a loss to understand how anyone could bring a body into the Tower of London without someone seeing something. Have the police interviewed everyone there? The wives of the guards? The ticket-takers? The —"

"The ticket-takers weren't there that day. The Tower was closed, remember. As for the wives, I saw no mention in the reports of anyone other than the guards themselves being questioned."

"That's where we need to go next, then," I said. "They live in the Tower, but they don't work there. The guards are each charged with particular tasks and duties; their wives, having no such occupation, are free to notice anything."

We called for the carriage and pulled on our coats. While I will privately admit that the carriage provided a more comfortable ride than Jeremy's Daimler, I still preferred the thrill of the motorcar. Yet this was not the appropriate time to broach the subject of purchasing one. Colin was in no mood for frivolous discussion. A cold rain had started by the time we reached the Tower, and the sun was slipping toward the horizon. The medieval fortress, squared next to the mighty Thames, was seen at its best advantage in this sort of weather. Lights from the windows flickered on the slick cobbles paving the streets, and one could almost imagine an armored knight inside William's White Tower preparing for battle.

Colin had a few quick words with the yeoman warder who greeted us as we breezed through Lion Gate. With a quick nod, he led us through the passage next to the Bloody Tower and onto Tower Green, where the Queen's House (which I suppose we ought now refer to as the King's House), built in the sixteenth century, stood across from the neatly trimmed grass. Render had long since covered its original half-timbered façade, and I regretted the change. It looked out of place amongst the sturdy, stone towers. The warder knocked on the door, and soon we were sitting in a pleasant parlor, accepting tea from the Lieutenant of the Tower's wife, Lady Anna Stirling. She was a charming hostess and, after expressing horror at the murdered body that had been left in Wakefield Tower, offered to introduce us to any and all of the other wives. More families lived in the Tower than I realized, and it was clear that speaking to them would be an enormous undertaking. This was where Lady Anna proved a more than capable assistant.

"My husband and I anticipated that some-one among the Tower residents might have noticed something of use that day, so he asked those with information to come forward," she said. "We have, of course, shared this with Scotland Yard, but they did not think any of it worth further investigation."

"Did you think any of it worth further investigation, Lady Anna?" I asked.

"Yes, I did," she replied. "One of the yeoman warder's wives, Mrs. Rillington, noticed a boat near Traitors' Gate early that morning, before the sun rose."

"But there is no access to the interior of the Tower from the river," I said.

"No, yet it is unusual to see someone at that time in that place. I would be delighted to take you to her."

St. Thomas's Tower, built by Edward I and later named for the martyred Thomas Becket, Archbishop of Canterbury, loomed above Traitors' Gate. As I followed Lady Anna up the winding stone stairs that led to Mrs. Rillington's home, I wondered what it would be like to live in such a structure. Darnley House, where I spent most of my youth, was comparatively modern, built mostly in the seventeenth century, and although Anglemore Park had sections that went back to the fifteenth century, it did not evoke history so strongly as the Tower of London. Imagine, if you will, looking out the window of your sitting room to see the Thames lapping up against the stones of Traitors' Gate! Would you suspect every noise heard under cover of night to be the restless ghost of some unfortunate soul imprisoned in this place? The very thought gave me the most delicious chills.

Mrs. Rillington, a pleasant middle-aged woman with bright eyes and hair styled in a manner popular during my childhood, greeted us warmly and welcomed us into her modest home. She might live in a castle, but tower rooms with no central heating and thick stone walls are far from cozy. She'd hung beautiful tapestries on either side of her windows, and a soft carpet underfoot gave the room a touch of color and warmth. It may seem incongruous to see a modern chintz divan in the middle of a medieval room, but what else is there to do? One must be comfortable at home. Lady Anna explained the reason for our visit, and Mrs.

Rillington was happy to oblige.

"It was quite odd, you see," she began. "I hadn't slept well that night. I suppose I had been affected by the queen's death, as we all were. I had decided not to try to see the funeral procession, as I knew the crush of people would be too much for me. Perhaps I was regretting that decision, or perhaps I was troubled by the loss of our monarch, but I sat up in bed at four o'clock in the morning, wide awake and unable to go back to sleep. Not wanting to disturb my husband, who hadn't come off watch until nearly two o'clock, I slipped out of our room and made myself a cup of tea. I tried to read for a while, but couldn't concentrate."

"Did you hear anything out of the ordinary?" Colin asked.

"I'm afraid, Mr. Hargreaves, that I wouldn't know what sounds are ordinary at that time of the morning. Furthermore, one can't hear much through these walls. They are far too thick! When the sun showed signs of rising, I decided to go for a little walk, just on the walls, you see."

"I can see the appeal," I murmured and went to her narrow front window. Astonishing to have such a view, and eerie to think of Traitors' Gate, just below.

"I was about to get my coat when I noticed something, just from the corner of my eye," she said. "It was a small vessel, an ordinary rowboat, with no distinguishing characteristics. I wondered who would be on the river so early — obviously, this wasn't a fishing boat — and then noticed that no one was in it."

"You're quite sure?" Colin asked.

"There is no question of it," she said. "It was most peculiar. I stood and watched for some time, but nothing else happened."

"Was the boat tied to anything?" I asked.

"Not that I could see," she said, "but the outer wall makes it difficult to tell."

"I want to be sure I'm clear," Colin said. "The craft was floating beyond the outer wall, far enough away that you could see it in its entirety?"

"Yes, just about," Mrs. Rillington said. "It occasionally bobbed closer, compromising my view."

"But you never saw anyone or anything in it?" Colin asked.

"That's right."

"What happened then?" I asked.

She sighed. "I'm afraid that's where my story becomes anticlimactic. The boat had distracted me from taking a walk, and by then I had started to feel drowsy again. I fell asleep on the divan. When I woke up, the boat was gone."

"Do you recall what time it was when you first saw it? And then when you fell asleep and woke?" Colin asked.

"I know the sun rose around half-seven," she said. "But the sky would have started brightening before then. I suppose it could have been as early as half-six, but I'm not sure. I don't know when I fell asleep, but I woke up a little before eight."

"I am most grateful that you took such careful notice of what was going on around you," Colin said. "Have you seen anything else unusual over the course of the past few weeks? Anyone coming or going whom you did not recognize?"

Mrs. Rillington shook her head. "No, life is quite ordinary in the Tower. More or less the same, day in and day out."

I found this statement a crushing disappointment, but I suppose one can get used to anything. "Have any of your neighbors or friends introduced you to new acquaintances? Someone who has, perhaps, started coming around to call on them recently?"

"No, Lady Emily, I have not," she said. "And at any rate, our visitors sign in and out at the gate. Not a good way to gain entrance to the Tower if one were bent on a nefarious errand." Her eyes glimmered just a bit, and I wondered if she shared my fondness for sensational fiction.

"What about secret passages?" I asked.

"There seem to be an infinite number of them," Lady Anna said. "Most aren't so secret any longer, of course. Didn't one of the other wives put together a little map of them?"

Mrs. Rillington nodded. "It was several years ago, I believe, and her husband is not stationed here any longer. I didn't pay much attention at the time, but if you'd like, Lady Emily, I can hunt down a copy and send it to you."

I thanked her profusely and we took our leave. Lady Anna reiterated her willingness to help us in any way possible and walked us back to Lion Gate. The rain had turned to sleet and then to snow and a vicious wind attacked us from the Thames. I expected Colin to bundle me into the carriage and take me home, but instead he took my hand and started for the embankment.

"We need to find a boat."

16
1415

Cecily dressed for the evening meal with extra care that night, not because she was desirous of impressing Father Simon, but because she wanted him to look kindly on her and have something pleasant to report back to William. The priest's arrival had distracted her from her concerns about Adeline, but only briefly, and before she went down to the hall to meet the others, she consulted the all-knowing Christine de Pizan for advice. She had debated consulting Father Simon. He was a priest, after all, who had offered his services as a confessor, and as he was one of William's dearest friends, she knew him to be trustworthy. But section twenty-six of *The Treasure of the City of Ladies,* titled *Of the young high-born lady who wants to plunge into a foolish love affair, and the instruction that Prudence gives to her chaperone,* guided her otherwise:

But she should not mention this situation for anything because of the perils and evils that could ensue from it. For whoever has a conscience and common sense ought indeed to dread making a report of such things to the husband or to friends or to anyone at all.

Of course, Cecily was not Adeline's chaperone. She was young and in a position that carried with it no power. Did this alter the situation significantly enough that she might reach out to someone else for aid and assistance? She closed the book and opened it again.

The second cause that gives rise to slander is a wrong impression formed in something like the following manner: one person will have the idea that another is bad or at fault in something or in everything . . . on the flimsiest grounds she will misjudge and slander . . .

Was this what she was doing? Misjudging Adeline, who, in the past few days, had begun to treat her with more kindness? Cecily had witnessed no sin in the forest. Adeline and Gabrieli were standing close, but not touching. It was Cecily who leapt to the conclusion — erroneous, she hoped — that there was some strong emotion between the two.

But what of her prayer? Of the clear feeling that her divine purpose was to protect Adeline? Could she have misinterpreted that experience? Unsure of what to think, let alone what to do, she debated telling her friend a headache had come on and that she would not be down to dine. But she recognized the scheme for what it was: cowardice. She would go to the hall, she would eat, she might even dance, but she would not let down her guard. If she witnessed anything that might threaten Adeline's reputation, she would intervene without hesitation. She would not, however, go looking for trouble.

She took her seat at the high table, Father Simon between her and Adeline. Gabrieli was at a lower table, but nearby. He paid no attention to his host's wife, and Cecily almost wondered if what she thought she had seen in the woods was nothing but a mirage. She had not, however, forgot the divine bargain she had made. She would keep Adeline on a righteous path, and God would protect her husband in France.

Thomas Morestede had not operated on the future king after he'd been wounded at Shrewsbury; his predecessor, John Bradmore, had that honor and more. He had developed the instrument necessary to remove the arrowhead buried in young Henry's cheek. But Morestede was capable of performing the operation; as a young man, he had watched Bradmore at work, holding his breath with wonder and fear as he waited to see if the physician's procedure would work. Never would he forget that miraculous day. Here, in France, he had tended to many battle wounds, but even more illness. He'd sent the king's brother the Duke of Clarence back to England only a few days earlier, as His Grace was suffering terribly from the bloody flux. The patient lying before him now, William Hargrave, gave him the opportunity to serve the king in a manner that might bring about a satisfying result in a more expedient manner. If the operation succeeded. Morestede said a silent prayer for the man-at-arms upon whom he was about to operate.

Hargrave's injury, though in the same place as that the king had received, was not so deep. The knight's recovery would be neither so agonizing nor so long as his sovereign's. Morestede worked carefully, extracting the arrowhead using the tongs and screw of Bradmore's invention. He cleansed the wound with wine and packed it with a mixture of flax soaked in a cleansing ointment, along with barley, bread, flour, and turpentine. The dressing would need to be changed regularly, but if infection didn't set in, Hargrave would make a good recovery.

But infection was rampant in a place like Harfleur, and the king's physician wouldn't be able to focus on one man's treatment. There was hope, though, that Sir William Hargrave would be left with nothing more than a scar that mimicked his king's and stories of the glorious battle that brought it.

17
1901

Colin's dash toward the embankment reminded me of the one I'd made previously, when I'd hired a ratty individual to take me out on the Thames during our first trip to the Tower. Sure enough, we were able to locate the same man with little effort. So far as I could tell, he had not moved from the spot on the dock where he'd tied his sad little boat when I'd last seen him. If he remembered me, he showed no sign of it.

I had assumed Colin wanted to take the boat to the approximate location where Mrs. Rillington had seen one moored the morning of the murder, but now I realized that we also could be looking at the very boat used by the heinous killer. Could that explain why the man had balked when I had asked him to take me to Traitors' Gate? Had he witnessed a gruesome scene that had haunted him ever since? Would he see we were trustworthy and that he could confide in us?

The astute reader may wonder that I did not suspect the man himself of the crime. I could not imagine any scenario in which an individual who exhibited so little gumption and who so well emulated a sloth could be actively involved in such a violent death. Furthermore, even an idiot, after committing such an act, would know better than to remain at the scene of the crime day after day. Unless, of course, that was part of his cunning plan, designed to throw suspicion from him. Further scrutiny of the man confirmed my original judgment; cunning was not in his nature, and he was no murderer.

Which is not to say he was of no use. Someone had hired his boat the night before the queen's funeral. He was paid half a crown and promised the vessel would be returned no later than three o'clock the next afternoon. He'd taken the money, given to him in advance, and slunk off to watch the funeral procession, staking out a position along the route not far from Buckingham Palace. He returned to his usual spot at a bit after one o'clock and found his boat already there. A few hours later, I had descended upon him.

I revisited every detail of that first trip I took with him, but must admit with regret that I had paid very little attention to the boat itself. There might have been some scrap of evidence still in it, and I had not even thought to look. I chided myself for the mistake, but knew self-recrimination would serve no purpose. I took Colin's hand as he helped me into the sad little vessel, and once again its owner rowed toward Traitors' Gate.

With the tide high, one could get right up to the wall where the water entrance to the Tower had been bricked up. Even so, a person would gain very little by making this approach. He would still have to scale the outer wall of the Tower — presumably while carrying a body — and then make his way, unseen, across the inner pavement and into Wakefield Tower. I looked at my husband and could tell from the saturnine expression on his handsome face that we were of one mind: consumed with frustration.

"I'm quite desperate for Mrs. Rillington to send us that map," I said, after the boatman had returned us to the pier. "I'm convinced it will help us enormously."

"What have you been reading lately?" Colin asked. "Malory? Sir Walter Scott? Perhaps we could find the Thames equivalent of the Lady of the Lake and ask if she noticed anything suspicious. Forgive me, my dear. I'm not ordinarily so easily flustered. But this case . . ."

I understood what troubled him. The king was under threat, and the responsibility of protecting him fell on Colin's broad — and, if I may say so, most extraordinarily capable — shoulders. There was no one in the Empire better suited to the job, but pointing that out would only put more pressure on him.

"Dismiss the idea if you'd like, but what would be a superior way to bring a body into the Tower than through a secret passage?" I asked.

"I know what it is — you've been reading William Harrison Ainsworth's ridiculous historical romance, *The Tower of London,* haven't you?"

"It's a thoroughly diverting book," I said, "and has no bearing whatsoever on my approach to this case. It's about Lady Jane Grey, after all, not Henry VI. Although . . ."

"You're about to make an appalling suggestion, aren't you?" he asked.

"We could go back to the Tower and persuade some of the yeoman warders not on duty to take us to their private pub inside. After plying them with ale, we would have no trouble persuading them to show us all the hidden —"

"No. No, Emily. We are not going to do any such thing. There were secret passages in the Tower, but none remain undiscovered. It's unlikely Mrs. Rillington's map will prove useful in the least. And don't you think the guards would already have mentioned any that could prove pertinent to the crime at hand?"

"How can you be so confident none remain undiscovered? Or discovered only by our murderer?" I frowned. "Modern man does not know everything. It's entirely possible there are tunnels forgot for centuries."

"If they're forgot, it's probably because they were bricked up ages ago, and hence, like Traitors' Gate, could have been of no use to our miscreant."

We had been walking along the embankment and stopped now, partway along the outside wall of the Tower in the direction of Tower Bridge. The snow had turned back to rain, but only a light mist. The golden reflection of the street lamps danced on the wet pavement, and the first hints of a freezing fog began to form over the Thames.

Colin took me in his arms. "You are even more stunning than usual in this light. I rather wish I were a medieval knight and could throw you over my shoulder and take you to the Tower." He kissed me, his lips soft. The rain started coming harder now, and he pulled me closer to him, his kisses more urgent. "I think I should get you home, unless you've solid knowledge of a secret passage that will take us to a hitherto undiscovered room in the Tower with a roaring fire and various, er, shall we say, material comforts."

"Home."

It was all I could manage to say. He had me thoroughly distracted.

I slept far later than I intended the following morning, but felt more refreshed than I had in weeks. Connubial bliss has that effect on me. Colin was nowhere to be found, but he had left for me on his pillow a note, rolled like a scroll and tied with a red ribbon:

Hear my soul speak. Of the very instant that I saw you, Did my heart fly at your service . . .

He always did prefer Shakespeare to all other poetry. With a smile, I climbed out of bed and rang for my maid. Deliciously addled or not, I had work to do.

My first task was to return to the Black Swan, this time without Jeremy, who I feared might come to fisticuffs with the establishment's new proprietor if he faced him again. I wanted to speak to Mary. Ideally, somewhere away from her place of work.

The same group of boys I'd seen before was hanging around in the street when I arrived in my carriage. They recognized me and lamented that I had not come in the motorcar. No person — particularly no mother — could help but feel a crushing pain in her heart at the sight of these children. Their clothes were tattered and dirty, their boots full of holes, and their coats entirely inadequate for the weather.

"Shouldn't you be in school?" I asked.

"We work, ma'am," the tallest said. "Too old for school."

I set a skeptical eye on the smallest of the group. "How old are you?"

"I'm eight," he said with a gap-toothed smile. One of the older boys smacked him in the arm.

"You're thirteen, remember?"

"But —"

"Thirteen or she'll send you off to school. You don't want that, do you?"

"No, I imagine he wouldn't," I said. "Who

would prefer a well-heated school and perhaps even a hot dinner to loitering here with you lot?"

"We're with the King's Boys, ma'am, and there's no better life to be had," the tall one said. "We're looked after proper and we can do anything we want."

"Is that so?" I asked. "I saw a bakery down the road. Why don't you go get yourselves something to eat?" I gave them a few coins, knowing this paltry assistance was nowhere near enough to make a real difference in their lives. They scattered, shouting thanks, and ran toward the shop. With a sigh, I marched into the Black Swan and demanded to speak to Mary.

Mr. Brown, who stood intimidatingly close to me, glowered. "You ought to take better care, Lady Emily. Your sort can wind up in a heap of trouble in this neighborhood. I'll get Mary for you, but I don't want to see you here again."

Mary appeared from the back room in a state of dishabille, a ratty dressing gown pulled around her shoulders. I told her I wanted to take her to lunch and that I would wait while she dressed.

"My time is quite valuable, Lady Emily," she said as she started upstairs. "I don't waste it dining with ladies."

"You will be compensated adequately," I said. When she came back down, she was wearing a catastrophically low-cut gown and more rouge than I would have thought existed in all of London. I made no comment. Obviously, she meant to goad me, and I would not fall prey to her tricks. Instead, I directed her to my carriage and asked the driver to take us to Harrods. My plan had been to go to a restaurant, so that she might be around civilized people and have a decent meal, but I feared the treatment she would receive because of her appearance — accompanied by disparaging looks and comments — would not help me further my cause.

"I don't like shopping," she said, when we had reached the store in Brompton. I ignored her and took her inside, marching her to the ladies clothing department, where, with the aid of a horrified shop assistant, I selected for her a modest dress of dark green serge that flattered her complexion. I then chose a pair of sturdy, practical boots, a warm wool overcoat, leather gloves, and a jaunty little hat that was more fashionable than strictly necessary. There is never an acceptable reason to resist a good hat.

Despite her protests, I rubbed the rouge off her cheeks with my handkerchief and we returned to the carriage, alighting from it at Brown's Hotel in Albemarle Street. After securing a table in the establishment's elegant restaurant, I studied my companion, who had fallen uncharacteristically quiet after we entered the hotel.

"No one's staring at me," she said, when I prodded her as to the cause of this change.

"That's because you aren't drawing attention to yourself by being deliberately provocative," I said. "I am no supporter of many of the rules of our society and firmly believe that people should be judged on their worth rather than their appearance, but it cannot be argued that observing some social mores does make one's life rather easier."

"The dress is nice," she said. "I'm sorry I barked at the shop assistant and said it looked like something a nun would wear. I've never even seen a nun."

"I accept your apology," I said. "As you know, I've brought you here to talk about Lizzie. From what little I've already heard about her, it is clear she did not want the life she had."

"She never put on airs, though," Mary said, wolfing down the soup a waiter had placed in front of her. "Truth be told none of us wants that life, but Lizzie, she tried not to live it. She could read, you know,

171

and almost got a job in service."

"So I've been told. Did she have any regular clients who seemed particularly attached to her?"

"Not really. In the beginning, of course, she caused quite a stir. You know what I mean, right? There's always a market for that." I had a fairly clear idea of what she meant and was utterly horrified at the thought. "But after that, she settled in like the rest of us. We all have some regulars, but no one special."

"No one who might have blamed Casby for her death?"

"No," she said.

"Did Lizzie have many friends?" I asked.

"At first none of us warmed to her. She was quiet and didn't much like a drink, but eventually we realized she wasn't trying to act better than us. She just didn't know what to do. Really, though, she should have. Her mother could've given her some guidance. She was a popular one, always —" She stopped. "Well, I doubt you're interested in those sorts of details. Still, if you're going to bring your girl into the business, you'd think you'd teach her how to navigate things."

I could feel color rushing to my cheeks and urged Mary to speak at a lower volume.

"So none of the rest of you were close to her?"

"I wouldn't say any of us is close to anyone. You can't trust people, you know. Everyone wants something, and nobody's going to look out for you but yourself."

She said this so matter-of-factly it was heartbreaking. "Did Lizzie have friends outside of the Black Swan? People she had known before? Someone whose surname was Atherton?"

"Atherton?" Mary wrinkled her nose. "Never heard her talk about anyone called that. There was some bloke, Ned, who she was quite fond of. He wasn't a customer, mind you, but someone who knew her from before. She used to take walks with him on Sundays when she first came to us, but he hasn't come around for ages."

"Can you recall his surname?" I asked.

She held her fork with her fist and tapped its handle on the table. "Traddles, I think, but I can't be sure. I hear a lot of names, you know."

"And what about you, Mary? I can't believe the Black Swan is where you've always dreamed of being. Do you want a better life?"

"Is this when you play noble guardian angel and try to rescue me from my life of vice? You great ladies like that sort of thing, don't you?"

"I don't want to play anything," I said. "But if you want a different sort of life, I would gladly help you find it."

"Thank you, but I'm quite content where I am," she said. The waiter returned to put a plate of roast beef and potatoes in front of her. I let her eat in silence, feeling altogether useless. What good was one decent meal and a new dress? I'd done even less for the boys in Ratcliffe Highway. The sensation of being overwhelmed by the poverty in which so many in London lived was not new to me, but I would never grow accustomed to it.

"Can you read, Mary?" I asked.

"No, and I don't want to," she said. "Seems like a waste of time."

I would have liked to have given her any number of things to read — the novel *The Story of an African Farm* sprang to mind — something unconventional and shocking that might give her the idea that there were, in fact, other ways to live and that women like her weren't the only ones looking for a better existence.

Her plate empty, she pushed it away from her. "I don't want you to think I'm not grateful for what you're doing. I appreciate it, in my way. But you have to understand

I'm comfortable where I am and I don't see a better way forward. If I remember anything else about Lizzie, I'll get in touch if you tell me how. But otherwise, there's nothing more to be done."

The fact that she said she didn't see a better way forward told me that if she did, things might be very different for her. I would not push her, but would leave open every door and window I could find for her. I pulled a calling card out of the silver case in my handbag and gave it to her. "You can come to me, anytime, day or night," I said. "You've been more helpful than I think you know. Lizzie had quite a friend in you."

18
1415

Early reports said that Harfleur had fallen to the king's army, but no detailed news had come yet from France. The baron, who had been short with everyone lately, distracted and irritated, didn't tell Cecily any of this. She learned it from Father Simon. A calm came over her as she listened to him, and she began to believe that if something dreadful had befallen her husband, she would be able to sense it.

She was starting a new project, a large embroidered wall covering, and was sitting at a table in Adeline's parlor sketching out the design — a group of ladies in a flower-filled garden, one of them holding a book and reading to the others — when Dario Gabrieli came and sat next to her. She bristled and scooted away from him on the bench.

"I do hope, Lady Cecily, that the way I spoke to you when I first arrived here did not put you off so much that we cannot be friends. I have conducted myself as a nobleman and would never dream of forcing my attentions on any lady. Yet I cannot help but notice how you have avoided me ever since. Hence, I apologize for offending your delicate sensibilities and pray you can find it in your heart to forgive me."

"There is nothing to forgive," Cecily said, relieved at his words. "I understand the precepts of courtly love and know better than to take offense at them. They are not, however, something that interests or entices me. Your friendship, Signor Gabrieli, I should very much welcome."

His smile lit up his entire face. There was no denying the beauty in his well-formed features. No wonder all the ladies on the estate vied for his attention. Adeline, who had been watching the exchange between the troubadour and her friend, approached the pair. He shot her a meaningful look as she stepped toward them and burst into joyful laughter. "It is all better now, is it?" she asked. "I have hoped for nothing else. Now my two closest friends will no longer be enemies."

"We were never enemies," Cecily said, wondering why Adeline would have drawn this conclusion. More astonishing was that she referred to Cecily as a close friend.

"Go, go, Dario," Adeline said, shooing him away. "We ladies must talk privately. There is much to discuss." He scuttled off, but not before kissing their hands. Adeline lowered herself onto the bench next to Cecily. "You are not angry at me, are you, my dear? I couldn't bear it if you were. But I saw how you and Dario flirted when he first arrived and could not help but notice when it ended badly. It's better to be friends again, though, isn't it?"

"I never flirted with him," Cecily said. "He —"

"I was a witness to those first overtures he made," Adeline said. "You followed the pattern set out by Capellanus so devotedly. I did not know you had read his work."

"I've read it, of course, we all have," Cecily said. "But it has never served as a guide for me."

"You need not worry," Adeline said. "I shall never reveal your secret to anyone and William shall never be the wiser. Do be careful around Father Simon, though. I believe he was sent to keep a careful eye on you. Had you given your husband cause to suspect your fidelity before he left for France?"

"I would never do any such thing," Cecily

said, putting down her pencil and feeling her heartbeat quicken. "I want only to be a devoted wife and to —"

Adeline put an arm around her shoulder. "You need not explain to me. I'm your oldest friend. I've known you your entire life. There's no one you can better trust, just as there is no one I can better trust than you. Come now. I'm planning disguises for tomorrow night. Will you join me in selecting who should wear what?"

Cecily nodded in answer and followed Adeline, but could hardly pay attention to anything around her. Something felt wrong, very wrong, as if she were being played for a fool, but she couldn't quite figure out why anyone — even Adeline — would do such a thing. She might have dismissed the notion altogether had she not, as they left the parlor, noticed Gabrieli slip a piece of paper into Adeline's hand.

If William's wound troubled him, he showed no sign of it. As soon as possible after the king's physician had extracted the arrow from his face, he was back with his fellow men-at-arms, ready to march across France. For that seemed to be the king's plan. Harfleur had surrendered, yes — Henry had sat on a magnificent throne and accepted the keys to the city — but a single victory was not enough to win all of France, and the king had no intention of returning to England without the prize he came for. The majesty with which he had taken control of the city would leave the citizens in no doubt of his power. He alone could offer and revoke mercy. He alone should rule France. And, in that vein, he wrote to the dauphin, challenging him to trial by combat, the victor winning the crown of France.

The dauphin never replied, proving to William and his compatriots that the man was nothing but a common coward, while King Henry was a model of chivalric honor. What better way to resolve the question of the throne? The soldiers might not comprehend the intricacies of Salic law, but they needed no other proof that their king had the divine right to rule.

But there was no trial by combat. Henry could not force the challenge and, hence, could not secure the crown of France in that way. Around him, he saw that the tattered remains of his army left much to be desired. The illness that had plagued them during the siege had thinned the ranks and had not yet run its course. Men continued to die daily. The king had no choice but to send home the sick and the weak, leaving him with a much-reduced force. Undaunted, he ordered those strong enough to march with him to Calais.

William heard grumblings that the king's advisors did not approve of this decision. They believed their numbers were too small to face the French. But Henry would brook no criticism and insisted they push forward. He told his men to prepare for an eight-day march and to abandon all superfluous supplies. They must travel quick and light. And then he told them they must behave with honor. Nothing was to be stolen, no woman would be violated. They would not destroy the land they crossed. The French army was his enemy, not the French people.

The latter he would govern; the former he would gladly annihilate.

19
1901

I admit to being frustrated by my lack of success with reforming Mary, but the knowledge that two more murders might happen at any time prevented me from brooding. All too aware that the wretched Inspector Gale and his colleagues at Scotland Yard were unwilling to share information with me, I embarked on an unorthodox method of research — unorthodox, that is, in the realm of police work. I set off for Fleet Street and the offices of *The Times.*

The newspaper kept a famously thorough index of its articles, and I hoped that I might be able to find some reference to any of the parties caught up in our investigation. If nothing else, there must be some mention of Lizzie Hopman's death. It could not have gone entirely unreported. The clerk sent to assist me was a congenial man, tall and wiry, sporting a bright turquoise pocket square. I explained to him what I sought and handed him a list of the names of every person connected to the case.

I waited, impatiently, as he searched the archives, distracting myself by reading *The Infidel.*

"That sort of book is literature at its worst," he said when he returned. "If one can even call it literature."

"You don't approve of Braddon?" I asked, readying myself to give him a stern lecture on the merits of her work. Not everything, after all, must be an exercise in the intellectual. One does require entertainment on occasion.

"Quite the contrary, Lady Emily," he said. "She's my absolute favorite. There's nothing I'd rather do than spend a fortnight in the gutter giving into guilty pleasure. I'll never forget the first time I read *Thou Art the Man.* I've never encountered a more thrilling story."

We had a pleasant, though necessarily brief, discussion of the lady's works, and then he handed me two back issues of *The Times* open to specific pages, explaining that he had found no other references to any of the people on my list beyond the current articles reporting on Mr. Grummidge's and Mr. Casby's murders.

To start, I was distressed to find there was

no mention of Lizzie's death. That a life can be violently snuffed out and no one bothers even to report it, shocked me. I brushed aside the inconvenient feelings consuming me and looked at what the clerk had found. The first paper contained an article with a horrific description of a disaster in a coal mine in Wales. Ned Traddles was listed among the dead. The accident had occurred four months ago and explained why he had stopped walking with Lizzie Hopman. Had she known about the accident and his death, or had she been left to wonder why he never came to see her again?

The report of the catastrophe was not directly pertinent to our case, but it gutted me nonetheless. Those poor men, working in abominable circumstances, doing their best to support their families! No one deserved to die like that. I swallowed hard, trying not to imagine what it must have been like in the dark tunnel after the collapse or to wonder how long they clung to the hope of rescue before the air ran out.

I sat for some time in silence, consumed with sadness for the dead men, and only came back to the present when the clerk asked me if everything was all right. I gave him a weak smile and thanked him for his concern before looking at the other paper in front of me. When at last I picked it up, I nearly shouted. It looked innocuous on the surface — a simple wedding announcement. But I know, Dear Reader, you will react with as much enthusiasm as I, when I share it with you:

Miss Violet Atherton to Mr. Edmund Grummidge on 15 December 1898 at St. Dunstan's, Stepney

Upon reading this, I thanked the well-read clerk and raced out of the offices of *The Times*. I hailed a hansom cab on Fleet Street and went directly to Marlborough House, where I expected to find my husband. Bertie's butler — that is to say, the king's butler — admitted me when I presented myself at the door, but rather than taking me to Colin as I had requested, he deposited me in one of Princess Alix's — that is to say, the queen's — sitting rooms, where I was left alone for nearly three-quarters of an hour. Twice I rang the bell; both times the liveried footman who presented himself to me apologized for not being able to assist me when I asked to see my husband. He seemed to think tea would rectify the situation. I am ashamed to say I disabused him of this notion in a rather unladylike fashion.

When the door opened again, this time without my having pulled the bell cord, I leapt to my feet expecting to see Colin. Instead, the wretched Inspector Gale entered the room, looking none too pleased. His pinched features seemed even more pinched than usual.

"Lady Emily, forgive me for keeping you waiting for so long." There was no way his tone could have been more condescending. "I gather it is difficult for you to understand the delicacy of the situation into which you keep trying to insert yourself. The life of our sovereign leader, the King of the Britons, is being threatened. My colleagues and I, your husband included, are doing our best to protect him and to bring to heel the insolent fool bent on destroying him. The late queen may have allowed your interference in palace matters on occasion, but she is gone and your presence will no longer be tolerated."

He went on at some length in the same vein. I stopped listening well before he stopped talking. This was not the first time I had encountered resistance from ignorant male persons. I could tell him what I had learned about Mr. Grummidge's widow, but he would pay it no heed. Furious that he was keeping me from seeing Colin, I weighed my options. It was obvious he wanted to upset me, so I decided the only way forward was to ignore the attempted insult. When his voice fell silent, I made no attempt to reply to him. Instead, without a word, I turned on my heel and exited the room.

The footman descended on me as soon as I entered the corridor, but I brushed him aside with a quick gesture. I marched straight out the front door, past the guards, and into Pall Mall, holding my head high. Even though no one in the house could see me, I felt that I ought to continue walking with purpose, even if I wasn't quite sure what that purpose was. In the end, I turned into St. James's Street and called in at Berry Bros. & Rudd. After asking them to deliver two particularly fine bottles of port to me in Park Lane, I felt much revived. I consulted my watch and determined it likely that I could find Jeremy in his club.

I continued up St. James's Street to Piccadilly, past the Ritz, and along Green Park until I reached Clarges Street. I had no illusions about being let into the Turf Club; the only place in the whole United Kingdom less likely to allow a woman to darken its hallowed halls would be White's, which

Jeremy had never joined because its membership was made up, so he claimed, of no one but his late father's friends. The Turf Club suited him much better. I went to the entrance and asked the doorman to fetch the Duke of Bainbridge for me, explaining that it was a matter of some urgency. Jeremy appeared, pulling on his overcoat, in fewer than five minutes.

"What a relief you came for me," he said. "I've been bored out of my mind for hours, Em. You can't imagine the worthless conversations that go on in these gentleman's clubs."

"I don't believe that for a second," I said. "If it were so tedious you'd never go. Still, I do appreciate you tearing yourself away from whatever it is you were embroiled in. I don't suppose you have your motorcar at hand?"

He didn't, but the doorman flagged down a hansom cab for us and soon we were on our way to Whitechapel to call on the newly widowed Mrs. Grummidge. En route, I caught my friend up with the latest developments in the case as well as the abominable treatment I'd received at Marlborough House.

"I shall have words with Bertie over this," Jeremy said. "I don't care if he's king or not. He will not be best pleased to hear what happened."

"That is far less important now than the conversation we are about to have with Mrs. Grummidge. I am convinced she holds the key to this mystery."

"Are you sure there's just one key, Em?" he asked. "Seems to me the whole thing would require at least three or four."

The cab pulled up in front of the house and Mrs. Grummidge's maid, who recognized me, admitted us without delay. Her mistress, who looked better composed than when I had last seen her, received us in the sitting room. I noticed she had removed the wedding photograph from her mantel.

"I apologize for barging in again," I said, after introducing Jeremy to her. As always, one could count on the good duke receiving a warm welcome wherever he went. "I have recently met a young woman with whom you share an acquaintance: Lizzie Hopman. I understand you were close?"

She all but started. "Yes, of course. Lizzie and I were bosom friends throughout our youth. When her mother fell ill . . ." She paused. "Eventually, we lost touch."

"We've come bearing sad tidings," Jeremy said. "I'm very sorry to inform you that Miss Hopman is no longer with us."

"What? You can't mean — was she ill?"

"Unfortunately, it was worse than that," Jeremy said. "Her employer . . . there was a most heinous incident with him and . . . she lost her life."

"No!" Mrs. Grummidge's thin face froze and all the color drained from her cheeks. "It cannot be. Lizzie?"

"I offer my deepest condolences," I said. "It is a terrible tragedy. It also appears that there is some connection between her and the death of your own husband."

"That is impossible," Mrs. Grummidge said, stiffening. "They never knew one another. Edmund would not have — that is to say, he did not approve — I mean —"

"We are all too well aware of the situation, both that Lizzie faced and that you did."

"I'm afraid I don't understand your meaning," she said. She was tugging at her cuffs again, just as she had done when I called on her before. This time, however, I could see no bruises on her wrists. I wondered how long it took for them to fade. "They never met, they weren't acquainted. If you are suggesting that he saw her in . . ." She was turning bright red now. ". . . in a professional capacity, I can assure you that is absolutely unthinkable."

190

"My dear Mrs. Grummidge, we would not dream of suggesting such a thing." Jeremy moved from his chair to the divan upon which the unhappy widow was perched. "All gentlemen have their faults, but no one believes your late husband frequented that sort of establishment. Can you imagine I would be calling if I thought otherwise?"

She looked at him, rapt. He was talking to her as if she were the prettiest girl at a ball, and I could see at a glance his strategy for getting her to open up to him was succeeding wildly. I appreciated the result, but had to resist rolling my eyes. Truly, I would never understand the sway a title — particularly that of duke — holds over women of every rank. "I cannot begin to express how much that means, your grace," she said, twisting a black-bordered handkerchief in her hands.

"Do not balk then at my next question," he said, his voice flirtatious, then serious. "It's very bad of me, but I have already mentioned that all of us gentlemen have faults, and I cannot help but notice the signs of the way you, his wife, suffered at his hand. Do not deny it to me; I know it all."

"But how?" she asked. "I have spoken to no one of it. I have borne the shame alone."

"You no longer need do that," he said,

resting his hand on top of hers. "He never needed your protection, and especially doesn't now. He ought to have been the one protecting you." Very gently, he took her hand in his. "It must have been awful."

"It was no more than what I deserved," she said. "I let him down in so many ways."

Jeremy's cheeks darkened. "It is not at all what you — or anyone — deserves. No man has the right to treat his wife in such a manner. It is a sign of consummate weakness and vice."

"He wasn't so bad, truly," she said. "He tried to stop, but then I would provoke him again, sometimes without even realizing it."

Now I moved next to her as well. "You ought not take any share of the blame for his actions. The duke is right. What your husband did was cowardly and wrong, and he alone bears responsibility for it."

Mrs. Grummidge pressed her handkerchief to her eyes and pulled herself up straight. "I apologize for breaking down in such an undignified manner. It is so much to take in. First Edmund, now Lizzie. Do you know of the details of the funeral? I'd very much like to go."

"I shall get the information for you and take you there myself," Jeremy said.

"Thank you, your grace," Mrs. Grummidge said. "I shall never forget your kindness. But, Lady Emily, you said Lizzie had a connection with my husband. What do you mean?"

"The connection comes through your friendship with Lizzie. As you know, two men have been murdered. The first victim, your husband, harmed his wife." I thought it best not to put it in any stronger terms. "The second victim is the man who killed Lizzie. Her death was murder, even if some might claim it to have been an accident. Can you think of anyone who knows both you and Lizzie who would have wanted to protect the two of you?"

"This is more shocking than I could have imagined," she said. "Of course, I haven't the slightest idea of who would do such a thing. Further, I don't believe there's anyone who would. No one knew what Edmund did to me. I never breathed a word of it to a soul." Her voice grew weak.

"Someone might have known, Mrs. Grummidge," I said, "even without you saying it. Your servants have probably noticed —"

"They would never have laid a hand on my husband."

I pressed my lips together. "You may be right, but one of them might have spoken in confidence to a friend of their own, a person who also knew Lizzie."

"My servants would not be cavorting with murderers." Tears pooled in her eyes. I could not help but notice she looked even prettier when she was upset, and I wondered if that was a quality much appreciated by her late reprobate husband.

"I am not suggesting they would," I said. "I believe that our murderer doesn't view his actions as a crime. He is seeking justice for the meek, lashing out against men doing violence to women."

She shook her head. "No, it can't be that. It's a coincidence, that's all."

"Did you know Ned Traddles?" I asked.

"Ned? Yes, when I was a girl, but I haven't seen him in years. He was killed not long ago in a coal mining accident. I hadn't thought about him in ages and was shocked when I read the story in the paper."

"Lizzie knew him as well," I said. "Who were your other mutual friends?"

"Please, this is very difficult for me. I must ask you to leave me in peace. I cannot take any more tragedy and horror. Forgive me, but I —"

Jeremy rose. "I know what we have said today was upsetting, and I offer my apologies for that. You need not say another word today. I shall send you a note with the details of Miss Hopman's funeral, and as promised shall escort you there. Until then, I do hope that you are able to find some measure of comfort in these onerous times."

20
1415

Disguising was a popular evening entertainment, and although no one doubted that the masked figures who swarmed into the great hall were members of the baron's household, that did not lessen anyone's delight at their game. Tonight, a tall man in a unicorn mask was pursued by six ladies, also wearing masks and dressed like fairies. Their impossibly tall headpieces swayed as they danced in a circle around the unicorn. Then, one more lady entered, her face hidden by a heavy veil fashioned from gilded netting. She approached the dancers, who, upon seeing her, fell to the ground as if playing a children's game. Thus freed, the unicorn took his rescuer by the hand and danced with her. When the music finished, he bowed over her hand, giving it an exaggerated kiss.

Cecily, seated next to Father Simon, laughed with the others who were debating the meaning of the scene and trying to figure out the identities of the masked performers. The joyful atmosphere in the hall was enhanced by servants bringing out more and more spiced honeyed wine, but that had far less of an impact on the guests than had the official news that came before they dined: King Henry had defeated the French at Harfleur. There was still no word from William, but that was to be expected. He would hardly be able to send messages at such a time, but his name had not been listed among those reported dead. Grateful relief consumed Cecily. She had room for no other emotion, which was probably why she paid so little attention to Adeline that night.

The disguisers gone, the minstrels started to play a tune, and much of the party got up to dance. Cecily declined however, preferring instead to talk to Father Simon, who had offered prayers of thanks with her after the news of the battle came. But when Dario Gabrieli approached her, Adeline by his side, and begged Cecily to join in the dance, she found herself whisked up with the others. The troubadour moved more gracefully than even the ladies, and when the dance finished, he called for the minstrels to stop playing and asked that someone bring him his lute.

He stared directly at Cecily as he tuned the instrument, his eyes still lingering on her when he began to sing, telling the tale of Lancelot and Guinevere. Cecily fidgeted in her seat, wishing he would stare at someone else. She looked around. Everyone else was focused on him, Father Simon included. For this she was grateful. She did not want anyone to think she welcomed Gabrieli's attention.

With a sigh, she poured more wine into her pewter goblet, but as she raised it to her lips, she noticed Adeline, her face still flushed from the exertion of dancing, watching her with a contented smile. She looked at Cecily and then at Gabrieli. Adeline, too, was holding a glass, and she raised it to her friend before she drank. Not wanting to draw attention to herself, Cecily slipped from her seat and went around the perimeter of the hall until she reached Adeline.

"When you accepted Dario's offer of friendship I did not suspect you had this in mind," Adeline said, leaning close and whispering to Cecily. "It is most exciting."

"You have misinterpreted entirely," Cecily protested. "There is nothing between us."

"I know how you like to emulate Christine de Pizan, so you are no doubt disappointed that I am not following her excellent advice and trying to dissuade you from your course of action," Adeline said. "You'll get no criticism from me, only a friend in whom you can confide anything. I shall never breathe a word of this to anyone."

"I assure you, there is nothing to hide," Cecily said.

"My dear friend, I shall not press you on the matter." Adeline's smile reminded Cecily of an extremely satisfied cat. "You must be careful, though. The other ladies are bound to be jealous. Thank goodness you have me to protect you."

"I saw Gabrieli give you a note," Cecily said. "If you mean to impugn me in an attempt to disguise your own behavior —"

"Do not speak to me like that," Adeline said. "You are a guest in my home. I have taken you in and stayed loyal to you despite your immoral leanings. Conduct yourself carefully, madam, lest you find yourself in a more uncomfortable situation."

On a crisp October day, King Henry and his much-reduced army — he now had fewer than a thousand men-at-arms, and the total number of his force was less than half what he had started with — set off from Harfleur. They were attacked only a few miles later, but rebuffed their enemy with little effort and continued their march. The men braced for another skirmish, but it did not come.

When they reached the town of Arques, the king demanded — and was given — free passage across the river. The same strategy worked again in other cities, but the soldiers began to hear rumors that the French were amassing a great army, swollen with the men who had not come to the aid of their countrymen at Harfleur. Was Henry's good fortune starting to change?

The king's plan to cross the Somme where his great-grandfather Edward III had after defeating the French at Crécy nearly a century ago could not be achieved. The French had anticipated him, and the English continued on until they could find a safer place to ford the river, forced to move deeper into the center of the country. They were still searching for an adequate site on the day they should have reached Calais.

William had grown weak during the march, and could no longer ignore the pain radiating from the wound on his face. He poured wine on it, as the doctor had instructed, and kept it packed with the prescribed poultice. Rain beat down on the army. Morale was low. It seemed France would destroy them.

And just when William started to believe things couldn't get worse, the unthinkable happened. A soldier had disobeyed the king. Not only had he stolen from a town they passed through, he had stolen from the church, removed the gilt — though not gold — pyx that held the bread for the Eucharist.

Would God support an army who stole from His house? Or would He turn His back on the English and their king? A dark gloom came over William. He pulled from his pack the diptych that matched the one he had given to his wife, fell to his knees, and prayed.

21
1901

As twilight's inky blue veil blanketed London, I retreated to the library after a quick visit to the boys in the nursery. Henry had constructed out of pillows and crates what I had to admit was a credible facsimile of a wooden fort. He'd persuaded his brothers to take the part of the settlers inside. Richard did not even pretend to be engaged in the activity — he was reading the book of medieval history he had taken from his father's desk — but Tom happily entered into the spirit of things, flinging projectiles at Henry, who was waving what I believe he intended to be a tomahawk.

When Colin arrived home, he was even less pleased than Jeremy at hearing what had happened at Marlborough House. "It is an inexcusable way to treat anyone," he said, so distracted that he had not lit the cigar he'd been holding in his hand for the past quarter hour. "Gale is —"

"Wretched," I finished for him.

"Quite."

"I don't understand why a Scotland Yard inspector — wretched or not — has such sway in this situation. Surely your own role, not to mention your extensive experience, puts you in a position of more authority."

"It would have during the previous monarch's reign," he said. "Gale, though, has smoothed over any number of scrapes the king got himself into when he was Prince of Wales, and you know how loyal Bertie is. The inspector's ambition is to become head of the king's security, and I say let him have it. It's not a position I would consider for even a second."

"Your expertise lies elsewhere," I said. "Discretion, cunning, and the subtle diplomatic manipulation of delicate situations are your specialties. They would be wasted in guarding the king." Still, I could not help but feel that it was unfair for Colin, regardless of his previous interactions with Bertie, to be forced to work under the wretched Inspector Gale. When I voiced this, he assured me I had misinterpreted the arrangement. Gale was investigating the murders. My husband was looking into the broader implications of the crimes, which meant he, not Gale, had the more important job. At least if one agreed it was more important to safeguard the king from theoretical threats than to bring a murderer to justice.

After leaving Mrs. Grummidge's house, I had parted from Jeremy and gone to the coroner's office, where I had been able to learn the details of Lizzie Hopman's funeral from the man who had examined her body. There was to be a simple service at St. Botolph's Without in Aldgate. He also shared with me the cause of death. She had been manually strangled. I could tell from the look on his face that there was more, but I did not press him to share it with me. I had heard enough. I went home and telephoned Jeremy to pass on the information. He promised to contact Mrs. Grummidge and arrange to escort her to the memorial.

"This is as good a lead as we've had in this case," Colin said, as I recounted for him the connection I'd discovered between Mrs. Grummidge and Lizzie Hopman. "You've done excellent work, Emily."

"I can't help but think that this suggests there is another meaning to the messages you have received," I said. "The murders look more and more like acts of vengeance, not like an elaborate scheme to put the king on notice."

"You may be right, but we cannot risk letting down our guard. If anything were to happen to the king —"

"I, of course, understand. But the messages must have some purpose, and if it is not to warn the king it might be something equally — or more — important."

"I suppose you have a suggestion as to both the meaning and the way to puzzle it out?"

On this count, he was wrong. I had nothing to go on but my intuition, and that told me that the messages and the murders were not so closely connected as we thought. The note Queen Victoria had presented to Colin — from the royal deathbed, no less — had been penned days before Lizzie's death, the event I was convinced served to catalyze the murderer's spree. Whoever wrote it could not have known that Lizzie would soon meet a grisly fate. More significantly, what on earth could it have had to do with the queen?

"You should see this," my husband said, producing a familiar-looking envelope. "I was beginning to despair that I would never find the next clue, but then I remembered the London Stone in Cannon Street."

"I'm ashamed I didn't think of it myself," I said. "The very stone from which Arthur pulled Excalibur."

"Unlikely in the extreme, my dear, al-though it's possible that Jack Cade struck his sword on it when he rose up against Henry VI. Regardless of the truth of any of the legends connected to it, you will want to read the message." He handed it to me.

. . . he caused proclamation to be made, that no person should be so hardy on pain of death either to take any thing out of any church that belonged to the same, or to hurt or do any violence either to priests, women, or any such as should be found without weapon or armor, and not ready to make resistance . . .

"It's from Holinshed's Chronicles," Colin said, "which Shakespeare used when writing his play. The passage describes Henry V's direction to his army before the siege at Harfleur, as soon as his ships had landed." A sketch of a chalice filled the bottom of the page.

At my request, Colin gathered the rest of the messages, and we laid them on his desk. He was standing behind me, still holding the unlit cigar. We studied the words, the handwriting, and examined both the paper and the ink, but could find nothing that offered any further illumination.

"The chalice is your next clue to find, but I am still at a loss to understand what the queen meant when she said this was an instruction," I said, picking up the first message. "*Une sanz pluis. Sapere aude.* One and no more. Dare to know."

"You can repeat it over and over. I doubt it will bring enlightenment."

"Funny that you mention enlightenment. It is the second phrase, *sapere aude,* that was used during the Enlightenment, correct?"

"Yes," Colin said, turning and sitting on the edge of my desk. "Kant coined it as the motto of the period, translating it, I believe, as *have courage to use your own reason.*"

"*Dare to know* is how you phrased it before," I said.

"That is another standard translation of the original Latin, often applied to Horace's original."

"Do we have the original?"

"Yes, of course." He crossed to the bookcase that held the Roman writers and pulled down a volume from one of the shelves, flipping through the pages before presenting it to me.

Sapere aude: incipe!
qui recte vivendi prorogat horam,

rusticus exspectat dum defluat amnis;
at ille labitur et labetur in omne volubilis
    aevum.

"How I wish Margaret were here! Not only would she take immense pleasure from chiding me for my substandard knowledge of Latin, she could give us a precise translation."

"I am not altogether incapable, my dear." He took the book back from me and read:

Dare to be wise, begin!
He who postpones the hour of living rightly,
a farmer who waits until the river flows;
but it still glides, and will glide into every
    kind of stream flows.

"This time you said *dare to be wise,*" I said.

"It's a small difference," he replied. "You of all people, who have spent years obsessing over various translations of *The Iliad,* should recognize that."

"You're quite right. I wanted a better feeling for the phrase, that's all. There's something striking about it, and knowing that it became a battle cry for the Enlightenment thinkers —"

"I'm not sure I would go quite that far."

"It doesn't matter," I said. "Let me finish what I am about to say before you criticize. What other movement gained momentum during the eighteenth century? The Freemasons. And doesn't *dare to know* sound like the sort of phrase that would be adopted by a secret society? Not the masons — I'm not suggesting they are behind your messages — but some other group. People dedicated to protecting the king at any cost."

"Who give a message to an aged woman on her deathbed in the hopes that she knows to whom it should be delivered?"

"No, not exactly. I don't have it all worked out yet, but you cannot deny that something along these lines could be possible."

"I most certainly can deny it." He crossed his arms. "You will never, ever convince me that Queen Victoria belonged to any secret society."

"A society of ladies, eager to defend their monarch —"

"Now you're getting carried away," he said. "You cannot think — even for a moment — that Victoria would have endorsed any such thing. She was all for a lady having power and strength when the lady in question was herself. She was not so generous to the other members of her sex."

His words, alas, rang true. Queen Victoria

had never offered even a hint of support to the women's suffrage movement. Quite the contrary. According to my mother, Her Majesty had once referred to the subject as a *mad, wicked folly,* and she never failed to make it clear to those around her that she supported the traditional roles of man and wife. Other than for herself, of course. I have never been able to tolerate hypocrisy. Perhaps that explains the cool relations I always had with the late queen.

I frowned and scrunched my eyebrows together. "I realize it sounds absurd and I quite agree that Victoria would not have joined any secret society — unless the Prince Consort had suggested it, in which case it no doubt would have pertained to something —"

My husband raised his hand to stop me. "Enough."

"Yes, well. As I was saying . . . the phrase itself, particularly when combined with the one that proceeds it, *une sanz pluis,* sounds like just the sort of rallying cry one would choose for a secret society. You cannot disagree with that."

"I absolutely disagree. To begin, would you be so kind as to elaborate for me on your experience — extensive experience, I assume — with secret societies and their rallying cries?"

"You can poke fun at me later, but this does —"

"What this *does,* Emily, is pertain to two murders, vicious and brutal, that were staged to send a message, a message it is not unreasonable to conclude is intended for the king."

"I cannot agree with you at all. If anything, I am more convinced than ever that the murders and the messages are wholly unrelated." I pursed my lips and stared into his flashing eyes. "Are you a member of a secret society?"

He cast those eyes, still flashing, to the ceiling. "Heaven help me. I should have known it would come to this."

"There's no need to answer the question," I said. "I am well aware that it would be unreasonable to expect an honest answer if you do belong to one. Either way, you would reply in the negative, and I would have no way of determining the veracity of your statement."

"I do not belong to any secret societies. However . . ." He pulled me to my feet and took my face in his strong hands. ". . . I realize that you cannot trust my denial and rather than subject myself to impertinent questions that could, in theory, compromise my integrity — particularly if I am indeed a member of some such group — I can think of no better way to distract you from your purpose than this." He kissed me with an intensity that would have made me lose my balance if he weren't holding onto me.

"I cannot believe you would think me so easily distracted —" He had moved his lips to my neck and the ensuing sensation was so pleasant I could not continue. He lifted me up so that I was sitting on the edge of the desk and had one hand firmly around my waist, the other resting gently on my cheek.

"What's a secret society, Papa?" Henry's voice came from under his father's desk on the other side of the room.

My husband and I both froze, our eyes open wide in horror. Colin straightened his cravat and then his jacket and strode toward the boy, whose head was now peeking up over the leather-covered mahogany desktop. "When a group of individuals share a common interest, they are sometimes moved to found a formal organization to pursue said interest," he said. "They can meet and discuss whatever is pertinent to the topic."

"Why do they keep it secret?" Henry asked. His father sat in his desk chair and drew the boy onto his lap.

"Because they believe — incorrectly — that keeping things secret makes them more interesting."

"That's all?" Henry frowned.

"That's all," Colin said.

"Bloody waste of time, I'd say."

"Henry! Where did you learn such language?" I asked. "You must not speak in such a vulgar manner." Henry shrugged, but agreed to my request and then apologized for having to rush off in a hurry.

"Nanny will want me to have my bath," he said, before picking up the cat — who had also been under the desk — and dashing from the room.

"I never heard him come in," I said. "He moves like a ghost."

Colin leaned forward and dropped his head into his hands as soon as the library door had closed behind our son. "I've never considered myself an overly religious man, my dear, but I should like to drop to my knees and thank the Lord above that the boy did not wait another five minutes to reveal his presence."

I shuddered and did my best to think of something else, picking up the message Colin had retrieved from Cannon Street and studying it for some time before speaking. "You cannot tell me this supports your theory that the messages pertain to the king's safety. If anything, it is a clear indication of what the king expects from the men in his service. At least if the king were a man like Henry V. I can't vouch for Bertie's standards."

"We ought, perhaps, be more careful about how we address such topics. Heaven knows who else might be hiding in here."

"Perhaps one of Mrs. Keppel's spies." I could hardly repress my laughter at the thought of Bertie's long-standing mistress directing a covert operation.

"I won't hear any words against that lady," Colin said. "She has been nothing but a positive influence on the king. I suspect even his wife would agree."

I could not argue with him there. Mrs. Keppel, so far as anyone could tell, was good for the king, but I could not help but feel sorry for the queen. She had spent much of her life having her husband's indiscretions thrown in her face; it must be an intolerable way to live. "In all seriousness, though, Colin, you cannot tell me that this latest missive supports your earlier theory —"

"Now it's *my* earlier theory. You have only just started to criticize it."

"I may have only just started to vocalize

my criticisms. I've had my doubts for some time. Perhaps you've been doing too thorough a job distracting me."

"Do you think so?" he asked. "I've half a mind to throw you over my shoulder, take you upstairs, and put that theory to the test."

"Do your worst," I said.

He did carry me up the stairs, but not over his shoulder. That, he explained, would have been far too uncomfortable for me.

22
1415

Cecily awoke the next morning consumed with a sense of dread. She heard mass as always, but today Adeline was there, too. Cecily did not sit with her, preferring a pew further back from the altar; it made her feel as if she could see better, and on days when the sun was out and its light streamed through the stained glass on the back wall, it was as if God Himself illuminated the space.

Adeline, who had waited outside the door when the service ended, took Cecily by the arm as she stepped over the threshold. "I must beg your forgiveness," she said. "I had taken too much wine last night and said some despicable things. Tell me I can still count you among my most treasured friends."

"How could I deny such a request?" Cecily said, but her heart hung heavy in her chest. She worked on her embroidery in a quiet corner of Adeline's parlor that afternoon, not joining the other ladies for a ride in the forest.

"You are quiet today," Father Simon said. "I've been searching for you and twice passed by this room thinking no one in it. Riding is a favorite pastime of yours, and you have denied yourself that pleasure. Is something troubling you?"

"I find staying on an honorable path not always so easy," Cecily said. "Even conversing with you could be misconstrued. Christine de Pizan warns against forming friendships with men."

"I am a priest, not an ordinary man, and would be honored to take the role of your confessor. No one, not even Madame de Pizan, would deny you the right to that."

"I thought I had finally achieved some measure of peace, the first I'd had since arriving here," Cecily said. "I see now, though, that one cannot escape the burdens of sin."

"What is the sin of which you speak?" Father Simon asked.

"I am not worthy to be the daughter of the holy woman my mother was."

"None of us is as worthy as we might be," he said. "God wants us to always strive to be better. Your mother miraculously survived the plague and spent her life serving the Lord. We are not all meant for that sort of contemplative life. To my mind, your mother's path was a difficult one, for she lived between the contemplative and active worlds when she wanted to stay only in one. I believe she resisted her adopted father's decision that she marry?"

"Yes," Cecily said. "She would have preferred the convent."

"God had other plans for her, and you were part of that plan."

"I killed her."

"No," Father Simon said. "Childbirth is inherently dangerous. Many women die during it, and it would be wrong to blame the innocent babe. Your mother was called home to the Lord. We are not meant to understand why."

"She would not have died were it not for me," Cecily said. "That is my burden to carry. I seek forgiveness through penance, but knew not where to begin until I came here. When I realized what I must do, I rejoiced, but I am finding the path treacherous and difficult."

"Do not let that daunt you," Father Simon said. "The most onerous journeys are often the most rewarding. Remember Christine de Pizan's wise counsel that *the good and proper active life cannot function without some part of the contemplative.* You must nourish your spiritual side. That will, in turn, feed the active. Never hesitate to call upon me for guidance. As I have said before, it would be my honor to serve as your confessor."

"I shall remember that," Cecily said, but even as she spoke she recalled Adeline's warning that Father Simon was William's friend, not hers, and that she ought to be very careful about trusting him. Yet it seemed to her he was far worthier of trust than Adeline. Surely, so long as she conducted herself honorably, she had nothing to fear. No one, no matter whose friend, could accuse her of wrongdoings then.

Until now, no member of the English army — from the highest-born man-at-arms to the lowest cook — had dared defy King Henry's order to leave unmolested the places through which they marched. No one had burned crops, interfered with women, or stolen even a mouthful of food. That a man had dared to do so now, and in a church of all places, sent a shiver of horror through the army. How could God be on their side now?

The king ordered the soldier to stand trial that very day, and the verdict of guilty of behaving *"in God's despite and contrary to royal decree"* surprised no one. The criminal was strung up on a tree, his body hanging before the gathered troops. No one else would dare violate the king's command.

The wound on William's face was still throbbing as he watched the execution and then as the body was cut down and buried. It was justice well-served and surely would be pleasing to God. But still, he felt a pall come over him, as if the shroud had been wrapped around him rather than the dead man.

They marched on, more slowly with each passing day. Their supplies were running short, and the extra effort of carrying the large sharpened stakes the king had ordered each archer to fashion and bring helped neither their speed nor their stamina. When they reached Nesle, they were denied food, and the citizens hung red cloths from the walls of the city.

"What does it mean?" his squire asked, but William could only shake his head and agree with the king's orders that the modest houses outside the walls be burned the next morning. They could not allow the French to get away with such open acts of defiance.

It had begun to seem as if they would never be able to reach the other side of the Somme, and the insult served them at Nesle made William fear their campaign was doomed. But then, as if by some miracle, the scouts found a crossing, a short distance away. The king rescinded his order that the village be burned, and the army set off once again. The crossing was not easy, but it was a success, and that night, at last, their morale began to improve.

Perhaps God was still on their side.

23
1901

Do not think, Dear Reader, that an interlude for the expression of connubial devotion distracted either Colin or me from our purpose. On the contrary, I found it cleared the mind. The next morning, I made a quick investigation (by telephoning my mother to tap into her infinite knowledge of everyone connected to the royal family) of the illegitimate descendants of William IV, the FitzClarences, and felt confident that none of them would attempt to usurp the crown. One was married to Princess Louise, our present king's daughter. Another — much to my surprise — had embarked on a career as a novelist, and under the name of the Countess of Munster, had penned a number of successful works. Her ghost stories would be much enjoyed by the boys when they were a bit older. Among the rest of the FitzClarences (there were quite a lot of them) one could find army officers, a vicar, and a rear admiral, but, alas, no one with pretentions to the throne.

I say alas, but, to be candid, did not consider this a blow. If anything, it supported my burgeoning view that Colin's messages were not meant as warnings to the king. I pointed this out to him in a most spirited fashion over breakfast that morning. He did not agree.

"However," he said. "You may be onto something. This is the first time we've had a message — since the original one — that does not appear to be sent in conjunction with a murder."

"No bodies dressed like Richard II or Harold Godwinson?" I asked.

"You shouldn't sound so glib, but, no, no bodies at all. I think Gale is a bit disappointed, but terrified at the same time. One is bound to turn up sooner or later. I've searched every church I can think of where I might find the chalice in the drawing on the last note — it looks remarkably like everyone's idea of the Holy Grail — but have had no luck as of yet. I'm starting on museums next."

Lizzie Hopman's funeral was scheduled for that afternoon. As Jeremy was escorting Mrs. Grummidge and Colin had to go to Marlborough House after breakfast, I planned to take the carriage and meet my husband outside the church. It was a dismal day, sleet falling from clouds so dark it looked more like dusk than day. St. Botolph's was at once a fitting and heartbreaking choice of location. Unfortunately, a not insignificant number of women who shared Lizzie's profession made a habit of plying their trade (or at least seeking potential clients) in the area surrounding the church, which had led some impertinent people to refer to the sacred building as the Church of Prostitutes.

Today, however, none of them stood outside, though half a dozen, Mary included, walked through the doors to mourn their friend. A handful of men came as well, but, not surprisingly, I knew none of them save Mr. Brown, the new proprietor of the Black Swan. As always, a swarm of boys appeared as if by magic the instant Jeremy pulled up in his Daimler. This time, when he selected one to watch the motorcar, I chose one as well, asking him to identify for me any of the persons he recognized entering the church. This strategy was not as fruitful as I had hoped. He knew the names of three of the women, but none of the men.

Colin arrived just in time for the service to begin, and had brought Mrs. Bagstock with him. After installing her next to Mrs. Grummidge — the two women appeared to be the only mourners genuinely grieving — he slipped into the seat next to me in the back of the church, where I had positioned myself in order to better observe the congregation's behavior. Despite the old clichés about murderers and funerals, no one revealed much of anything. Truly, it was a sad little gathering.

"Mind-boggling to think that Sir Isaac Newton lived just across the street, isn't it, my dear?" Colin whispered to me during the vicar's sermon. "How the neighborhood has changed."

"You shouldn't talk during a funeral," I whispered back.

"I've never liked a long sermon, and it's perfectly clear the reverend didn't know Miss Hopman," he said. "Furthermore, I object to him sounding so judgmental. He doesn't have the courage to accuse her outright of being a prostitute, but he's making it very clear that he does not approve of the life she lived. As if she had much of a choice in any of it. No one offered her a comfortable vicarage for a home."

When, at last, the service ended — Colin's words may have been inappropriate for the situation, but he was quite right about the sermon — pallbearers carried the coffin to the churchyard, where the body would be lowered into a pauper's grave, a layer of lime between it and those buried earlier. The motley group of mourners stood near the hole in the ground, but not quite around it, their heads bowed as the reverend recited a final prayer.

I had suggested to Colin that we host a small tea after the funeral — not at our house, of course, but in the private room of a suitable neighborhood tavern — but he howled at the mention of the idea. His objections were numerous, the strongest being that there was something unsavory about using such an occasion to glean information from those mourning a death.

At the time, I could hardly disagree with him, but after having observed the decided lack of emotion around us, I wished I had insisted on putting my plan into action. It was too late now, however, so I was left with no choice but to introduce myself to the others after the burial. Lizzie's colleagues, if I may call them that, bristled when I approached them. Mary alone gave me more than the barest greeting and a rote exchange of sympathy. I noticed that she was wearing the outfit, overcoat included, that I had purchased for her.

The men were even less interested in speaking to me than the women, so I left that task to Colin, but observed each of them carefully. None engaged in any suspicious behavior and none stayed for long after the reverend had gone back into his rectory. Mr. Brown, not surprisingly, was the first to leave, but not before pulling me aside and reminding me that I was not safe in this neighborhood. His breath stank of ale. Only one of the others, a well-dressed older man with a barrel chest and a neatly trimmed white beard, approached me.

"Your husband assured me you would not be offended if I introduce myself. Prentice Hancock. I did not know Miss Hopman well, but she grew up not far from my haberdashery and I have many fond memories of her. Always seemed a bright little thing. I'm sorry to see that her life took such a sad direction."

"As am I, Mr. Hancock. Are you acquainted with Mrs. Grummidge as well?" I asked, gesturing toward her.

He squinted and shook his head. "I don't recognize her."

"You might know her by her maiden name, Atherton."

"Can't say it rings a bell. Also can't say I'm much surprised to hear Casby was responsible for Miss Hopman's death. Terrible man. I tried more times than I can count to set the authorities on him, but they never could quite catch him. Such a pity. I grew up in the East End and have spent my life doing whatever I can to improve the opportunities available to my neighbors. Not all of them share my good fortune. But I find so few willing to accept even the smallest changes. People like what they know, even when it's not good for them."

"Where is your shop, Mr. Hancock?"

"Oh, I retired years ago and sold the place."

"But you still live in the neighborhood?"

"I do indeed, Lady Emily," he said. "Can't rightly claim to want what's best for it if I'm not willing to be there myself, can I?"

"That's very good of you," I said. "I should very much like to speak with you about your efforts. I'm quite keen on doing whatever I can to improve opportunities for the poor as well. Perhaps we could combine forces."

His broad smile revealed a row of uneven teeth, but it warmed his whole face. The cold wind and pelting sleet had turned his cheeks and nose a rosy color, and I could not help picturing him as a benevolent Father Christmas. "That would be most welcome, Lady Emily."

I gave him one of my cards, told him to call on me at his convenience, and turned back to the rest of the little group. Mary had disappeared and the weather appeared to be having a debilitating effect on the elderly Mrs. Bagstock. It was time to take her home. I spoke briefly to Mrs. Grummidge, who was clinging tightly to Jeremy's arm, but did not think this was the time to pepper her with any further questions. Grief was writ all over her pale face.

"I had hoped the funeral would prove more useful," I said, after we had returned Mrs. Bagstock to her home. "I'll give Mrs. Grummidge a few days before calling on her again, but given what she has already told us, you must agree that there is now solid evidence that she suffered terrible abuse at the hand of her husband. His murder could absolutely have been motivated by revenge, as could that of Mr. Casby's."

"I do not deny the possibility," Colin said. "But we need more, Emily, much more."

"I hate feeling so frustrated," I said. We rode in companionable silence back to Mayfair. He leapt out at Marlborough House and I continued on to Park Lane. As Davis took my outer garments, he told me that Nanny had taken the boys to the Natural History Museum, leaving the house wonderfully quiet. Much though I would have liked to curl up with *The Infidel* and a cup of tea, I instead applied myself to going through the mail, which was piling up in the library after we had neglected it for the past several days.

There was very little of import. We had no invitations, as most of Society avoided London during the winter, preferring instead the comfort of their country houses. Indeed, it was only the queen's funeral that had drawn us here from Anglemore Park. I had a note from one of the keepers at the British Museum asking me to come see a new piece recently acquired by the Department of Greek and Roman Antiquities. It was a fifth-century (BC, I need hardly add) marble bust of a young athlete he thought I would greatly appreciate. I replied to him with delight, promising to come as soon as I could manage.

Below this in the stack were the usual sorts of bills, the latest edition of *The Strand Magazine* — which had several promising-looking short stories in it — and a note from my mother. Knowing full well that her missive would be less satisfactory reading even than the bills, I opened it first, always preferring to dispatch with the unpleasant as quickly as possible. She opened by chastising me for not allowing her to discuss this when we had last spoke on the telephone and continued with a detailed criticism of my behavior at the queen's funeral. There was too much jet beading on my dress. My veils were not heavy enough. I had not looked appropriately pale for such a sad occasion. The bulk of her remarks, however, dealt with the disgraceful manner in which I followed my husband out of the luncheon, without so much as a thought for how this would have horrified Her late and much-lamented Majesty.

Naturally, this led to her favorite form of rhetoric, the scolding lecture. She devoted six full pages of stationery (which sported a wide black border) to an attempt (vain, I need hardly say) at stopping me from any and all involvement with detectives, murderers, and other unsavory characters. While I admit to agreeing with her judgment that the wretched Inspector Gale was not a fit acquaintance for me, I would go further, saying he was a fit acquaintance for neither man nor beast. But, unlike my mother, I reached my conclusion as a result of observing his character, not by passing judgment based solely on his occupation.

She finished by sending her warmest regards to Colin and the boys. I crumpled the pages into a small ball and flung it into the fire. I had no intention of favoring her with a reply, but did wonder if she would ever grow tired of her relentless barrage of criticism. No doubt that was too much to hope for. I prodded at the burning paper with a brass poker and returned to my desk. When I reached the final envelope in my pile, I found inside a note from Mrs. Rillington, the helpful yeoman warder's wife, and the map she had promised to send indicating the locations of hidden passages in the Tower. She reiterated that one of the wives had made a project of exploring the passages, but no longer lived in the Tower. Her husband had retired and they were now living abroad.

I admit to giving way to a number of thrilling flights of fancy about what I might find in these tunnels, and was in such a state of reverie when my husband entered the room that I did not immediately respond to the derisive comment he made as he looked at the map over my shoulder.

"I suppose it would be too much to hope that you won't insist on going yourself to explore every dank nook and cranny you can find," he said. "As I've warned you before, do try not to irritate the yeoman warders. The raven master in particular."

"You know perfectly well that we must follow up on this," I said. "We still have no idea how the murderer entered the Tower. Mrs. Rillington has offered to accompany me."

"You should take Bainbridge with you as well. No one would mistake him for someone involved in a criminal investigation, and he's likely to charm the guards. I'll ring him myself and arrange for him to collect you."

24
1415

Cecily considered Father Simon's words carefully. It was true that her mother would have preferred a contemplative life, but that was never what Cecily desired. She would have to better balance the active and the contemplative, just as Christine de Pizan recommended. She vowed to give more alms and to spend more time visiting those less fortunate than herself. And she promised she would be a better friend to Adeline.

This proved simple enough for the next week. The weather had turned cooler, and the ladies spent less time riding and more in the castle. Cecily bent over her needle-work, having completed the figure of the first of the ladies in her scene — the one holding the book. Adeline took to sitting with Father Simon. The baron and a large group of friends had embarked on a hunting trip the day after Cecily had heard him arguing loudly with his wife, and in his absence, Adeline behaved like a model of propriety. On some nights, she refused to let Dario Gabrieli perform, instead insisting Cecily read aloud. On the third day after the hunters had set off, Adeline asked Father Simon to hear her confession, telling him that she felt so terrified by her husband's priest, that she could not escape the worry that she would make a bad confession whenever she knelt before him, not deliberately, but because she was too scared to speak with an open heart.

And so, Father Simon became Adeline's confessor, and she spent hours with him each afternoon, discussing spiritual matters. She began to display a piety apparently more sincere and of greater depth than she ever had before. When she saw Cecily preparing alms, she added to them and pledged to visit any ailing tenants on her husband's estate. The next morning, the ladies together went to the village and distributed alms, and the day after that, Adeline asked to borrow Cecily's copy of *The Treasure of the City of Ladies.*

"I know I sometimes do not conduct myself in the best manner," she said as Cecily placed the book in her hands. "I can't even claim that I always try to, but I do very much want to do better, and as these words seem to have brought you strength and guidance, perhaps they can do the same for me."

So Cecily embroidered while Adeline read, night after night. The other ladies of the household complained at the lack of entertainment, but Adeline only scolded them, imploring them to use the time to improve their own characters. She retired early to her chamber, explaining that she wanted to pray.

One evening, Cecily, consumed by a complicated floral section of her needlework, remained downstairs long after Adeline had gone to bed. When at last she cast her work aside and started up the stairs, the house was quiet, everyone else already asleep.

Or so she thought.

As she crossed the corridor near Adeline's room en route to the small staircase that would lead her up to her own chamber, she heard soft laughter and then the click of a latch. She pressed herself against an alcove in the wall, hiding herself in the darkness, and watched as Dario Gabrieli emerged from Adeline's door, a satisfied smile on his face.

Now Cecily understood the change in Adeline's behavior since her husband left for the hunt. The baroness had cynically designed her attempts at leading a more admirable life to cover up her affair, so that no one would suspect her of wrongdoing. There could be no question that Cecily must intervene, must attempt to stop her from continuing on this evil path, but she knew not where to begin. Alone and helpless, she knew that only God could guide her now.

Due to the location at which they crossed the Somme, some in the English army began to hope that the French, who had expected them elsewhere, would not force a battle. Instead, heralds delivered a message from two great French dukes and the constable of France to King Henry, offering to fight at a mutually agreeable time and place. The king, proving again of far greater honor than the dauphin, showered the heralds with gifts and sent a reply informing the French that they were welcome to fight him whenever and wherever they wished. The English would not hide from the challenge and did not consider it necessary to arrange the details in advance.

From then on, the army had to be always at the ready, dressed and armed, displaying their coats of arms. Henry visited his men, to rally them and remind them that he, too, was a soldier. They would not be fighting for him, but with him.

Every day now, William saw more signs that the French were close, but he never laid eyes on a single member of their army. The English kept marching, on and on, through rain and mud, as the weather grew colder. So focused was the king on making forward progress, that on one night he neglected to stop at the town in which he was to lodge. When he realized his error, he made no move to correct it. Rather than go back, even this small distance, he continued on. He would not let anyone see the king of England, bearing his coat of arms, retreat for any reason at all.

Then, on 24 October, the army crossed the river at a town called Blangy, and the word they had anticipated at last came: they were but three miles from the French, who had amassed an enormous army. When they reached a hilltop, the sight of their enemy pouring into the valley below, banners streaming, brought home to William the disparity in the size of the forces. One could not even compare the two. It was as if a scrappy group of wanderers was to face the strongest military in Europe.

The king, undaunted, stood before his

men. They dismounted, and Henry began to speak, giving them his battle plan, putting them in formations, and in all ways encouraging them, down to the lowliest soldier. This was a man who could turn even a scrappy group of wanderers into a formidable fighting force. This was a man who understood the way both the desire to fight and fear consumed them. Bravery, after all, required a certain amount of fear — or at least the recognition and acceptance of the danger one was about to face. No man, if he was honest, could claim to be entirely free of fear before battle. If that were the case, there would not be so many of them lined up, waiting to offer a last confession before the bloodshed began.

William made his peace with God and looked again at the French, wondering if they would fight. Would it not be wiser for them to let the English continue on to Calais? Once King Henry and his men had crossed the channel and were home, the French could attack Harfleur, and if they won it back — which William thought they could, knowing all too well the sad condition of the forces left there — the English victory would be erased, and their campaign in France meaningless.

There were so many French soldiers, led

by the finest knights in their realm. Could such an army be persuaded not to fight? They would follow orders; all good military men did. But could their leaders resist slaughtering what, to them, must seem a feeble enemy? God would decide.

William thought the battle might come that very day, but the French made no move. They might think the English weak, but William knew better. He and his brothers-in-arms would fight for their king, for their wives and sweethearts, for their land. They would fight with the strength and fury of men who knew the day would end in either glory or death. No English soldier had forgot what the French had done to the captured archers at Soissons: they cut off their bow fingers, gouged out their eyes, and gelded them before massacring them. The tales of their brutal treatment still filled William with rage. Who would not fight to the death rather than be subjected to such an ignoble end?

Still, one could not altogether ignore the fear. As the sun sank low in the sky, William knew there would be no fighting until the morrow. The night that stretched before him would be the longest of his life.

25
1901

As Colin had suspected, the yeoman warders balked when Jeremy and I arrived at the Tower. The wretched Inspector Gale had ordered them to keep me away from his investigation. Jeremy, in his most pompous drawl, explained that we had come to call on Mrs. Rillington for tea, after which he hoped to see some of the more gruesome bits of the place.

"You know, Sir Walter Raleigh is an ancestor of mine," he said to the guard. "I figured it was time I took some interest in his imprisonment and execution."

"Is that so, your grace?" The guard stood up a bit straighter and looked rather impressed. "If you'll just sign the register here, you can go straight to Mrs. Rillington."

We did as instructed. As we walked toward the Rillingtons' rooms, I took Jeremy's arm and leaned close to him. "I had no idea you were descended from Raleigh."

"Oh, I'm not. It's just that he was the only person I could remember who had been held here who embodies any of my own dashing qualities. I knew the guard would like it."

"You are a terrible person."

"Thank you for noticing."

We paused for a brief tea with Mrs. Rillington before the three of us set off on our exploration. Many of the passages marked on the map were now so well-known that they could hardly be called secret, but others so thoroughly disguised, I wondered how anyone could find them. There were trapdoors leading to long underground corridors that joined the buildings within the Tower and cunning mechanisms that opened hidden tunnels. Jeremy was particularly taken with a clever system that revealed a staircase behind what looked like a solid stone wall, while a tunnel that went all the way beneath the now-empty moat fascinated me.

"The staircase is much more interesting," Jeremy said.

"Yes, but the tunnel proves that there are still ways into the Tower that allow one to avoid detection by the guards," I said.

"Except that the end of that passage is now locked," Mrs. Rillington said. "If we follow it all the way, you'll see that an iron door prevents anyone from entering through it."

"That does not mean there can't be another that remains accessible." Undaunted, I gripped a candle firmly in my hand and set off to make a methodical exploration of the passages that went from tower to tower, below the ground. For the most part, this proved straightforward. The tunnels allowed for access primarily to dungeons and prison cells, but further scrutiny revealed less obvious branches of them. The mechanism that hid Jeremy's beloved staircase was used down here, too, and careful inspection of the tunnel walls enabled us to discover three paths not on our map. The first took us to a rickety helical staircase that led to the undercroft of the White Tower. The second ended abruptly at a wall of dirt, as if the medieval excavators had tired of the project and abandoned it.

The third, however, stunned and horrified me.

We had already burned through two candles apiece. Jeremy, who had brought with him an electric torch, brandished it with pride, but unfortunately had to shut it off periodically so that the batteries would not die. I preferred the flickering candlelight to its steady glow — it felt more authentic — but as the tunnel narrowed and patches of damp appeared on its stone walls, I began to wish for more illumination.

Mrs. Rillington paused. "I wonder if we should keep going. We've come awfully far, haven't we?"

"It feels that way," Jeremy said, "but we aren't more than a ten-minute walk from the entrance to the passage. I think we're near the river now, hence the water."

The sound of constant dripping accosted us, and puddles dotted the ground, but the walls remained immobile when I pushed against them with my hand. I had been keeping track of our location as best I could, using a compass and the map as my guide, but could only guess at the distance we had traveled. It appeared that we were, as Jeremy suggested, quite close to the Thames, beneath the outer walls, somewhere between the Cradle Tower and Henry III's water gate.

Jeremy, who had gone ahead of us ladies, called out, "There's quite a lot of water here. I'm not sure we should continue."

I went toward him, and soon had to hold up my skirts to keep them from getting wet. My boots and stockings were already soaked. I lifted my candle close to the walls, looking for any sign of a hidden door or another passage. By the time the water reached close to my knees, Jeremy was pleading with me to turn around.

"Em, my trousers are ruined, I'll be scandalized if you raise your skirts any higher, and I'm convinced I stepped on something that used to be a rat. There's nothing for us here."

"Not quite," I said. I pointed to a stone in the wall. The mortar around it did not quite match the rest in the vicinity. I pressed hard against it, but nothing happened. Putting all my weight behind the effort, I tried again and the stone began to move, the sound of scraping echoing through the tunnel. Mrs. Rillington, not wanting to get wet, had remained some distance back and now cried out in alarm. Jeremy rushed to her side, leaving me alone to see a door open.

Its position, several feet above the floor of the tunnel, had kept most of the water out of the room into which it led. My candle in one hand, I used the other to grip the wall as best I could and climbed into the dark chamber.

"Jeremy, stay with Mrs. Rillington," I said, once my candle had lit the space. The floor was damp and a dark splatter of blood stained the walls. A crude table stood to one side. On top of it I found two clippings from *The Times:* the same article I had already read reporting the coal mine disaster in Wales that took the life of Ned Traddles and a piece lauding a factory in the East End as a model of safety and modernization.

Now a feeling of hideous claustrophobia engulfed me. The room, no more than ten feet by twelve, felt even smaller, and I imagined I could hear the sounds of a struggle. The blood on the walls most likely belonged to Mr. Grummidge. But how had the murderer brought him to this place? I examined every square inch of the walls, my stomach roiling when I came to the bloody patches, but I could not let myself look away. And then, partway up the wall I saw a smear that looked like a handprint in the dried blood. Cringing, I pushed against the spot, and another door opened, this one three feet above the floor.

"I'm afraid I require your assistance, Jeremy," I called. He was at my side in an instant.

"Bloody hell." His voice was low and husky. "Literally and figuratively."

"Boost me up so I can better see what's beyond the door," I said.

"Let me go first."

"It's my discovery," I said. "And there's no danger. If anyone was on the other side waiting for us, he would have already made his presence known." My friend didn't look happy about it, but he did as I instructed. The door led into another tunnel, this one steeply sloped and even narrower and wetter than the other. It went south for approximately twenty yards, ending abruptly at an archway that opened into the river, not far from Tower Bridge. We'd come further west than I had realized.

At high tide, the arch would be completely under water, invisible from the river. The angle of the passage kept the room from flooding with water, but it would have been extremely difficult to get an unwilling person into the space. Then I remembered that Colin had told me the coroner found river water in Mr. Grummidge's lungs. He might have been unconscious and inhaled the foul stuff when the murderer brought him here and dragged him into his little chamber, where he could finish his evil deed without being disturbed.

I was now completely soaked and starting to shiver, but it had been necessary to poke my head out through the opening to see where, exactly, I was. That done, I retreated up the tunnel, stepping carefully on the steep, slick stones. Jeremy, who had followed me, provided a steadying hand, and we returned to the room, where I collected the newspaper clippings and then went back to Mrs. Rillington. She gasped when she saw me.

"I must get home and warm as quickly as possible," I said, "but not before we discover if there's a direct way from this tunnel to Wakefield Tower."

"No more exploring for you," Jeremy said. "Mrs. Rillington, please get her into a cab. I'll send word to Park Lane as soon as I've finished here, Em. Hargreaves will murder me if you wind up with pneumonia."

I was too cold to argue. When Davis opened the door for me, he actually swayed on his feet. I've never seen him so discombobulated. He called for Colin, who, without a word, stripped off my wet coat and dropped it on the floor before scooping me into his arms and carrying me upstairs. He ran the bath, and while it filled, removed the rest of my soaking clothes before lowering me into the water. Davis sent a maid up with tea. Between that and the all but scalding water in the tub, my teeth had soon stopped chattering.

"I would have gone with you myself if I'd thought you'd get into this much trouble," he said. "All the details, please."

After recounting the story, I sent him to get the clippings from *The Times,* which I had thrust at Davis upon returning home. By the time Colin came back upstairs with them, I was warm and dry. Shortly thereafter, our butler brought a message from Jeremy. I tore it open.

"The passage not only leads to Wakefield Tower," I said, "but directly into the chapel where Grummidge's body was left. We have found the murderer's lair."

"So it seems," Colin said.

"The article about the mining disaster connects him, via Ned Traddles, to both Lizzie Hopman and Mrs. Grummidge."

"I recall reading about it when it happened," he said, looking it over. "Dreadful business. Those poor men. No one should die like that. It's diabolical, really. Safety standards have got to be improved — the miners complain about them constantly, as they should. This disaster proves that. I assume the second article is meant as a comparison — a place that is safe rather than one that is not."

"Most likely," I said.

"I shall ring Gale to update him and Scotland Yard with what you have learned. He will want to investigate the passage and the room, but I doubt he will find anything that escaped your notice."

"You must agree that none of this points to the murders having anything to do with the king."

He ran a hand through his tousled curls. "I will admit to giving serious consideration to your idea that they are not meant as a warning to the king. The content of the last note — I still haven't located the chalice — has given me pause. Which is not to suggest that I, in any way, have warmed to your notion of a secret society."

That did not trouble me in the least. He would come around to that idea when I found further proof of it. We took tea in the nursery with the boys, after which Henry, who had tied a feather around the cat's neck, recruited his father to play Red Indian alongside him. I went back to the library determined to pull down every volume I could find that might discuss secret societies. Unfortunately, I found only two: one, a history of architecture that included a section on markings of the Freemasons, the other Wilkie Collins's spectacular novel *The Woman in White*.

While the latter is one of my favorite books, even I could not help but draw the conclusion that I was unlikely to be able to adequately research secret societies in general or particular. This did not mean, however, that I had abandoned my suspicions about Colin's messages. And should someone else turn up dead, with the letter *T* carved onto his arm as did the villainous Count Fosco in the novel . . . well, then I would be able to convince even my husband to reconsider his position.

I turned back to the messages still spread out on Colin's desk, but I could draw no precise conclusion from them. I opened a biography of Henry V, thinking that if I read it I might be in a better position to understand what the sender could be trying to communicate, but before I had reached the end of the first chapter, I closed the book and returned to my husband's desk. I did not think I would find my answers in history.

I reread the article about the mining disaster and was more convinced than ever that Ned Traddles was the key. I lifted the telephone receiver from its cradle. In the span of a few minutes, I was connected to the offices of *The Times,* and soon was speaking with the reporter who had written the article in question.

He was eager to be helpful and provided a number of details not included in his report, but I could not see how any of them might relate to the murders. I asked him about the man who owned the mine, a Mr. Crofton, and he told me that he had never seen a businessman so aggrieved in the face of an industrial accident. He had provided each of the miners' families with a generous bequest. A poor substitute for husbands and fathers, but better than nothing.

The journalist remembered nothing about Ned Traddles, so I determined that I would find the man's family. Mrs. Grummidge claimed to have had no contact with him in years, but perhaps Mrs. Bagstock would remember him. I told Colin of my plans, called for the carriage, and was soon knocking on her door.

"Lady Emily!" she exclaimed. "This is not a fit place for you to be after dark."

"The sun sets so early these days I'm afraid I had no choice," I said. "I've come on a matter of some importance. Do you recall a friend of Lizzie's, a man called Ned Traddles?"

"Ned? Oh, yes, an affable enough boy, but always in trouble," she said. "You will take tea, won't you?"

"No, thank you, I mustn't stay too long."

"Your handsome husband will worry, I suspect." She sat in her rocker. "Ned was

252

caught up with a bad lot, pickpockets, most of them. Not surprising, I suppose. He didn't have many options, but still, that's no excuse for crime. He managed well enough when he was small, but you know how it is when a pickpocket starts to grow. I believe he was nicked more than once and eventually thrown in jail, but I can't say I remember the details. I rather hoped he wouldn't come around when he was released, but he did, and Lizzie walked with him, saying he was reformed. He did go to Wales and work in that mine, so I suppose there was some truth to the claim. He still came to see her, once a month. Quite a distance to travel for a walk. It's a pity he died, if he truly had changed his ways."

I rather felt it was a pity regardless of whether he'd changed his ways. "Do you know any of his family?" I asked.

"No, I never met any of them. Had a pack of siblings — eight or so — and they lived somewhere near the docks. Can't imagine any of their lives turned out well."

I thanked her for her help and ordered my driver to take me to Mrs. Grummidge's, but she was not home. I was about to return to Park Lane, when an idea struck me. So far as I could tell, the wretched Inspector Gale was spending far more time at Marlborough

House than Scotland Yard, and at this late hour, he was even less likely than usual to be in his office. I decided it was time for me to see what I could learn from the police.

My name and courtesy title (there are benefits to being the daughter of an earl) gained me entrance to the redbrick building on the Victoria Embankment, but I did not expect a warm welcome at New Scotland Yard. After explaining what I was after, the dour constable to whom I spoke disappeared for several minutes and then, returning to where he had left me waiting, motioned for me to come behind the counter that separated him from what could only be described as a waiting room. I followed him through a maze of corridors until we came to a small office. Its occupant, a man of ordinary height with mouse brown hair that curled rather nicely and a pair of spectacles perched on his narrow nose, hovered in the door.

"Thank you," he said to his colleague. "I'll take it from here." He waited until his colleague was out of sight before offering me a chair across from the desk that nearly filled his room.

"Fenimore Cooper Pickering is a most unusual name," I said after he had introduced himself.

"My mother is American, Lady Emily," he said. He paused briefly, but before I could wonder if that was meant to be a complete explanation, he continued. "She was a great fan of the writer James Fenimore Cooper, particularly his Leatherstocking Tales, and was convinced that Nathaniel Bumppo is the greatest of all fictional characters. I'm grateful she didn't try to call me Hawkeye."

"She sounds like the sort of lady I should very much like to meet," I said.

"I'm afraid we lost her years ago. But you have not come to discuss my family history. I understand you are interested in the murders currently plaguing my colleague Inspector Gale. How can I help?"

There was something in his voice — just a hint of sarcasm, perhaps, in the way he mentioned the wretched Inspector Gale — that caused me to warm to him. Could it be that I had finally encountered a police detective who might prove useful? I gave him a brief description of what I had learned about Ned Traddles, including his acquaintance with Lizzie Hopman and Mrs. Grummidge. I did not mention my expedition to the Tower. I had, after all, first learned of the mining accident in the offices of *The Times.* There was no need to share more information than strictly necessary when I had, as yet, no idea how trustworthy young Inspector Pickering would prove.

"I can have his record pulled up in a matter of minutes," he said when I'd finished. "Have you time to wait or would you prefer that I deliver a summary to your home?"

Again, there was something in his voice. Was he suggesting it would be better for me to speak to him in the privacy of my home? The idea tantalized me, especially as I knew all too well from past experience that — until possibly now — no one in Scotland Yard had warmed to the idea of my assisting in any sort of investigation.

"I am perfectly happy to wait, but would not like to put you in the awkward position of assisting me before you've finished any other work you have at hand. What is most convenient for you?"

"I am rather involved in another matter at the moment," he said. "Might I call on you in an hour or so?"

"It would be a pleasure," I said, and offered him my hand, which he grasped and shook firmly.

"I look forward to it, Lady Emily. If I may be so bold, your reputation precedes you."

It was nearly eight o'clock when I reached home and Colin listened, his head cocked to the side, one of his eyebrows ever-so-slightly raised, as I recounted for him what I had achieved.

"I have not met Inspector Pickering," he said when I'd finished, "and can't claim to know anything about him. Do you really believe he will come here, my dear? Is it not more likely that his knowledge of your reputation combined with a cleverness I admit we have not often encountered among his brethren inspired him to send you away in a manner that did not require an argument?"

"In theory, yes, I would agree with that assessment, but there was something about him that makes me think he will prove trustworthy. If I'm wrong, so be it, and tomorrow you will have to get the records from Scotland Yard."

"You might have left it to me in the first place," he said. "It would have been simpler."

Except that it would not, in fact, have proved simpler. Three-quarters of an hour after I arrived home, Davis knocked on the library door.

"An Inspector Pickering to see you, madam. Shall I bring him here or would you prefer to receive him in the sitting room?"

26
1415

When the baron and his compatriots returned — successful, of course — from their
hunt, the atmosphere at the castle brightened at once. Lord Esterby's mood had
quite improved, and he had brought with
him a newcomer, Hugh de Morland, another dear friend of Cecily's husband.
Adeline arranged for a feast to welcome
them back, and the ladies were aglow at
having another handsome gentleman to
fawn over. If the troubadour regretted losing some of their attention, he did nothing
to show it, and Adeline went out of her way
to shower her husband with affection. She
did, however, ask Gabrieli if he meant to
finish the tale he had started before the
hunters had left, that of Lancelot and Guinevere. He demurred to her request — for
that was what he considered it — with a
handsome smile.

After the assembled company had stuffed

themselves with roast pheasant, broiled venison with pepper sauce, and a great pie stuffed with chicken and rabbit, they turned their attention to sweets and then to spiced wine and cheese. Well-sated, the baron called to Gabrieli, inviting him to begin the entertainment.

The troubadour gave Cecily a smile as he prepared his lute, but he did not keep his focus on her. Instead, he let his eyes linger on Adeline, but only for a moment, and then began to sing. As he performed, his rich voice filling the hall, he played to the entire crowd, never focusing on anyone for more than a short while. His behavior was altogether different than it had been before, when he had stared so blatantly at Cecily. She knew that she might be misguided, but she was convinced that his early ploy was meant as a distraction. Everyone had noticed him favoring her, and that was what they would remember, should anyone ask about his behavior.

Now, though, he had found a willing partner in flirtation, which meant he had to be more careful. Cecily knew little of love, but she did recognize the warmth in Gabrieli's eyes in those brief instants he looked at Adeline. William had gazed on her that way, on the day of their wedding. The realization made her miss her husband in a most unexpected way that made her heart beat too rapidly and her cheeks flush. This caught her unaware, and she hardly knew what to think. Surely a husband would not think of his wife in the way a lover did of the object of his affection? Cecily clenched her hands together as she realized that her fingers had started to tingle.

"Are you well?" Hugh de Morland asked, coming to sit next to her on the bench near the fire. She had selected the spot as it gave her the best vantage point from which to simultaneously watch the troubadour and Adeline. "You've come away from your friends and look rather worried. In fact, I've never seen a countenance so clouded."

"That is not a fair charge," she said, turning to him. "I'm not worried in the least. I can't quite put my finger on the emotion coursing through me at the moment, but it must come from the sad story to which we are listening. Lancelot's hopeless love, Guinevere's betrayal of Arthur."

"You feel no sorrow for her?" he asked, his eyebrows shooting up nearly to his hairline. "She did not choose her husband. Do we blame Iseult in the same way when she forsakes King Mark for her Tristan?"

"I cast no blame," Cecily said. "But you

cannot claim Guinevere's actions brought happiness to anyone, herself included."

"Surely they brought her — and Lancelot — some measure of happiness, if only temporarily."

Cecily did not like the way he was studying her face, and she feared he was misinterpreting her words. "No lady would want that sort of happiness. Not ever, Master de Morland."

"You need not be so formal with me, Lady Hargrave." There was no mistaking the emphasis he put on her title.

"We have only just met," Cecily said.

"Yet we are bound to become the closest of friends. William would have it no other way." Truly, his smile was charming and made his blue eyes shine. "Do you insist on having no sympathy for poor Queen Guinevere?"

"None at all. Iseult did not marry King Mark, did she? Guinevere was Arthur's wife."

"Guinevere had no choice in the matter. She was all but bartered as part of a political alliance. And Merlin warned Arthur that if he married her, she would fall in love with his best knight."

"How can a true knight, supposedly full of virtue, love his king's wife?" Cecily asked.

"It is true then," de Morland said. "You have no sympathy for the lovers."

"No lady could." Cecily looked straight ahead, unwilling to meet his eyes. When she could feel that he was no longer looking at her, she risked a glance in his direction. His lips curled in a half smile as he stared at the troubadour.

After sitting quietly for some time, he turned to her again and spoke. "Yet Guinevere remained ever loyal to her Lancelot, did she not? Malory tells us she had a good end because she was a true lover."

"Malory saying it does not make it true," Cecily said.

To this, de Morland replied with a laugh. "Truly, you are young and your innocence is most fetching." Spotting Father Simon not far away, he waved the priest over. "Come, Simon, and sit with us. William has got himself a fine wife."

William could hear the French all night. They called to their servants, they drank wine, and they conversed in tones that sounded, to him, full of arrogance. Not that he could pretend to make out the words. King Henry, unable to risk missing the first signs of attack, had commanded his army to observe a strict silence. William wondered what their enemy thought, what they made of the quiet across the line.

The weather had taken a grievous toll on his armor. The march from Harfleur had provided little opportunity to rub away the rust that came after so much abuse, but as William bent his arms and knees, he could feel that it had not degraded to the point that it would inhibit his fighting. Unable to sleep, he wandered among the Duke of Gloucester's men, up and down the line, ignoring the heavy rain pelting him that soaked his padded jerkin through the joins of his armor.

His compatriots did their best to keep the king's order of quiet, but they still whispered among themselves, careful to modulate their voices. William started when he heard someone behind him and turned to see one of the company's priests.

"Shall I hear your confession, Sir William Hargrave?" he asked.

"I've already made it," William replied. "What have any of us to fear, though, if our cause is just?"

"And do you believe our cause is just?"

William did not recognize this new voice, which came from behind the priest. Nor did he recognize the hooded figure, when it stepped toward him.

"The king says it is, and I do not argue with the king," William said.

"That does not mean you believe he is right," the man said.

"It is not my place to draw any conclusions on the matter." William pulled himself up to his full height. "He is my lord and I shall fight for him — and die for him, if that is what God wishes — as any Englishman would."

"You care so little about the fate of your soul?" the stranger asked. "If the king's cause is not just, you will be condemned for your role in the bloodshed."

"I have made my peace with God," William said. "And as for the king . . . do you not think he envies us our position? Tonight, we struggle with the anxiety that comes with the anticipation of battle, but the king wrestles with the fate of all of our souls. We will follow him wherever he bids us to go and owe him our respect and our confidence. Where do you think he will reside in hell if he leads us in a cause that is not just? I would much rather be a simple soldier, fighting for my king, than to have that weight on me."

The man nodded and walked away, his bearing regal, and then was engulfed by darkness. There could be no doubt it was the king. The priest made the sign of the cross in front of William and offered a blessing. William nodded thanks and remained there, standing, until the first light of dawn struggled through the heavy clouds in the sky.

It would not be long now.

27
1901

Naturally, I directed Davis to bring Inspector Pickering to us in the library. After introducing him to my husband, there could be no mistake that Colin's reputation had preceded him far more than mine. The young man shook his hand with a vigor and enthusiasm that nearly exceeded the effusive praise he offered to accompany the act. I told him to sit and offered him a glass of whisky.

"I have the information you requested, Lady Emily," he said, taking the whisky but looking almost afraid to drink it. "And I must say again, Mr. Hargreaves, what a very great honor it is to meet you, sir. Your acumen and intellect, combined with endless courage and physical strength unlike that possessed by any of your colleagues —"

Colin silenced him with a motion of his hand.

"Yes, of course," the inspector said, pushing up his wire spectacles, which had slid down his narrow nose. "Forgive my fervor."

"What can you tell us about Traddles?" Colin asked.

The direct question appeared to calm down the other man, but he still took a deep breath and paused, collecting himself, before continuing. "He was arrested once as a youth, but not held accountable for his crime because the victim refused to press charges — he was, it appears, averse to seeing a boy so young punished in too severe a fashion. Felt that the lad deserved a second chance at an honest life. The rest of his file contains page after page of incidents in which his participation was suspected, but never proven. When he was seventeen, however, he was arrested again, this time not for petty theft, but for stealing a horse. He was convicted of the crime and served out his sentence in Newgate. Upon his release, he must have gone to Wales. I am not quite sure how a man with his record managed to get a job, but somehow he did, and that's how he wound up in the mine."

"Was there any mention of where he lived when he was a boy?" I asked.

"No," Inspector Pickering said. "In fact, he refused to give any address, saying only that he lived on the street. No doubt he ran with some gang or another."

"I've been told he had numerous siblings," I said. "As many as eight. Would it be possible for you to locate any of them?"

"I did, Lady Emily, take the step of searching for information we had on other persons with the surname Traddles," he said. "A Robert Traddles was arrested during the Trafalgar Square riot on Black Monday in 1886. Two leftist organizations planned protests for that day — something to do with the unemployed, if I remember correctly; it was before my time — and pandemonium broke out afterwards in Pall Mall. There was a great deal of window smashing and looting. Traddles was part of a group cited for drinking brandy they'd stolen from a shop. At the time, he was an unemployed dockworker. I made note of the address he gave when he was arrested." He passed a slip of paper to Colin, who nodded thanks. "According to baptismal records, he does have a brother called Ned."

"This is good work, Pickering," Colin said. "Shows initiative."

The younger man's cheeks flushed. "Forgive me if I am too bold," he said, turning to me, "but I understand that you have, Lady Emily, often faced difficulty when seeking information from my colleagues. My mother would have disowned me if she thought I stood in the way of a lady trying to pursue meaningful occupation, so I should very much like to offer my services, limited though they are, to you. To you both, of course, although I know you, Mr. Hargreaves, have unfettered access to anything you want. It just strikes me that there may be times, like today, when it isn't convenient for you to come running to Scotland Yard. Furthermore" — he paused and his cheeks flushed even darker — "a lady ought not to have to rely on her husband for everything. In the way of, as I said before, pursuing an occupation, that is. I hope you don't think I meant —"

"There is no need to explain," Colin said. "The offer is understood as intended. Emily, what say you?"

"I should be delighted to consider you a colleague," I said, and offered my hand to Inspector Pickering.

"That's very good of you, madam, I'm thrilled to be of service," he said, his boyish exuberance once again being expressed through the vigorous shaking of hands. "I hesitate to say this, but should you ever wish to reach me by telephone at the Yard, you might have your butler ring. The other fellows are more likely to come fetch me if they don't know you're the one looking for information. It's just that —"

"I am all too well aware of how your coworkers feel about me," I said, "and shall heed your excellent advice." We thanked him again, and after he'd spent several more minutes expressing his deepest admiration of Colin's abilities, he took his leave.

"That's quite a conquest you've made," I said when we were alone again. "He all but worships you."

"I should be flattered, I suppose, but I don't do my work in the hope of receiving compliments," Colin said. "I do it out of duty to my country. I am, nonetheless, pleased that his rather absurd admiration of me has led you to, at last, have a source at the Yard. Perhaps someday, young Inspector Pickering will rise through the ranks, become commissioner, and hire female officers."

"I suspect we are a long way from that happening," I said.

"Sadly, I must agree." He leaned back in his chair and shot me a meaningful look. "It is too late to go to anywhere near the docks, and it's unlikely Robert Traddles is still at an address he gave fifteen years ago. What would you say to a game of chess? We can search for Traddles in the morning."

The sparkle in his eyes told me he had no intention of playing chess. I will only say that he did, indeed, make me feel like a queen.

The next morning, much to our surprise, we found the Traddles family still in residence at the address given by Robert all those years ago. Their building stood in a street with rubbish-filled gutters that produced a shocking stench. The malodorous environment appeared to go wholly unnoticed by the children who played there, their faces streaked with the smut residents of London know all too well. Mrs. Traddles, who opened the door for us and hesitated before inviting us inside, was a middle-aged woman with thin lips and kind eyes, and exuded the exhaustion brought on by a lifetime of hard work. She explained that her husband was at the docks.

"But don't go searching for him," she said, motioning for us to sit on a settee that looked as if it might collapse at any moment. Her tidy front room, warmed only by a small stove, was chock-full of worn furniture, some of it in obvious need of repair. No one, however, could fault her housekeeping; there was not a speck of dust to be seen. "We don't need that sort of trouble.

It's hard enough finding a job these days. People like you in your fancy duds showing up to talk to him would just make tongues wag."

"We are not here to cause any sort of trouble," I said. "Rather, we are seeking information about your husband's brother Ned."

"A pack of nothing good was all anyone ever got from Ned," Mrs. Traddles said, picking up the knitting on the table next to her chair. The undyed wool looked home-spun. "Never wanted an honest day's work, that one. My Robert, who was the oldest in the family, tried to help him, you know, when they was young. But Ned would have none of it. And what more could Robert do? There was eight of them then. Their parents died — cholera, it was — and left them with nothing. Robert did his best."

"I'm sure he did, Mrs. Traddles," I said. "No one should shoulder so much responsibility at such a young age."

"Only someone who lives in your world would say that."

I could not argue with her on that point. "Perhaps your husband did have an impact on Ned. He eventually got a good, respectable job."

"Only because he had no other options.

272

He'd been nicked, you know, and went to Newgate. Not even his old gang wanted him after that, although I'm not quite sure why that would be. Jail always seemed to be a badge of honor among them, so far as I could tell. That's what they do, those gangs, seduce boys into thinking the life's full of fun and excitement and then make it impossible for them to earn a decent living. They know nothing but crime."

"Do you know which gang Ned belonged to?" Colin asked.

"He ran with the King's Boys, and if you ask me there's none that's worse."

"The King's Boys?" I asked and turned to my husband. "The boys outside the Black Swan mentioned belonging to that group."

"You make it sound like a gentleman's club," Colin said, which caused Mrs. Traddles to laugh.

"Well, they'd like to think it's something of the sort. Don't realize what they're getting themselves into, do they? Too young and too stupid."

"Did you have any contact with Ned after he went to Wales?" Colin asked.

"Yes, he came to town once a month or so and always showed up here all apologetic and acting like he'd reformed," Mrs. Traddles said. "Maybe he had, but I wasn't

273

about to trust him and neither was Robert. We'd fallen for his tales of woe too many times before and weren't about to get pulled into his sordid world again. I do feel a bit bad, though, given how he died. When the news came, Robert was near beside himself. And then, when we got word that he'd named us as next of kin and we received the settlement paid by the mine, well, it was even worse for my poor husband. He tried to refuse the money, but they wouldn't have none of it. So, in the end he gave it to the Salvation Army, every last bit. Maybe some good will come from that, but who's to say?"

"Did you know any of Ned's friends?" I asked. "Either a Lizzie Hopman or Violet Atherton?"

"Oh, he was quite taken with that Lizzie when he was young, I do remember that. Never met her, though. Violet Atherton I've never heard of, but that don't mean a thing. Ned could've married her for all we'd know."

"He didn't," Colin said.

"Well, I suppose that's true, or she'd have got the settlement from the mine, wouldn't she?"

"Where do your husband's other siblings live?" I asked.

"Most of them is gone. Three went to

Australia, one died at least ten years ago now in some sort of fight, and little Victoria, she didn't make it to her fifth birthday. Johnny, he was the one just above Ned, he went off to sea. We haven't heard from him in ages. Ned was the youngest."

"Did Ned ever tell you anything about his life in Wales?" Colin asked. "Do you know if he had friends there?"

"I'm sorry, Mr. Hargreaves, I truly am, but I just don't have answers to your questions. Like I said, we didn't want nothing to do with him anymore. Robert didn't have the heart to refuse to see his brother, but we kept his visits as short as possible."

"I understand and appreciate your being so generous with your time," Colin said, rising from his seat. "Furthermore, despite your brother-in-law's many failings, I am most sorry for your loss."

"Thank you, sir," she said. I could see a touch of moisture in her eyes. "I do wish . . . but, there's no point in thinking about that anymore."

Back out in the street, the children were still playing, their laughter and games no different from those of children one could find anywhere in England. Only the diabolical conditions in which they grew up set them apart. "It is not right for children to live like this," I said.

Colin took my hand and squeezed it. "You can't save everyone, Emily, but I know how it pains you."

"This gang, the King's Boys —"

"It's notorious," Colin said, navigating his way around a particularly nasty-looking heap of trash and helping me into our waiting carriage. "They bring them in as children when they're quite young — most of them start as pickpockets — and as they get older they serve other purposes, if the leaders decide they can be trusted. Enforcing the gang's territory, running protection rackets, that sort of thing. It gets rather violent, I'm afraid."

"What a pity so many get caught up in it," I said. "These children need a better option. It's filthy here and completely devoid of hope. I can see how a gang that provides some sort of income and a position that makes one feared, if not respected, would seem preferable to muddling through life in such a place on one's own. If you're not a member of the gang, no doubt you're a victim of it." I sighed. "You're correct to say that I can't save everyone, but I must do something."

"And I've no doubt you will," he said.

"In the meantime, however, do you think

we ought to speak with Robert Traddles? Not at the docks, but later, when he's home?"

"He's unlikely to know anything beyond what his wife has already told us."

"Are there girls in the King's Boys?" I asked. "Despite the organization's name? Could Lizzie have been a member?"

"Not so far as I know." The carriage lurched forward.

I dropped my head against my husband's shoulder. "What would do the most good, do you think? A school, perhaps?"

"No. These children would benefit more from medical care and a decent meal," Colin said. "They have options if they want to go to school — and they are supposed to, you know, up to a certain age. Not that anyone seems to be trying to stop truancy here."

We were both somber when we reached home. I refused luncheon, as I could not shake the stench of the gutters, and instead went upstairs for another very long, very hot bath while Colin retreated to his study. The thought of our boys, happily ensconced in the nursery, almost made me feel guilty. How lucky they were not to share the fate of those in the East End.

After toweling myself off and drying my

hair in front of the fireplace in my dressing room, I pulled on my favorite tea gown, fashioned from the softest azure silk and with a high net collar. Delicate Venetian lace formed the sleeves and trim, and a darker blue silk sash gently cinched the waist. Best of all, it required no corset, so I could breathe deeply and slouch to my heart's content. It was one of the pieces I had bought at the House of Worth on my last trip to Paris. Meg, my maid, twisted my hair into a Gibson Girl pompadour, all the while telling me the extremely convoluted plot of a novel she'd been reading, but I was too distracted to follow the story.

When she finished, I went down to the library, where Colin was sitting at his desk, speaking into the telephone.

"Yes, quite," he said. "I'll be there at once. No, no, don't bother. I have the matter in hand." He rang off, returned the handset to its cradle, and looked up at me with serious eyes. "There's been another murder. Richard II."

28
1415

Laughter, dancing, and song filled the days that followed Hugh de Morland's arrival at Lord Esterby's estate. He loved — and demanded — constant entertainment, and delighted in the attention of Adeline's ladies. At last, there was someone to compete for their interest with Dario Gabrieli. Cecily, too, enjoyed his company, but she found him more challenging than alluring. After their conversation about Lancelot and Guinevere, she had asked Lord Esterby if she might borrow his copy of Malory's *Le Morte d'Arthur.*

She was familiar with the story, of course — what girl in England wasn't? — but she found that returning to it as a married woman made it a different book altogether. Truth be told, she had paid little attention to Lancelot and Guinevere on her first reading, being more interested in the adventures of the Knights of the Round Table. Now, though, she began to believe that the entire work hinged on the illicit relationship between the queen and her husband's favorite knight.

She was sitting next to Adeline by the fire, embroidering a rose on the wall hanging she'd been working on, when de Morland strode into the room and took the seat across from her, on the other side of the mantel.

"You have given me a great deal to think about, Master de Morland," Cecily said. "I have revisited Malory and cannot agree with your assessment of Lancelot and Guinevere."

"Hugh, you must call me Hugh. I had no idea my words would stay with you for so long."

"Do not make what I say something it is not." Cecily frowned. "How could a true knight — which Lancelot is called again and again — betray his king in such a personal matter?"

"He is noble and honorable in every other way, is he not?" de Morland said. "Perhaps we are meant to forgive his one sin."

"That is for God to do, not us."

"You are a very serious young lady. I hardly know what to make of you."

"Need you make anything of me?"

"Perhaps not, but I find I want to."

Adeline looked up from her own needle-work. "Truly I have never heard two people engaged in so murky a conversation. I suspect your interest lies not in Arthur's knight and his queen, but in persons far closer to home."

"Whatever can you mean by that?" Cecily asked, wondering if Gabrieli had seen her in the corridor when he was leaving Adeline's chamber that night not so long ago.

Adeline did not reply because the troubadour had entered the room and was bowing in front of her. She gave him her hand, which he kissed, and her silvery laughter filled the space. "My dear Gabrieli, would you be so good as to escort me to the stables? I have a sudden desire for a ride through the forest. Perhaps you do as well?"

"I am a guest in your house, madam," the troubadour said. "I could deny you no reasonable request."

Cecily felt strange watching them leave together, and from the look on de Morland's face, he shared the sentiment. "They are close, are they not?" he asked.

"Not in an inappropriate way, I'm sure," Cecily said, nearly choking on the words.

Her companion once again raised his

eyebrows. "Perhaps now is not the best time to discuss Lancelot and Guinevere."

By the time the sun brightened the horizon, the rain had stopped, leaving behind it a mess of thick mud nearly impossible to walk through. In the hazy light of dawn, William could make out the French taking up their positions, row after row after row of meticulously outfitted fighters, led by the flowers of their nation's aristocracy. Their armor gleamed and their numbers seemed to go on forever.

King Henry, who had already heard three masses that morning, also wore armor that gleamed, and he sat on a small, modest steed before his gathered men, helmet in his hands. This man, William's sovereign, never tried to hide his identity on the battlefield. His bascinet, which he always wore with the visor up, was bejeweled and encircled with a crown, the Black Prince's ruby taking pride of place in the center front. Henry's bravery and confidence inspired all around him. And when he spoke that day, reminding his soldiers that his cause was just, and that, as always, he would fight with them, there was stirring amongst the men.

"We fight for England and for all those things we hold dear," the king said. "But you do not need me to remind you of that. Instead, recall that the French have threatened to cut off the bow fingers of every one of our archers. And recall what they did in Soissons. Today is the feast of two noble saints: Crispin and Crispinian, who suffered mightily at the hands of the Romans before their martyrdom at that very same Soissons. Can any of us doubt that on this holy day we will avenge the horrors of Soissons and show the French that they may not cut anything from the hands of our archers?"

The soldiers' voices united in a cry, low at first, but building in urgency and volume. The king waited, drinking in the enthusiasm of his men.

"I am a man of honor," he said, motioning for them to quiet. "So I will offer one last parley. If the French are reasonable" — his men all but howled — "they will meet our demands. If not, they face nothing but destruction on a battlefield of their own choosing."

The soldiers cheered again, shouting their wishes that Henry would live a long life and lead them to many victories. But no one doubted what would happen next. The French would reject all of the king's demands and before the sun set, the field near

Agincourt castle, above which the English army stood, would be soaked with blood.

29
1901

I expected Colin to order me — not, mind you, that he would harbor even the slightest belief that I would obey — to stay home and wait for him to send word from the scene of this latest murder. Instead, his only direction was that I change into something more suitable than my lacy tea gown as quickly as possible so that I might accompany him. He had already hailed a hansom cab when I all but flew down our front steps, still buttoning my overcoat, my gloves nearly falling out of my pockets.

We did not take the carriage because he did not like to make our driver wait indefinitely, and one never knew how long this sort of grim errand might take. Despite the fact that Society had abandoned the capital for the winter, the traffic was horrendous, as the bulk of London's inhabitants did not have the luxury of retreating to the country. A mess of carriages, cabs, and the occasional motorcar entangled us for most of the way to the Savoy Chapel, just south of the Strand.

A crowd had gathered around the modest church, but Colin pushed his way through, keeping me close. The constable guarding the entrance to the building opened his mouth, no doubt to protest my presence, but Colin shut down any objections before the man could speak.

"Not a word from you," he said. "I am in charge here."

The scene inside was not at all what I had expected. Richard II, after all, had died in the dungeon of Pontefract Castle in West Yorkshire, nowhere near a chapel of any sort, so far as I could tell. The Savoy Chapel, originally built as part of a hospital, was, perhaps, more modest than other places of worship, but nothing about the royal peculiar called to mind the dank prison in which the former king had been cruelly left to starve to death.

The body lying on the tiled floor in front of the altar did not look emaciated in the least; quite the contrary. But no one could deny that Mr. Carson, the costume maker, had done an admirable job in constructing the outfit in which it was dressed. The clothing looked straight out of the portrait of

Richard II in Westminster Abbey: a long robe, trimmed with ermine (rather, a good copy of it, as genuine ermine would have cost a pretty penny), over a medieval-style gown embroidered with gold thread. On the man's head, fastened firmly in place, was a golden crown, and in his hands, plaster of Paris copies of the scepter and orb.

"Look, here, Hargreaves, what do you mean by bringing her here?"

I recognized the voice as it boomed through the chapel, so did not bother to turn around to see the wretched Inspector Gale.

"Not another word from you, Gale," Colin said, in a tone I had never before heard him use, the sort of tone from which strong men shrink and weak ones flee. "She's here under my authority and with my permission. Need I embarrass you in front of your men by reminding you that I outrank you considerably? I don't work for Scotland Yard, man, I work for the palace, and my orders will always take precedence over yours."

Apparently, the wretched Inspector Gale was a weak man rather than a strong one. I heard the thud of his boots as he made his way back up the aisle and out the door. Only when it banged shut — behind him, presumably — did I turn around.

Colin raised a single finger. "Do not say a word."

I pressed my lips together. Smiling would have been inappropriate. When I looked at the body again, a hideous glimmer of recognition coursed through me.

"I know that man," I said. Obviously, when Colin had implored me not to speak, he meant about Gale, not the case in general. "Not personally, but from the newspaper. It's Neville Crofton, the man who owned the mine in which Ned Traddles died."

"Yes, my dear, it is," Colin said. "And that is precisely why I insisted on your presence here."

"Have we any clue as to the manner of death?" I asked.

A constable, who was standing nearby, replied. "It's a funny thing, ma'am. There's no sign of injury on him. Not that we disturbed the body, sir, we left things just as we found them."

In the absence of an obvious wound, it would be impossible to ascertain how the man had died without removing his clothing. All we did know was that, like Mr. Grummidge and Mr. Casby, he, too, had been staged to appear as a dead king. But unlike Henry VI and Edward II, Richard II was not felled by a weapon.

"We'll need the autopsy report to determine cause of death," Colin said. "I assume you organized a canvass of the area? Did you or the others find anyone with something useful to say?"

"No, sir, we did not," the constable said. "We secured the chapel first, of course, and then questioned everyone we could, but learned nothing of interest."

Colin and I began to walk the perimeter of the interior, taking note of each way in and out of the building. "This is a crowded part of the city. It would have been difficult to carry a dead man in without drawing anyone's attention."

"Could Mr. Crofton have come in himself?" I asked. "Perhaps led by the murderer? They would have drawn no attention if he was dressed in an ordinary suit. If he'd been poisoned —"

"He would have been unlikely to go anywhere voluntarily with the man who administered the poison," Colin interrupted.

"Assuming he knew the man's intentions," I said. Despite its location, the chapel, tucked into a small garden between the Victoria Embankment and the Strand, did not receive many visitors on any given day, increasing the odds that the murderer might have slipped in unnoticed. I recalled the last time I'd walked by here, seven years ago, in the midst of solving another crime. Like most passersby, all I'd noticed then was the lovely garden. "At any rate, it's all irrelevant until the coroner can tell us the cause of death. What I don't understand, though, is why this place? It has nothing to do with Richard II. Wasn't the chapel originally built by Henry VII as part of the Hospital of St. William? That's far too late to have any connection to the dead king in question."

"You are very nearly correct, my dear," Colin said. "However, before the hospital's construction, the Savoy Palace stood here. Edward I's wife lived in it, and in the fourteenth century it was the London residence of John of Gaunt. John of Gaunt, of course —"

"Was Henry Bolingbroke's father," I finished for him. "And when he returned from exile in France to inherit his dukedom — I can't recall which one it was —"

"He was the Duke of Lancaster, Emily. I should think you'd remember that."

"Yes, quite," I said, scrunching my eyebrows together. From that time, Lancaster became the personal dukedom of the monarch, not linked to the possessions of the Crown. "A rather significant one, particularly in light of what happened next. But you know my expertise lies in history rather more ancient."

Colin smiled. "Henry threw Richard into the dungeon of his Yorkshire estate, Pontefract Castle, leaving the deposed monarch to starve to death. He took the crown for himself —"

"And his son was Henry V."

"Yes, although I'm not certain that matters at the moment," Colin said. "Right now, the significant connection is that this is the location in London that has the closest tie — slightly convoluted though it may be — to Henry Bolingbroke and the murder of Richard II."

We spent the next hour inspecting every inch of the church, but this task, as it had at the prior crime scenes, left us unsatisfied. Whoever had so carefully placed the body had been equally careful to leave behind no sign of his presence. This did not trouble me so much as it had in the past, because there were myriad other things to consider, most of all the identity of this latest victim and his connection to Ned Traddles. There could be no doubt of the ties between this group of East End friends and all three murders.

Colin had the unhappy task of notifying Mr. Crofton's wife, and I offered to accompany him, despite my dislike of delivering that sort of news. I had done it too many times in my life, but I knew that the presence of another lady might be a comfort to Mrs. Crofton. I steeled my nerves and climbed into a cab beside my husband.

The Croftons lived in an ostentatiously large house not far from Belgrave Square. As I have already explained, most of Society fled London in the winter, making me wonder what had drawn the Croftons into town at this time of year. The glow of electric lights brightened the windows of their home, and, as always in such circumstances, I felt a pang in my stomach, knowing that the news we were about to deliver would forever divide Mrs. Crofton's life.

It could not be helped, though, and delay was no kindness. I took Colin's hand and mounted the marble steps that led to their bright red front door. My husband rang the bell, and we waited. After a length of time Davis would have considered outrageously unacceptable, a butler in an ill-fitting suit opened the door. Colin gave our names, explained that we had come on behalf of the palace, and asked if we could see the lady of the house.

"I shall see if she is at home," the butler replied. He let us inside, but only just, abandoning us in the entrance hall without so much as offering to take our coats. He was gone long enough that I began to count — in Greek, as was my habit — the ticks of the tall cabinet clock that stood at the foot of the curved staircase. Nearly a quarter of an hour later, the butler returned.

"Mrs. Crofton will receive you in the gold sitting room."

He opened the door to the chamber in question — it was not six feet from where we had been standing — and we stepped into a room that would have made Louis XIV faint dead in despair. It is quite common for rooms to be referred to by their color, and I had seen countless gold sitting rooms. In general, silk of that hue covered the walls, but in this case, they were covered with elaborate plaster panels, every inch of which was covered in unrelenting gold leaf. The effect was dizzying, as the twelve electric chandeliers hanging from the ceiling cast a glow that reflected again and again off the gilt surfaces. It was as if the Empress Elizabeth of Russia had more money than sense and had rejected the Amber Room for its tackier cousin.

The furniture that filled the space — and I do mean filled; there was so much it hardly left room to walk — did not improve the ambience. Alongside a delicate suite of exquisite Louis XIV pieces stood hulking, chintz-covered chairs and sofas that looked as if they had been plucked out of a middle-class nightmare. Reclining on one of the sofas in a pose I can only imagine was meant to imitate a pre-Raphaelite painting was the amorphous form of a lady of indeterminate age, dressed in a cascade of ruffles and lace unlike anything I'd seen before.

She did not rise as we entered, and I took no offense at this. Given her position, I would have been shocked to find she could move without spilling onto the floor. She lifted a white ostrich feather fan to her face so that all we could see were her eyes.

"Lady Emily, Mr. Hargreaves, it is a pleasure. Do sit. May I offer you tea?"

"No, Mrs. Crofton," Colin said, lowering himself onto the sofa directly across from the one upon which she was sprawled. "I'm afraid we've come on official business —"

"Yes, yes, I cannot say I'm surprised," she said and started to squirm unattractively. I suspected that the arm attached to the elbow upon which she was leaning had fallen asleep. "It was only a matter of time before I was summoned. Alix and I have never been close, mind you, but I knew the moment I met her that we had a connection. Of course, I am happy to serve as a lady-in-waiting. It is an honor."

"Mrs. Crofton, I'm afraid you misunderstand," Colin said. "We are not here on behalf of the queen. I'm more sorry than I can say to have to bring such dreadful news, but your husband has been found —"

"Dead?" She managed to fling herself into an upright position.

"Yes," Colin replied. "Please accept my deepest condolences. He —"

"Don't say another word." She threw her fan on the floor and covered her face with her hands. "I had a premonition something awful was going to happen today."

"Did anything in particular cause you to feel like that?" Colin asked.

"I am a very sensitive soul," she said. She reached up and tugged at the bell pull on the wall behind her. "I feel more than most."

"I am truly sorry for your loss," I said. "Your husband —"

"It is a blow from which I am unlikely ever to recover," she said.

A footman in red and gold livery opened the door. "You rang, madam?"

295

"Yes, my fan is on the floor. Return it to me."

The man did as instructed and exited the room.

Mrs. Crofton did not fool me. I noticed the way her lips trembled, ever so slightly, as she reopened the fan and then closed it and how her face, underneath the rouge on her cheeks, had gone pale.

"Of course, you will want to know what happened," I said. "Would you object to my sitting beside you as Mr. Hargreaves explains? I, too, am a sensitive soul, and don't know that I can bear hearing the dreadful words." She nodded. I crossed to her and took her hand.

"We are not certain yet how this terrible thing came to pass," Colin said. "Mr. Crofton's body was discovered in the Savoy Chapel and it is certain that his death, if you will forgive me for speaking so bluntly, was the result of an attack on his person."

"He was murdered?" she asked. The fan, once again, was flung to the ground. I know one ought not give inanimate objects human characteristics, but I swear it looked exhausted.

"Yes," Colin said. "I can give you as many or as few details as you would like — that is entirely up to you. Unfortunately, we will need someone to confirm his identity."

"Does that mean there is a chance it isn't him?" Her voice sounded small now.

I squeezed her hand. "No," I said. "It's a necessary formality. I myself recognized him from a picture I'd seen in the newspaper."

"Is there anyone I can fetch for you? Do you have children?"

"No," she said. "We were not blessed in that way. Why was he in a church?"

Colin drew a deep breath and then, very gently, explained both the way her husband's body had been posed and how his death fit with the previous two murders. When he finished, Mrs. Crofton pried her hand from mine.

"So he died like a king? I suppose there are worse ways to go. We must take comfort where we can. Have I offered you tea?"

It was nearly two hours later when we managed to disentangle ourselves from Mrs. Crofton. As our cab pulled away, Colin took a last look at the façade of the house.

"That dwelling, my dear, neatly encapsulates every reason your mother has for despising the nouveau riche."

"The interior is an absolute travesty," I said, "but I find less fault with its occupant. Mrs. Crofton is an odd woman, of that there can be no doubt. Yet she was fond of her husband. She did, eventually, make that clear."

"Yes, by sobbing in your lap. The poor thing was in shock when we first told her."

"Which is no surprise. I expect Mr. Crofton was killed as a result of the mine accident, not because he mistreated his wife."

"Unless one could argue that everything about that house constitutes mistreatment," Colin said.

"*De mortuis nil nisi bonum*," I said. But I could not argue that he made a fair point.

30
1415

From that day forward, Adeline and Gabrieli went riding together every afternoon. She always took at least two of her ladies along as well, but never once did she ask Cecily to accompany her. On three separate occasions, Cecily confronted her friend, begging her to consider her behavior. Each time, Adeline shot her a sinister glare and reminded her that, as a guest, she ought not aggravate the mistress of the house.

After hearing mass one morning in October, when the weather had turned cold and rain fell hard against the stained-glass windows of the chapel, Cecily, who, as was her habit, had stayed behind to pray, felt someone sit on the pew. She did not open her eyes, nor rise from kneeling. She paid close attention to the calendar of saints, and every day prayed to the holy person whose feast day it was. Today, she implored Crispin and Crispinian to look after her husband

and protect him in France. Only when she had finished and crossed herself did she turn to see that it was Father Simon who had nearly disturbed her peace.

"Forgive me for intruding," he said, his voice low and gentle. "I wanted to speak to you privately. I am concerned about certain things I have seen, and I believe you know to what I refer."

Cecily felt her stomach plunge to her knees. She nodded, but found she could not speak.

"I cannot claim to have the right to interfere, but someone must," he said.

Cecily found the strength to speak. "I have tried, but my efforts bore no fruit."

"You must be stronger," Father Simon said.

"I cannot force her to listen," she said.

"Her?" Confusion was writ on the priest's face for a flash, but was then replaced with calm determination. "I am speaking of you, Cecily. I have seen how you and Hugh take yourselves off together to converse, and I know that it is Lancelot and Guinevere whom you discuss. As your confessor, I must implore you to tread carefully. Courtly love is not always wrong, but —"

"There is nothing between Master de

Morland and me. Nothing. Courtly or otherwise."

"Adeline came to me, Cecily. She told me what she saw."

"What did she see?"

Father Simon shifted uncomfortably. "You were in the forest. Embracing."

"I have never done any such thing! I wouldn't." Her heart was pounding and she felt beads of perspiration on her forehead despite the cold damp of the stone church. She had seen Adeline and Gabrieli in the forest, weeks ago. Did Adeline know this? She started to tell this to Father Simon, but realized that she would be no better than Adeline if she did. Well. A little better, as she would not be lying, but she could not claim to have a firm knowledge of what was transpiring between the two when she had observed them. Their meeting might have been innocuous. "Speak to Master de Morland. He will confirm what I say. Yes, we have discussed *Le Morte d'Arthur,* and he can tell you that he chided me for having no sympathy for Lancelot and Guinevere. He spoke with me most severely on the subject, but I held my position firm. A wife must guard her fidelity and never stray from the path of righteousness. He wanted to compare Iseult, but I —"

"These are not topics to discuss with Master de Morland," Father Simon said. "Let me hear your confession, Cecily, and I will help keep you on the path of righteousness."

After King Henry offered his last parley, there was nothing to do but wait. William could just barely see the envoys who met in the center of the field, far below where he stood. He did not try to imagine what words they exchanged, because he, like the rest of his fellow soldiers, knew the day would end in a bloody battle. He looked past the negotiators, into the lines of the French army, row after row, seeming to go on forever, and offered one more prayer that God would look after him as he fought. It would take nothing short of a miracle for him and his comrades to survive.

The stench of dysentery filled the air around him, no one willing to move from battle position. The envoys parted and returned to their respective ranks, but nothing else happened. Neither side started to fight. William could feel the restlessness of the men around him, daunted by the sight of the enemy. How long would the French wait to attack?

Everyone expected they would move first.

They were better prepared, better fed, better armed, and rude speculation said that their nobles were eager to finish the fighting so that they might get down to the business of collecting ransoms for any high-ranking prisoners they took. Rumor said that eighteen of the best men in France had pledged an oath to kill King Henry, but the English sovereign still refused to disguise his identity on the field. He would fight in plain sight with his men.

But when? A shrewd commander would know that a small army of men suffering from disease could lose their nerve if they were kept standing and staring at their enemy. King Henry was nothing if not shrewd. He turned to his men and barked a command. Obeying at once, each soldier dropped to his knees and, after kissing the ground, pried up a piece of the wet earth upon which he fell, and put it in his mouth.

Now, they could fight.

William's place in the line was behind the archers, whose deadly war bows were poised to decimate any approaching enemy. Amongst them protruded the sharpened stakes they had fixed in the ground, ready to cause mayhem should any mounted knight approach the English line, but given that the French were not attacking, let alone approaching, the stakes, and the archers, would have to move.

And then, William heard the king's voice:
Felas, let's go!

And then trumpets sounded and drummers beat out a tattoo as the English army started to advance.

Still the French did not move.

The English archers repositioned their stakes in the thick mud, close enough now that their arrows could reach the enemy, and protected by the dense forest on either side of the field.

Now William heard English battle cries and he watched as the arrows of five thousand bowmen darkened the sky, flying so close together they all but blotted out the sun. Then came the shrieks of men and horses as the bodkins hit their targets.

And then the fighting began in earnest.

William and his fellow men-at-arms hung back at first, letting the archers and their long war bows do their work. The French were charging now, but their horses, weighed down by the armored men on their backs, fumbled and got stuck in the thick mud covering the field. Some made it to the English lines, but many who did met their demise at the sharpened ends of the wooden stakes.

As the French men-at-arms advanced, their burnished armor, the armor William had taken note of the night before, became all but a weapon against its wearers. The heavy plate dragged them down into the mud, but those who could free themselves from the muck continued on, and it was against these men that the English fought. Their line was not so deep as the French, and they were initially pushed back some feet, but they rallied and with a loud cry, pulled out their poleaxes and swords and faced their enemy in close combat.

William saw bodies heaped one on top of the other near the king's standard. There must have been a certain amount of truth to the rumor that eighteen Frenchmen swore to kill the English king. Henry was fighting valiantly, delivering blow after blow, not losing ground even after a Frenchman managed to hack one of the fleur-de-lis from his battle crown. William moved forward, wielding his sword with skill and strength, cutting down more men than he cared to count.

And then he saw, not far away, his lord Humphrey, Duke of Gloucester, brother of the king, surrounded by enemies, Henry fighting beside him. William ran toward them, dispatching three of the men-at-arms attacking Gloucester, but he feared his efforts were too late. A tall knight thrust his sword forward into the duke's groin. With a fearsome cry, William fell upon the Frenchman, his sword piercing the slit in the man's visor and sending him to a bloody death. He turned and saw the king himself was standing beside his fallen brother, fighting more furiously than ever. William bettered four more knights and then, seeing the enemy was weakening, he picked up Gloucester and carried him away from the worst of the carnage, managing to fend off two more attacks on the way.

Satisfied that the duke was no longer in danger, he returned to the melee. Blood covered his armor, but he could not tell if it was his or someone else's. He kept fighting, on and on, hardly aware of anything around him except the clash of metal and the sound of men dying. And then, all at once, he noticed the enemy no longer came in such thick waves and that his compatriots had started taking prisoners, looking for those who would bring the best ransoms. Soon it seemed there were more prisoners than soldiers and the fighting had all but stopped.

But the confusion had not.

Word came that their baggage train had been attacked. Were French reinforcements behind them now? Was the English army all but surrounded? King Henry did not have the time to watch and wait. He ordered all prisoners killed, unable to risk that they might pick up the arms of the fallen dead and join in the fight. So far as anyone could guess, they far outnumbered their captors.

And then, at last, King Henry called for the heralds and asked who had won the battle.

"You have, sire," came the answer from the most senior of the Frenchmen holding that position.

"Proving, then, once and for all, that our cause was just," the king said.

"Yes," the man replied.

"What is the name of this place?" Henry asked.

"Azincourt."

"Then forever shall it be known that here, at the Battle of Agincourt" — he pronounced it like an Englishman, not in the French way — "we soundly defeated the French and proved our right to their throne."

31
1901

So far as I was concerned, Mr. Crofton's death certainly threw into question — even more question, that is — the idea that the murders were in some way meant as a threatening message to the king. Colin, however, was not altogether convinced. He could not deny the connections between Lizzie Hopman and her friends, but he insisted this did not mean the murderer was not also using his crimes to make a larger point — or a threat. We were arguing about it in my dressing room, where I was preparing for bed. I had dismissed Meg as I did not require her assistance when my husband was ready to lend a helpful, if diverting, hand.

"The predominant impact of each of the murders — aside from the tragic loss of life and the impact on families, etcetera — is the message sent by the elaborate staging," Colin said. He'd traded his perfectly tailored suit for a pair of claret silk pajama trousers. Their matching top was nowhere in sight, but he had pulled on a paisley silk dressing gown, not bothering to tie it closed. The effect, if I may say, was more than a little distracting as he leaned elegantly against the wall and watched me brush my hair. "What message do you take from the crime scenes, my dear?"

"I know what you are trying to get me to admit," I said.

"The staging of the bodies all but shouts that no one, not even a king, is safe from violent death. Who, then, would not assume the perpetrator means to threaten the king?"

"I cannot deny the logic in your thinking, particularly given the timing of the first murder," I said. Finished with my hair, I laid my silver-backed brush on the dressing table. "Yet I am still unconvinced that your messages tie in the way you think they do."

"And I cannot deny the logic in your thinking," he said. "Before you utter a single word, I must make it clear that I categorically refuse to entertain your notion about secret societies."

I shrugged. "I won't bother to argue."

"That's more alarming than your forcing the idea on me. What are you up to?"

"Nothing, darling," I said. "I shan't trouble you with my silly little thoughts until I've uncovered enough overwhelming evidence to convince even you."

"I have never, ever accused you of being silly." His cheeks darkened and his eyes flashed.

"One must, on occasion, draw one's own conclusions," I said. "At any rate, what's most important now is to determine which of the men who died in Mr. Crofton's mine left behind a family with murderous impulses. And then we shall have to see if he knew either Lizzie Hopman or Mrs. Grummidge."

"And how do you propose doing that?" he asked.

"By going to Wales, of course."

By morning, Colin had convinced me that a trip to Wales was not necessary, although I must admit to regretting it just a bit. I'd always wanted to see the Brecon Beacons. Not, mind you, that I would have included a sightseeing excursion as part of a murder investigation, but if one is in the area, one might as well take advantage of the scenery. Rather than go ourselves, he put Inspector Pickering on the case, ordering him to liaise via telephone with his Welsh counterparts in the village where the mine was located and get them to conduct interviews as appropriate. The village being nowhere near the Brecon Beacons had no impact whatsoever on my agreeing to this scheme.

That settled, Colin went off to Marlborough House, leaving me at loose ends until a message arrived from Mrs. Crofton, asking if I would call on her at my earliest convenience. I had hoped for the opportunity to speak to her again, after the initial shock of her husband's death had passed, but had not dreamed she would reach out to me, especially so quickly.

Her butler was not quite so rude to me as he had been the previous day. I credit this to the icy stare I gave him when he opened the door. The tone in which I demanded to see his mistress might have played a small role, too. He seemed the sort of man who reacted to a firm hand rather than kindness, an observation that made me feel a bit sorry for him.

Mrs. Crofton received me in a chamber so unlike her gold sitting room I could hardly reconcile the two spaces being contained in the same house. This, she explained, was her sewing room, although I saw no sign of any of the implements required for that task. Nonetheless, it was a pleasant little space, its walls painted a rosy pink, with a collection of charming watercolors hanging on them. I complimented her on the paintings, and she blushed so fiercely I wondered if she had painted them herself.

She had abandoned her ruffles and lace for a simple mourning gown, but here, again, she surprised me. I would have expected her to select something covered in a profusion of jet beads, but instead the black crêpe was unadorned except for a simple black braided trim around the high collar and the cuffs of the sleeves. Yesterday, her hands had been covered with rings — one a diamond so large it would have been better suited to a royal crown — but now the only jewelry she wore was a thin gold wedding band and an oval pendant that contained a clipping of what I assumed was her late husband's hair.

The absence of rouge and pearl powder from her face revealed her to be much younger than I had guessed when I first met her. She was past the first flush of youth, but could not have been more than thirty years old. Mr. Crofton, if I recalled correctly, was sixty-three at the time of his death.

I gave her my condolences and accepted her offer of a cup of tea. Her hands were shaking as she lifted the pot.

"Thank you for coming, Lady Emily," she said. "I am afraid you might have formed an incorrect impression of me when you called yesterday. You must understand that Mr. Crofton was a gentleman with very specific tastes, and as he has always been good to me, I was quite content to give him what he wanted. No doubt you have noticed that he was substantially older than I, but I assure you that in no way mattered to either of us. Ours was a marriage based on affection."

"There is no question you were fond of him."

"I loved him, too," she said, swallowing hard. "In a way."

"You need not justify anything to me," I said, not entirely sure what to make of her appearing so unlike the lady I had seen yesterday. If it weren't for the murders of Mr. Grummidge and Mr. Casby, it would be tempting to wonder if she had killed her husband so that she could live a less vulgar life. My mother, certainly, would have approved of that motive for murder. "I am pleased that you wrote to me, although I admit to being surprised by your message. Is there something I can do for you?"

"No, I don't need anything. I'll be comfortable enough for the rest of my life. My husband made sure of that. I just didn't want you to think that I was . . . that . . . I should not have said what I did about the queen yesterday."

"That is of no consequence whatsoever." I wondered what was really worrying her. Surely an offhand (and, admittedly, tacky, embarrassing, and wholly unrealistic) comment about wanting to be a lady-in-waiting made to a total stranger was not the sort of thing over which one would obsess after one's husband had been murdered. "I would have got in touch before long regardless as I had hoped to ask you some questions that might help us find the person who did this to Mr. Crofton. Did he have any enemies?"

"Only every person in Wales after the mine disaster," she said. "But why should he be held responsible? He'd never even been to the bloody — excuse me — place, and I'm sure he did whatever one is supposed to do to make a mine safe."

It was not the fact that she cursed that tripped me up, but the slightest hint of an accent I had not noticed before. Her vowels, just for a moment, made her sound Welsh. "Do you know Wales well?" I asked.

"I've never been there and have no interest in going." Her voice was back to the upper-class drawl she had affected before.

"Had anyone contacted him recently about the disaster? Some of the miners' families, perhaps?"

"No, that's all done and dusted," she said, her tone clipped and callous. "He paid them off, you know. What else could he have done?"

"It was good of him to offer the families compensation," I said. "Not everyone would have done. It is possible, however, that someone amongst the victims' families still bears a grudge and wanted to do to him what he — or rather, the mine — had done to his loved one."

"That's absurd." She shrank a bit in her seat. "Isn't it?"

"Not necessarily. I'm sure that at the moment you are experiencing a tumult of emotions you can hardly make sense of. The miners' families would have gone through something similar when dealing with their grief, and now, months later, one among them may have decided he wanted revenge."

"An inspector from Scotland Yard — Gale was his name — was here yesterday and went through all Mr. Crofton's papers but said there was nothing pertinent to his . . . to his . . . to anything."

That the wretched Inspector Gale would

reach an unsatisfactory conclusion came as no surprise. The man was probably interested in nothing that did not mention Bertie by name. "Did you notice anything unusual in the past few weeks? Was your husband behaving differently? Did he seem troubled by anything?"

"I told him Mr. Crofton had been at his club most of the day that he died, but apparently he never actually went there. Other than that, I know nothing. We've only been in London for a bit over a week, having planned to stop briefly en route to Egypt, where we had arranged to spend the rest of the winter. I'm fascinated by Cleopatra and want to see her tomb. We were to sail from Southampton tomorrow."

I didn't have the heart to tell her that no one has been able to determine the location of Cleopatra's tomb. The famous queen was exactly who I would have guessed inspired the Mrs. Crofton I met yesterday, but the widow sitting in front of me now struck me as someone who would prefer copying the elegant paintings found on the sepulcher walls in the Valley of the Kings. Realizing I was letting my imagination run away with me — I had not, after all, confirmed that she had done the watercolors in her charming sewing room — I shook myself back to the present. "How many people knew of your plans?"

"I haven't the slightest idea. Our staff, of course, and our friends."

"Would you object to me taking a look at your husband's papers, just as Inspector Gale did? I find I often notice things that men overlook."

She reacted to my pointed tone exactly as I'd hoped she would, with a flash in her hazel eyes and a quick grin. "Come, I'll take you now."

Mr. Crofton's wood-paneled study was more in keeping with the gold sitting room than his wife's sewing room. It was evocative of the stereotype of a gentleman's club, with leather chairs and a marble fireplace, but a hulking suit of armor — far too large for any man to ever have worn; it was at least seven and a half feet tall — rather spoiled the effect. A large desk stood in the center of the room, and it was there that I focused my efforts. I went through every sheet of paper on its surface and everything in each of its drawers, but found nothing that even my fertile imagination could connect to his death.

"I don't see anything related to the disaster at the mine," I said. "Did he have an office as well, not in the house?"

"Oh, no, Mr. Crofton wasn't much interested in business," his widow said. "The mine was an investment, that's all. All part of how he kept me in the manner to which he wanted me to be accustomed. That and a host of other things he mentioned from time to time — something about the 'change, I believe — were how he made his money, but he was not involved in the day-to-day operation of the mine or anything else. He was a gentleman, Lady Emily."

I appreciated the nuance of her choice of word, but at the same time understood that Mr. Crofton could not, in the most technical sense of the word, have been a gentleman. He earned his money. For although I saw no documents referring to the accident, I did see numerous letters, memos, and reports about the mine that made it clear he was at the center of decision-making for the business. This added support to my theory that someone from the mine was involved with his murder.

But who? The connection between Ned Traddles, Lizzie Hopman, and Violet Grummidge could not be anything less than critically important. I thought of the fourth and final costume Mr. Carson had made for the elusive Mr. Smith. Who, posed as Harold Godwinson slain in battle, would fall victim to our vigilante next?

After making note of a few details concerning the running of the mine, I thanked Mrs. Crofton and asked her to reach out to me if she thought of anything further that might shed light on her husband's death.

"Of course," she replied. "May I ask your advice on a point that has been troubling me? Would it be too bad of me to go to Egypt as I'd planned? There's nothing more I can do here for poor Mr. Crofton, and I do hate to let the steamer tickets and all our arrangements go to waste."

I need hardly say that I managed to hide my absolute astonishment at her words. Not that I judged her for her unusual behavior; I understood all too well that we all mourn in our own ways. Furthermore, I believe the restrictions forced on new widows by Society are excessive. Yet I could not help being shocked that she wanted to rush off to Egypt so quickly. It was impossible Mr. Crofton could be buried before the boat left Southampton.

"My only advice would be to stay in London until Scotland Yard have released your husband's remains for burial. After that, if they need nothing further from you, I don't see that anyone can keep you from your trip."

She nodded, her eyes narrowing. "I shall ring Inspector Gale at once and ask him to hurry things along. Thank you, Lady Emily."

My carriage was waiting outside the house, but I sent it home without me in it, preferring to walk back to Park Lane. I've always found a brisk constitutional clears the mind and allows for more efficient ratiocination. On this occasion, however, I had not managed to reconcile my thoughts about Mrs. Crofton by the time I reached my house. I made two superfluous circuits of the block without being able to come to a satisfactory conclusion about her contradictory nature. As I approached my stoop and prepared to continue around the block yet again, I saw Colin standing in the library window. He waved and motioned for me to come inside, holding up an envelope as an added incentive.

32
1415

For two days after Father Simon confronted her in the chapel, Cecily moved like a ghost through Lord Esterby's castle, hardly speaking to anyone. Her conscience was so troubled she nearly turned to the baron's terrifying priest, but she was not so far out of her wits that she could believe him capable of giving sound advice to a young lady. Even as she thought this, she said a silent prayer and crossed herself. Who was she to judge a man of God?

She turned to Christine de Pizan for consolation, but found nothing that made her feel better.

. . . the women of the court ought likewise never to rebuke or defame one another . . . as for the fact that whoever would slyly defame another is herself defamed. For assuredly the person who knows that someone is defaming her will also slander that person, and she may even make up stories. Nor is any man or woman so upright that he or she ought to say, "I am not afraid of anyone. What could anyone say about me? I know I am blameless, therefore I can talk fearlessly about other people." But it is foolish for those men and women who say that sort of thing to believe it, for there is always something, somewhere, for which one may be reproached.

The words stung, and Cecily cowered at the cutting knowledge that she was far from blameless. Had she not prayed for clarity? Had she not sought release from the burden of her sins? For her role in her mother's death? And had she not known, without doubt, that to atone she was meant to guide Adeline? Her efforts to do so had been too scattered and too feeble. She would not let any distraction keep her from doing what she knew she must.

That afternoon, she asked Adeline if she might ride with her, but her friend refused. "Work on your embroidery," Adeline said, a sly smile on her face. "I've other plans for today."

The carnage of the day was evident in a

glance to anyone on the field at Agincourt, but only when the roll call came did William realize how significant a victory the English had won. Not only had they lost very few men — so few, he could hardly reconcile it with the blood soaking the ground — but thousands upon thousands of the French, the mighty French, in their burnished armor and seeming endless numbers, lay dead. Not just their ordinary soldiers, but their nobles. It was said the flowers of French chivalry were destroyed that day. The English, gathering up the armor, weapons, and valuables from the corpses of their defeated enemy, were soon overburdened, and King Henry ordered no man to take anything more than he needed to rearm and resupply himself.

It took days to bury the dead. Only the bones of the most noble among them — boiled and boxed for transport — would be returned to England. Families of some of the Frenchmen came to search through the corpses, but aside from a very few, English and French alike were buried in the field in common graves, the land hastily consecrated by the local bishop.

The aftermath of battle was never pleasant, and even the king wept over the fallen. Yet no one could deny the enormous significance of the fighting. God had stood with the English, and whispers of miracles ran through the ranks of soldiers. William gave little credence to one of his comrade's insisting that St. George had appeared next to him on the field and vanquished the Frenchman who was about to run him through with a sword. The king himself gave all credit for the victory to God, our Lady, and St. George, but no one doubted that he knew how tirelessly and with what courage his men had fought.

As the sun hung low in the sky that evening, rain began to fall again, but it would not be enough to cleanse the field of its blood and gore. While the army rested, King Henry would receive the noble French prisoners captured that day. William knew he would treat them with the humility and grace chivalry demanded, and he knew that he should try now to sleep. On the morrow, the march to Calais would resume.

33
1901

"It looked as if you planned to circle the block all day," Colin said, after I'd returned to the house and rushed into the library, not even pausing to hand Davis my coat and gloves. "So far as I could tell, the enticing prospect of a new envelope was my only hope of bringing you back inside."

I was disappointed to find that it was nothing more than a ruse. He had not located the chalice, and hence, no other message. After admonishing him for playing this little trick on me, I gave him a detailed account of my strange meeting with Mrs. Crofton, being careful not to let my shock at some of her behavior — that is, her desire to go to Egypt as planned and the wholesale shift in her personality — color my narrative. He agreed that the change in her was odd, but did not suspect her of nefarious motives regarding her husband.

"Admittedly, if we were looking only at

this one murder, things might seem different," he said. "But I cannot believe that Crofton's death is unrelated to Grummidge's and Casby's."

"I concur." I had flung my coat over a nearby chair. He was sitting behind his desk and I now perched on the top of it, my legs dangling. "We know of Ned Traddles's connection to Lizzie and Mrs. Grummidge, but is it possible that he also had ties to Mrs. Crofton? I detected something in her accent —"

"She may be an eccentric woman, but I doubt very much that she has ties to either Wales or the East End."

"Why?" I asked. "We know almost nothing about her. Mr. Crofton did not grow up a gentleman, did he? If so, he would be unlikely to be so involved in the details of running a coal mine, as the papers I read in his study confirmed. She, too, might have a humble background. In fact, he could have seen her somewhere — perhaps in Mr. Grummidge's greengrocery — and, captivated by her beauty, vowed to remove her from a life of poverty to a life of ease."

My husband leaned back in his chair and crossed his arms. "Pray, continue, my dear. It's been weeks since I've had time to lose myself in a work of fiction."

"What if Mrs. Crofton was best of friends with Lizzie and Violet?"

"Have you even a shred of evidence to connect them?"

"No." I had, before leaving Mrs. Crofton, asked her if she knew either of them; she had denied it.

"And have you any hint — beyond a momentary fluctuation of accent — that suggests Mrs. Crofton grew up poor?"

"Well . . ."

"You raise interesting possibilities, my dear, but without anything to back them up —"

"I know, I know," I said. "Truth be told, much though I like the theory, it doesn't hold together too well. Lizzie died at Casby's hand, and Mr. Grummidge beat his wife. Although her behavior is somewhat eccentric, I detected no hint that Mr. Crofton was anything but kind to his wife. If revenge is our murderer's motive, which I firmly believe it is, the mine disaster must be the catalyst, in which case, I stand by my earlier conclusion that we are searching for a vigilante, particularly given that a friend of Lizzie's and Mrs. Grummidge's died in the accident."

"It is less ridiculous than many of your earlier speculations," Colin said. "However,

I would prefer to discuss actual facts, and I have some new ones for you. The coroner's report has come in. Mr. Crofton died from eating death cap toadstools."

"Good heavens!" I said. "Death cap toadstools? That sounds like something straight out of the Brothers Grimm."

"Apparently, they are easily disguised in food, as they don't look all that different from mushrooms, once chopped and cooked. Furthermore, they take approximately ten days to cause death. The coroner admitted that if it weren't for the manner in which the body was found, he would probably have thought Mr. Crofton died of natural causes."

"What an intriguing choice," I said. "Our murderer could not have spared the time to starve Mr. Crofton to death, in the mode of Richard II, but by choosing a slow-acting poison, he stays true to the spirit of the king's murder. He cares very much about ensuring that he keeps his scenes as accurate as possible."

"Which strengthens the importance of the message he is sending with each crime," Colin said. "Kings can be murdered."

"Would you care to speculate as to what he has planned next?" I asked. So far as we knew, he had one costume remaining: that of Harold Godwinson. "Harold died in battle. Perhaps he means to assassinate Bertie with an arrow through the eye. Only imagine the impact he could have if he could do it during the coronation procession —"

"The coronation has not even been scheduled and is unlikely to occur for another year," Colin said.

"I am well aware of that, but you cannot deny it would be quite spectacular. Not for poor Bertie, of course. I may not be one of his devoted supporters, but I wouldn't wish him such an ignominious end."

"You're generosity itself, my dear." I could see it took a not inconsiderable effort for him to keep from rolling his eyes and gave him a little whack on his arm before he continued. "It would be useful for us to consider poor Harold. What location in London could stand in for the Battle of Hastings?"

Never before had I felt so handicapped by having the bulk of my knowledge of history restricted to the ancient. Beyond the bare basics of that fateful day in 1066, I knew very little. "What if he doesn't plan to stage his next victim in London? He could set the scene at the site of the battle."

Colin shook his head. "I don't think so. It

would not have the immediate impact he has achieved with his other victims. Battle is a small, out-of-the-way town."

"And the people who live there are probably rather accustomed to seeing tourists re-create the battle."

"I myself charged up the hill as a small boy and am confident that most tourists do not leave bodies in their wake. Particularly bodies with an arrow in the eye."

"I was being facetious," I said. "There's not a Hastings Square in London, is there?"

"There's a Hastings Street near St. Pancras in Bloomsbury," he replied. "I've got men watching it around the clock. It ends in Cartwright Gardens, which has a pretty little green space, but it would not bear the obvious connection to Harold that Berkeley Square did for our Edward II. Thus far, our murderer has been shrewd about choosing his locations, even when doing so must have proved a challenge."

"Yes," I said, remembering how the Savoy Chapel connected to John of Gaunt, and, hence, Henry Bolingbroke, King Henry IV after the murder of Richard II. At first glance, one might not realize the significance of the site, but when it was explained, one could not deny not only the appropriateness of it, but also the cleverness of it.

"Surely he would want his last murder — assuming, of course, he only has one further planned . . . a dangerous assumption, I might add — to be the most spectacular of them all."

"Assumptions are always dodgy," Colin said, "but in this case, we aren't assuming. I've had constables calling in at costume shops and they have uncovered no other suspicious orders for outfits meant to mimic kings."

Considering the scenes our dramatic miscreant had already staged, I found it difficult to believe that he could top what he had already achieved. A full-scale reenactment of the Battle of Hastings in Hyde Park? Unlikely in the extreme. "Harold's death is different from the rest. Being killed in battle is a far cry from being murdered."

"Quite right, my dear. So what could that mean? Does it tell us something about the intended victim?" He blew out a long breath. "William the Conqueror felt he had a legitimate claim to the throne of England after Edward the Confessor died. I believe they were cousins."

"I'd say that's not a particularly good claim."

"You're not alone in your thinking," he continued, "and it illustrates one of the myriad reasons that it is preferable for a king not to die without an heir. If Harold's death symbolizes a succession crisis —"

"We must look again at the FitzClarences!"

"No, Emily, that is nothing but a blind alley. I am, however, more concerned than ever." He pulled out from his top desk drawer the messages. "I feel like I am missing something of grave significance. It's all well and good for me to have men watching Cartwright Gardens, but that is not an attempt to stop the murder, just to catch the perpetrator after the fact. I'd prefer to prevent another killing."

"Then you're not convinced Bertie is the intended victim?" I asked. "If so, keeping him protected wouldn't be impossible, would it?"

"I'm not entirely convinced, no, but I do think that in light of the evidence, it's the most likely scenario. If I could, I'd lock the king up to keep him safe, but that would be impractical for a number of reasons. I am reasonably confident that we are taking every precaution. But if I'm missing something . . ."

I could see the tension on his handsome face. His well-cut lips pressed in a hard line, and his strong jaw clenched. He might not approve of Bertie, but he would never let his personal feelings stand in the way of doing his duty. I took his hand. "Well, then, we shall just have to work harder. I'm going to call on Mrs. Grummidge and see if I can inspire her to remember something — anything — about Lizzie and Ned that might lead us to a reasonable conclusion as to who our man might be after next. Care to come with me?"

"She's taken quite a shining to Bainbridge. Why don't you ring him and ask him to take you in that ridiculous motorcar?"

"I'm surprised by your attitude," I said. "I should have thought a man like you would be eager to embrace new technology, as reflected in your insistence on having that dreadful telephone installed the moment it was possible."

"The telephone provides convenience without negative impact. I don't see that loud vehicles spewing noxious fumes will enhance life in our new century. Is not London filthy enough?"

"You can't say they aren't convenient. Only think how fast they are! We could drive to Anglemore Park —"

"In approximately the same length of time it would take us to reach there on a train in a compartment that, if I may be so bold, is far more comfortable and allows for far more interesting ways to pass the time during the journey than any motorcar ever could. Furthermore, the condition of the roads and the presence of other vehicles, many of them slower than —"

"Enough! I'll hear no more. You have, however, piqued my curiosity. Elaborate, if you will, on these far more interesting ways to pass the time on a journey."

"I believe I showed you in detail on our wedding trip when we were en route to Constantinople," he said, looking deep into my eyes. "Surely you have not already forgot?"

"That was nearly a decade ago."

He put his hands around my waist and pulled me across the desktop until I was directly in front of him. "Perhaps I should order a special train to Anglemore and remind you of the possibilities."

"I can think of nothing I would better enjoy," I said, and bent over to kiss him. "You're quite certain Henry isn't hiding somewhere in here?"

"I now make it a habit to inspect every room when I enter it, just to be sure." He pulled me off the desk and onto his lap. The interlude that followed left me focused and refreshed and in such an agreeable frame of mind I did not object to using the telephone to summon Jeremy. When he arrived to collect me, I all but floated down the steps to the motorcar.

"This cold air suits you, Em," he said, passing me a pair of goggles. "Your cheeks are all aglow and your eyes are sparkling. Winter must be your season."

34
1415

Cecily felt ashamed of those days she spent wandering through the castle like a ghost. On the third morning, a message came with news from France. The English had soundly defeated the enemy in a victory described as nothing short of miraculous. Lord Esterby ordered a mass of thanksgiving and a celebratory feast, and the castle all but vibrated with excitement. Father Simon, telling her that the rolls of the dead did not include William's name, was beaming, and Hugh de Morland, standing beside him, let out a joyful yelp and stepped forward as if he would embrace Cecily.

She moved aside and reached for the priest's hand instead, neatly avoiding any contact with de Morland. That she had to do this angered her. Master de Morland had never given her even the slightest indication that he was flirting with her. He had always behaved with honor, but she could not risk anyone — least of all Father Simon — coming to an evil and erroneous conclusion about their friendship. After expressing her relief and delight that her husband would soon return, she excused herself and went in search of Adeline.

The baroness was deep in plans for the feast. Cecily, her voice serious, asked to speak to her privately, and this time, rather than dismissing her, Adeline acquiesced to the request. They went into her bed chamber, Adeline closing the door behind them.

"I am most disturbed by what I have seen happening in this house," Cecily said, not waiting for Adeline to invite her to speak. "I have tried to be a good friend to you. I recognize that you did not appreciate the words of advice I offered regarding Signor Gabrieli. You could argue that your interactions with him are none of my concern, and, in truth they wouldn't be if I cared not for you. We were not close as children, despite being much thrown together."

"You always despised me," Adeline said.

"I did not. I half envied you and half feared you. You had a vivacity that I did not understand."

"You were always too holy to tolerate, dedicated to preserving the memory of your saintly mother."

Cecily all but laughed. "You have misunderstood me from the beginning, and no doubt I have you. But that is no longer of any consequence. We are grown now, both married ladies, and we owe it to ourselves — and to each other — to speak honestly. I do not know what has transpired between you and the troubadour. Yet I cannot, in good conscience, keep from warning you of the danger I see. You know the peril you would put yourself in by entering into an affair. You risk the happiness of your household, but more deadly is the risk to your immortal soul. I shall speak no further on the subject. I have made my feelings and worries clear to you and only want to say, in the strongest terms possible, that I do this not only because it is right, but because I care about you."

"Haven't you some clever phrase from your beloved Christine de Pizan to throw at me? I had not thought you could hold an opinion separate from hers."

"You may mock and insult me as you wish," Cecily said. "But know that I am an honest and loyal friend. I cannot force you to do anything and would not try. But my warnings and cautions are genuine. William will return from France soon and take me away, so you will not be burdened with me

338

for much longer. Until then, I shall keep out of your way and never again speak of this matter. Should you, however, decide not to pursue this affair, I would once again open my heart to you and offer any support you might need."

Adeline's eyes flashed and her pretty face colored a dark crimson. "You disgust me. Accusing me of the very crime you are committing. Your husband shall hear what I've seen, and you will regret forever having tried to slander me."

"I have never slandered you," Cecily said. "If anything, it is you who has resorted to such tactics, in what I can only believe is an attempt to distract your husband from your own behavior. If you think —"

But Adeline did not let Cecily finish. She opened the door and shoved her into the corridor with such force that Cecily slammed into the hard stone wall. Her shoulder would be bruised, but her conscience, at last, would be clear.

The dead buried, the English prepared to resume their march to Calais. Before Agincourt, they had expected battle every day. That was no longer the case; the French defeat was absolute. The king did not even insist that they wear their coats of arms. As

William prepared to leave camp, a man approached him and ordered him to follow him to the place where the king was lodging.

"King Henry would have words with you."

William followed in silence until he was brought before his sovereign. He fell to his knees and bowed his head.

"We are most grateful, Sir William Hargrave, for the service you offered our brother, not only through your skillful fighting that kept the enemy from causing him even more grievous wounds, but also for carrying him to safety. As a gesture of our thanks, we grant you a tract of land in Derbyshire, thirty thousand of the prettiest acres in all of fair England. Rise, then, and prepare to return home."

"I am most humbly obliged, my lord. Your generosity is without parallel."

"Our generosity is never unearned." The king held out a scroll that documented the transfer of land. "We will require your services again, no doubt, and we know that we can count on you to serve us with as much courage as you have shown on this campaign. Tell us, does your wound still trouble you? We know all too well the pain caused by an arrow in the cheek."

William still kept his head bowed and

could not see the king's face, but he thought he detected a note of good humor in this last comment. "It is much better, my lord, and I owe you thanks for ordering your own physician to attend to me."

"It is what physicians are for," the king said. "Go finish your preparations for the march, Sir William, and do not forget to continue to pray. We are not back in England yet, and our enemy, though vanquished, should not be dismissed from our minds."

By the time William returned to camp, the march was about to begin. King Henry's words stayed with him, and he did not let down his guard. They could not ignore the possibility of a French attack, even if it seemed unlikely. But no attack came, and the army, unmolested, covered the miles to Calais, where fresh supplies awaited them. The king arrived a day later and entered the city to the cheers of his supporters, stopping at St. Nicholas' church to offer prayers of thanksgiving to God for having remained at his side.

They would remain in Calais for some weeks, while the king dealt with his prisoners from the campaign; there were ransoms to be determined. No man of honor would fail to come, not after having surrendered. William had taken two captives of his own.

The ransoms he collected for them would support his wife and, God willing, the children they would have, for years.

He waited to leave Calais until the day of the king's departure, and by the time he saw Dover's white cliffs thrusting through the blue twilight, snow had started to fall. The next morning, he joined the king and his retinue as they trekked through Canterbury en route to London. After the royal party left the cathedral, William ducked back inside. He stood before the tomb of the Black Prince, and studied the effigy, offering a prayer on behalf of the mighty warrior. He then turned his attention to the legendary fighter's funeral achievements. His eyes passed over the bascinet, on top of which was mounted the prince's crest, a mighty lion statant, and then the shield and the surcoat, but he could not tear his gaze from the prince's gauntlets. He might have been wearing them as he wielded his sword in battle, defeating the French at Crécy nearly seventy years earlier.

And now, William, too, had helped defeat the French. Agincourt, he believed, would come to be even more significant than Crécy. King Henry's victory was nothing short of a triumph, and England would forever celebrate the day her army conquered France.

35
1901

Before setting off with Jeremy to call on
Mrs. Grummidge, I had telephoned the
clerk at *The Times.* In short order, he rang
back with the information I had requested:
Mrs. Crofton's maiden name. Much to my
disappointment, however, Mrs. Grummidge
insisted that she knew no one called Mabel
Walding and that she had never been acquainted with either of the Croftons.

"I'm more sorry than I can say to be of so
little use." She squirmed in her chair, next
to the fireplace in her snug parlor. "Are you
quite certain you won't take tea?"

"I should love a cup," Jeremy said. He rose
to his feet and crossed toward her, resting
his arm on the mantel. "You've made a most
comfortable home here, Mrs. Grummidge.
I hope I can manage to find a wife who can
create such a cozy nest."

"I'm sure your home is too grand to ever

be cozy, your grace." She blushed as she spoke.

"Too right," he replied. "Did you grow up nearby?"

"Not far away," she said. "After my adoptive parents took me in, that is. I spent my early years in an orphanage."

"I'm so sorry," I said.

"There's no need to apologize. There were some there who were kind," she said, "and once the Athertons chose me, I was very happily settled. They picked me because I'd taught myself to read. Their house was full of kindness and love. I was far luckier than most of the other children I knew."

"Like Lizzie?" Jeremy asked.

"Yes," Mrs. Grummidge said.

"Who else were you close to growing up?" I asked, certain the clue to the murderer's identity lay somewhere in Mrs. Grummidge's past.

"Oh, there were loads of children around. Most of them had to work, and none of us went to school, but there was still time to play."

"Ned Traddles was one of them?" I asked.

"Yes, and his friend Gilbert. And there was a boy called Rodney whom Ned and Gil all but worshipped."

"Can you recall their surnames?"

345

"Gil Barton. I knew him well. But Rodney was not someone my parents wanted me to associate with. Like Ned, he ran with the King's Boys and was always organizing confidence games. He was quite a big man in the gang. I wouldn't be surprised if he wound up running the whole thing. That was always his goal."

"What about Gil?" Jeremy asked.

"Oh, yes, he was a King's Boy, too, and an orphan like me. No one wanted to adopt him, though," she said. "He never knew what happened to his parents, but one day they never came home. I think he was four years old. A chimney sweep found him wandering the streets in search of food and took him in. He was awfully skinny, Gil. Could squirm down the narrowest spaces. That's why the sweep wanted him, of course, but when he grew too big, the man abandoned him. The King's Boys were like a new family to him."

"A criminal family," Jeremy said.

"Yes, I suppose you could describe it as such," Mrs. Grummidge said. "But what else was a boy in his position to do? He hated the orphanage — only stayed there for a few weeks, and then went out on his own. I never did know where he lived. Lizzie and I suspected he drifted from place to place and slept on the street. His clothes were always in tatters."

"And Rodney?" I asked.

"I never knew him well. He was older than us and not interested in silly girls who made lace."

"Did you make all this?" I had noticed the lace doilies and tablecloths the first time I'd come into Mrs. Grummidge's parlor. The work was exquisite.

"I did," she said. "My mother taught me. She thought it would give me an occupation that would keep me inside and out of trouble. Our neighborhood, as you already know, was not the best. A ladylike skill, she always said, helps make a lady."

"Quite right." I smiled at her. A picture had begun to form in my mind, of a group of youngsters being pulled in different directions, each of them trying in their way to rise above their circumstances. Lizzie had not escaped the squalor around her. Ned had, but had still died a horrible death. Violet, who had appeared to have a comfortable life, had married a man who battered her. What had become of Gil? And how did Rodney factor in with the rest? Violet may not have known him well, but Lizzie could have.

Most important, I decided, was the continuing mentions of the King's Boys. It will have escaped no one's notice that a gang with such a name was no doubt run by a person who considered himself a king. I no longer believed Bertie to be in the slightest danger, but as for the odious individual who lured boys into lives of crime? He should not be resting easy.

Realizing I had stopped paying attention to the conversation between Jeremy and Mrs. Grummidge, I shook myself back to the present. The young widow was blossoming under my friend's attention. Her husband had most likely never been kind without expecting something in return, and his notice had brought her more pain than happiness. She was not flirting with Jeremy, but her relief at speaking to a gentleman who would not hurt her was palpable. I hoped her future would contain no more violence.

"It's astonishing how quickly she started to trust you," I said, after we had left the house and were back in the motorcar. "Given her past experience, I should have thought she would despise all men. Yet with you . . ."

"It's the dukedom, Em," he said. "All the ladies trust in it."

"You can be glib all you like, but it's not

that. There's something about you that inspires . . . well, not confidence precisely —"

"I should hope not!"

"But trust," I finished. "You may pretend to be useless, but you cannot hide your decency."

"I've not the slightest idea what you're talking about." He pulled the lever next to him, stomped on a pedal, and our speed increased. "I'm a profligate wastrel."

I studied his face. There was no denying he was attractive — not breathtakingly handsome like Colin, but his well-formed features, bright eyes, and easy smile were appealing. He did his best to appear useless and fast, but I knew his heart was kind and true. Never before had I felt such a strong urge to play matchmaker. Jeremy deserved to find someone who would recognize the golden character hidden beneath his well-curated foppish exterior.

He glanced over at me. "I don't like the way you are looking at me, Em. Either you're considering kissing me, which seems unlikely in the extreme, or you're thinking about trying to marry me off. I recognize the signs all too well. Don't tell me you've become one of those wretched matrons bent on ensuring the girl of her choice will provide me with a suitable heir."

"How on earth could you know?"

"In my not inconsiderable experience, those are the only two explanations for a lady pulling such a face. I much prefer the former and have, on occasion, taken brash action in an attempt to keep from having to deal with the latter. Even old matrons like a good kiss now and again, and it generally keeps them from being too keen on marrying off a chap."

"Good heavens, Jeremy, you can't tell me that you've been going around —"

"Kissing mothers who want me to marry their daughters?" He laughed. "No, not quite. I only kiss the ones who don't have daughters. To do otherwise could bring nothing but disaster."

I stared at him, my mouth open.

"Rendered you speechless, have I?" He grinned. "Now promise me you won't start searching for a suitable duchess for me or I'll have to kiss you. Hargreaves would not be happy and I'd rather not have to meet him with pistols at dawn. I object on principle to all appointments before noon."

This absurd statement deserved no reply. He dropped me in front of my house, making a great show first of helping me down from the motorcar and then of kissing my hand. As he leapt back into the driver's seat, there was an exuberance about him I had not seen for some time, and I resolved to abandon all thoughts of marrying him off. He enjoyed being the Bachelor Duke too much.

Colin was not home, so I asked Davis to telephone Inspector Pickering. Once my butler had passed the handset to me, I made a simple request of my new colleague: bring me everything he could find that relates to the King's Boys. He did not question what I asked, and promised to come to me within two hours. I passed the time reading *The Infidel* and wondered if our heroine, now that her mortal soul was saved, would abandon the deathbed promise she had made the night of her marriage. When, at last, the inspector arrived, I hardly heard him, so caught up in the story was I. He was carrying a file box, tall enough that I could hardly see his face above it. He swayed, and I feared he might drop it, but he steadied himself, deposited it onto my desk, and took the seat I offered.

"I brought everything," he said, "so you can read for yourself, but I am also prepared to offer what I hope is a thorough summary of what I have learned. The King's Boys is a notorious gang, as you already know. They have been a presence in the East End since the middle of the last century. Like so many others, their leaders recruit children — primarily young boys — and train them as pickpockets. When they're too big for that, they move onto other targets, like the tills in West End shops. They also run a far-reaching protection racket, but we've never been able to hold them accountable for it."

"Who are the leaders?" I asked.

The young man pushed up his spectacles, which had begun their usual descent down his narrow nose. "We don't know. Other gangs are not so reticent about their organizations. It's considered a position of honor to be a captain or junior officer, as some of them call themselves, and we keep close tabs on a number of individuals we know to be at the top. But the King's Boys never refer to their master, if I may use the word, as anything other than *The King.*"

"I encountered a number of them when I went to the Black Swan," I said. The color drained from his face; he pushed his spectacles up again and opened his mouth to speak. I stopped him before he could. "I shall brook no criticism from you, Inspector, for the way I choose to handle my investigation. I shall not be put off from finding the truth simply because doing so involves visiting a brothel."

"I beg your pardon, Lady Emily," he said. "I meant no criticism. It was just that, as you spoke, your tone reminded me so very much of my late mother, it was almost as if I were standing before a ghost."

I was not sure I liked a man of his age comparing me to his mother. I was not, after all, nearly so old as she would be now, had she lived. Deciding the best course of action was to ignore his explanation, I continued. "The boys I saw were all wearing emerald green scarves around their necks. Does that serve to mark them as members of the King's Boys?"

"Yes, quite," he replied. "They call them *stooks*. Most unruly youths wear white ones, but not the King's Boys. I found the file on Gilbert Barton, but none that references anyone who could be our Rodney. Barton has been in and out of jail more times than I can count, but his record ends about five years ago. I have not been able to find an address for him."

"How long do I have to read the files?" I asked.

"I'll need to return them by tomorrow morning before eight o'clock."

"Then I have my work cut out for me, don't I?" I smiled at him and gave him my thanks. He kept glancing surreptitiously at the door, and I knew he was hoping to see Colin. "I don't expect Mr. Hargreaves back for some time, but if you'd like to stay and help me go through these, I would welcome the assistance."

"That's very kind of you, Lady Emily. Where would you like me to set up shop?"

I directed him to one of the long tables parallel to the library's bookcases and gave him a blank notebook and a pencil. We divided the files — all of which, presumably, he had already read — and set to work. I admit the task was disheartening. Page after page of crimes committed by boys too young to be out of the nursery. As they got older, they became more brazen, their acts more and more audacious. A group of three of them had descended upon a respectable lady in Hyde Park and managed to make off with her watch and handbag before anyone could come to her aid.

As Inspector Pickering had said, they all seemed to be in and out of jail with a dizzying frequency, and not one of them ever gave the name of the man — or men — at the head of their organization. Their loyalty to their king appeared to know no bounds. Fascinating — and horrifying — though it all was, I found nothing that shed further light on the murders except that I took it as further evidence that Edward VII was not the target of our killer's ire. Growing frustrated, I started to pace — a habit I had picked up from my husband — and soon had drifted over to the table at which the inspector sat. One of the files next to him caught my eye. I reached for it and started to leaf through.

"Here!" I said, my voice full of building excitement. "I should have thought to ask this before, when you told me about Ned Traddles. Look — the man who did not press charges when the boy was arrested — Prentice Hancock!"

"I'm afraid the name means nothing to me," Inspector Pickering said. "Ought it?"

"Yes, well, no, you weren't at the church. Prentice Hancock came to Lizzie Hopman's funeral, you see. He grew up in the East End and has done all he can to improve conditions there. He knew Lizzie and obviously did what he could to set Ned on a better path —"

"No, no, Lady Emily." My colleague was growing excited now, too. His spectacles fell right off as his face glowed with enlightenment. "He didn't want the boy on a better path, he wanted him in his control —"

"Of course. What better way to lure a

vulnerable child into his clutches? How could I be so foolish not to have thought of it myself?"

"It is a credit to you that you did not," he said.

"Mr. Hancock didn't give Ned a second chance, he recruited him," I said. "Which means that Mr. Hancock could be the so-called king —"

Inspector Pickering rose to his feet. "If you are correct, he is in a great deal of danger." I half expected him to rush off in search of the man and realized I ought to rein in his enthusiasm.

"It is too soon for us to draw any firm conclusions. We don't know for sure what Mr. Hancock's motives were. It is entirely possible that he was engaged in nothing nefarious, but we need to interview him as soon as possible and can start by going to the address he gave after Ned picked his pocket."

"Ought we wait for Mr. Hargreaves? I wouldn't want him to think I had led you into danger."

"Mr. Hargreaves knows better than to try to keep me out of danger," I said. I led my companion back into the hall and asked Davis for our coats and hats. "And at any rate, we have no reason to think Mr. Hancock will view us as a threat, should he prove to be a criminal mastermind. He asked me for my assistance in his charitable work after Lizzie's funeral. We shall let him think my enthusiasm for his cause has got the better of me." I raced down the steps and hailed a cab in Park Lane. My young friend matched my pace, but the look on his face betrayed his emotions. He was very, very concerned at taking his idol's wife into a rough part of town.

36
1415

Cecily received one letter from William after the English victory at Agincourt. It was brief — terse, even — but he signed it *your devoted husband* and said that he would be in Sussex soon. Surely Father Simon would not have been able to get word to him of Adeline's foul accusations, but Cecily could not help but worry. She kept to herself, afraid to so much as speak to Master de Morland, and worked on her embroidery. She had covered nearly two-thirds of the panel she had started, but no longer could take pleasure in the scene she had chosen. The lady holding the book was complete, as was the circle of friends around her. They were sitting in a forest with trees and flowers all around them. Off to one side, she had sketched the form of a knight returning from battle, his standard flying high above him. She had styled him after William, but now whenever she looked at the drawing, she worried that he would not be pleased to return. Not if he could be persuaded that his wife was not guarding her virtue with care.

Worry now her constant companion, she found she could hardly eat. Alys, her nurse, the only servant she had brought with her from Lord Burgeys's house, ordered her to bed, and fussed over her, believing she had fallen ill. But when she came upon her young charge and found her in tears, Alys coaxed the truth out of her.

"My poor child," she said, drying Cecily's eyes. "You have fallen victim to your own innocence. Anyone could see Adeline's scheme — she wanted to create a false scandal that she could use to hide her own affair. No one will be looking at her behavior if they're busy gossiping about yours. I know you too well to need to ask if you engaged in any flirtation, but is there anything she might have seen and misinterpreted?"

"No, nothing at all," Cecily said. And then she confessed what she had witnessed in the forest. "I know, Alys, that I have failed her as a friend."

"She is no friend, and the sooner we leave this place the better. Sir William will be here before long, and that will put an end to all of this nonsense."

"No, I cannot leave until I have saved her from the treacherous path she is following. It is my penance. I made a sacred promise."

Alys frowned, but said nothing for some time. "I cannot force you to act against your wishes, but I promise you that interfering with Adeline will bring you nothing but misery. God would not ask such a thing of you."

"I took the life of one He favored, my mother. There is nothing He cannot ask of me in return."

The old nurse recognized the stubborn set of her charge's jaw and knew argument would prove futile. A few judicious words to the visiting priest, however, might be just the thing. Father Simon should not have been so easily taken in by the charming mistress of the house. But Alys never got the chance to speak to him. The next morning, the baron ordered her and Cecily to leave the castle, without even giving them time to gather their belongings.

William was less than a day's ride from Sussex when he heard Hugh de Morland hailing him. The knight's retinue was small — only his two squires, his prisoners, and a handful of men he had fought with in France, who, having heard of the king's commendation and gift of land in Derbyshire, had pledged their loyalty to him. It was time for him to form a household and set up his fief. He waved to Hugh and called back to him, dismounting from his steed and embracing his friend.

"Your face —" Hugh blanched at the sight of William's wound.

"It is not handsome, I know," William said. "I can only hope my bride does not run from me when she sees it. I see the shadow cross your countenance. She is not ill, is she?"

"No, my friend, she is not, but she is no longer at the baron's estate. There was a controversy and Lord Esterby flung her out. He would not let me, nor anyone else follow. She had only her old nurse with her. I knew you were en route and that I could find you on this road. I came without delay."

"There is no controversy shocking enough to merit such treatment of a lady. I shall deal with him after my wife is safe." He scowled. "What is she accused of?"

"Corrupting Lady Esterby, it would seem," Hugh said. "Enticing her by example."

"Speak not like that to me, Hugh. What is the specific nature of the accusation?"

"Well, William, he thought that Lady Hargrave's attachment to my humble self might give his own bride ideas she ought not have."

William felt heat building in his chest, and recognized it as kin to the rage that had consumed him during battle. He looked at his friend, handsomely dressed, his face unmarred by an ugly scar. He remembered the sweetness of his wife's kisses. "I would never doubt you, nor her. It would seem someone in the baron's castle is a liar. He'll have no more to say when I finish with him."

He swung himself back onto his horse with an impossibly fluid motion and urged the steed forward at a gallop. Hugh followed suit, though without his friend's elegant skill. He would do whatever was necessary to match his pace. William must not reach the castle alone.

37
1901

No sooner had Inspector Pickering and I set off in search of Prentice Hancock than I regretted not having asked the man in question to give me his card after I had presented him with mine at Lizzie Hopman's funeral. This feeling was compounded when we reached our destination. The building in front of us was not a residence, but a laundry. Upon inquiring with the current proprietor of the establishment, a rather intimidating-looking woman who stood nearly a foot taller than my young companion, we learned that she had converted it from a haberdashery.

"Which is precisely what Mr. Hancock ran," I said, turning to Inspector Pickering.

"He told me I could do whatever I wanted to the place," the laundress said. Her voice, both in tone and volume, would have shamed a fishmonger's wife. "It's not my fault he weren't asking a fair price. If he don't need money, what business is it of mine?"

I recalled that Mr. Hancock had mentioned selling his shop upon his retirement. This, combined with the woman's continued shrieks proclaiming her innocence regarding the details of the transaction, lent credence to his claims that he did what he could to improve the lives of those who dwelled in the East End. Inspector Pickering, pushing up his spectacles, stepped directly in front of her and gripped her firmly by the shoulders.

"I've no interest in Mr. Hancock's business transactions," he said. "But I have a great deal of interest in his current whereabouts. Tell me where I can find him. If I'm successful as a result, you'll receive a handsome reward."

She pursed her lips and looked down at him. "Well . . . I suppose there's no harm in it, is there? He lives six blocks over, beyond the Black Swan. Wouldn't take *her* that way if I was you." She scowled at me and then held her hand out to the inspector, palm facing up.

With a quick gesture, he pinned her hand behind her back. "The reward comes only if I'm successful." I cast a sideways glance at him, shocked that he could sound so authoritative, and then glared at the laundress. I would have liked to have barked out a sharp retort of my own, but confess that, in the moment, none came to mind. Instead, I let Fenimore Pickering bustle me back into our waiting cab.

"Well done, you," I said, after he'd closed the door.

"I find that appearing meek often keeps my opponents off guard," he said. "Not that I would say our laundress constitutes an opponent. Still, I do like to stay in practice." His grin was that of a naughty schoolboy who has just pulled off a grossly inappropriate scheme.

After a short drive, we reached the modest terrace house that stood at the address the laundress had provided. We knocked on the door and were told by a pert young maid, her uniform starched almost to snapping, that Mr. Hancock was not at home.

"Oh, dear, how perfectly dreadful," I said, doing my best to imitate a female version of Jeremy's favorite drawl. "Whatever am I to do now? Fenimore, dear, give me your arm, I'm afraid I'm feeling a bit unsteady." I swayed to lend verisimilitude to my words. The inspector, not missing a beat, caught me and propelled me up the stoop closer to the door.

"Out of the way, girl," he said. "Can't you see she's about to faint?"

Flabbergasted, she stepped aside and let us into the house. Once there, I flung myself onto a settee and called for water. The inspector prodded her to produce it, and she flew out of the room. He closed the door behind her.

"What do we do now?" he asked.

"Search the place, of course," I said. "See if you can find anything that might prove a connection to the King's Boys, or any other criminal activities. Or to Harold Godwinson."

"King Harold?" he asked. "Of the arrow in the eye?"

"Yes."

He did not question me further, but made quick and efficient work of inspecting every inch of the room. I was doing the same, of course. Neither of us found anything of interest. When I heard the click of the maid's heels in the corridor, I returned to the settee and draped an arm over my face. She handed me a glass of water, but I pushed it away, insisting that I was no longer in need of refreshment. "Fenimore, go to the study and fetch me some paper. I will have to leave a note for Mr. Hancock."

The maid did not stop him when he left

the room. I took this to mean that there was, in fact, a study, and that Mr. Hancock did not, if I may be permitted a naval analogy, run a particularly tight ship. "Do you need anything else, madam?" she asked.

"How long have you worked for Mr. Hancock? It's so good to see what he's done for the old neighborhood."

"The old neighborhood? Surely you didn't used to live here, did you?" She was blinking rapidly. Knowing that I would not be able to convince her that I had been reared in the East End, I took a different tack.

"No, no, of course not," I said. "But he's told me so many stories of the place that I feel like I know it as well as he. I've helped him find work for —"

"That's so very kind of you, madam," she said. "I should've known when I saw you at the door. Your hat told me you're a lady of fashion, if you don't mind my saying so."

"How long have you worked for Mr. Hancock?" I asked.

"Only three months," she said. "He rescued me from a far worse life."

Her cheeks colored and I decided there was no need to inquire further about her previous employment. "And he is a good master?"

"The best. Kind and generous."

"How large is his staff?"

"There are five of us, all from the old neighborhood, as you say."

A small number, but more than nearly anyone else had in this part of town. Mr. Hancock's house was no larger than those surrounding it, but it was in far better condition. No peeling paint or broken windows here. The furnishings were modest and tasteful, almost as if they had been selected in a deliberate effort not to be showy.

Inspector Pickering returned to the room with a sheet of paper and a pencil, which he handed to me. A quick and subtle shake of his head told me he had discovered nothing of significance in the study. I penned a note, asking Mr. Hancock to call on me at his earliest convenience, thanked the maid for her assistance, and we quitted the house.

Stepping back into the street, the smell of something rotting assaulted us. Mr. Hancock had succeeded in creating a haven for himself, but it would not be so easy to do the same for his surroundings. A pack of boys ran past us, all of them sporting emerald green scarves. I reached out to stop one of them, but they were too quick.

"You won't get anywhere with them, Lady Emily," Inspector Pickering said.

I pulled a face. "True, but I know someone who might."

Back home, after I'd dropped the inspector at Scotland Yard, I found my husband in his study, where, beneath a cloud of cigar smoke, he was poring over a stack of papers that pertained to hypothetical threats against King Edward. He looked relieved to push them away, explaining that he had been over them twice already and could find no connection between any of them and the murders.

"Perhaps I can present an alternative possibility," I said. He listened attentively when I detailed my theory about the King's Boys.

"It's a reasonable idea," he said, leaning back in his chair and clasping his hands behind his head. "I read through Pickering's files as well — I assumed that's why you left them on my desk downstairs — and find it striking that there is no information about the leaders of the gang. That's quite unusual. Ordinarily, those in charge are happy to reap the rewards of their positions. They command a great deal of fear and respect, and are careful to never be implicated in any criminal schemes. They're dashed difficult to arrest."

"I suspect Prentice Hancock is the king in

question. And before you ask, no, I have no evidence to support my claim," I said. "So far as I can tell, he's a model of propriety and a beacon of light in the East End. It is his very sincerity that gives me pause."

"How very cynical of you, my dear. I should have thought you'd be singing his praises."

"It is wholly out of character for me, I agree. But he is the man who gave Ned Traddles his second chance — a second chance that never amounted to anything at the time. So far as I can tell, Ned joined the King's Boys immediately after the police let him go. If Mr. Hancock is the king, he was in the perfect position to get Ned under his control. The child would have been so grateful not to have been sent to jail that he'd do anything his savior asked."

"And by maintaining a reputation for goodness, who would suspect him of anything nefarious? But what does Hancock gain from it all? Based on your description of his domestic arrangements, he's hardly living a life of luxury. What does he do with his ill-gotten gains?"

"Perhaps he prefers power above everything," I said. "Which would explain why he chooses to be called king, not captain. Furthermore, he could be a miser."

"I take it you want to warn him that he may be in danger?"

"I don't see how I can do otherwise. He may be a vicious reprobate, but I cannot stand by and let him be slain."

"Quite," he said. "However, you haven't confirmed whether he is, in fact, running the gang. Warning him could put you in a great deal of danger. It would tip him off to your interest in the organization. Even if he's not in charge, word might get back to their so-called king. On another subject, I have news of my own. In my ongoing quest to find the chalice illustrated in our last clue, I went to your favorite spot in London today, the British Museum. And there, behind a case holding a rather magnificent Anglo-Saxon vessel very like the one in the drawing, I found this." He passed me a sheet of paper sheathed in an envelope bearing the Hargreaves coat of arms.

"*The brother of the king, the noble Duke Humphrey, was wounded in the groin. Gore flowed down from the sword. Having fallen to the ground, the king stood over him to assist him. He was in this battle the defender of his brother.* Your much-loved Tito Livio Frulovisi again?" I asked, studying the sword sketched at the bottom of the page.

"No," he replied. "This is from a chronicle

penned by a monk in Canterbury, Thomas Elmham. Humphrey was wounded at Agincourt."

"I don't see how this fits with any of our theories," I said. "Let us consider the broader implications of the messages. All of them refer to Henry V, correct? Why would Queen Victoria have wanted to turn your attention to him in particular?"

"Perhaps she believed her own son would prove as disappointing a monarch as Henry V's did."

"Henry VI wasn't all bad," I said. "He founded Eton and King's College, Cambridge, which to my mind has one of the most beautiful chapels in all of England."

"Don't ask a Trinity man to start lauding King's, my dear." He motioned for me to return the letter to him, which I did. He picked up a magnifying glass from his desk and scrutinized every word on the page. "There's nothing in the handwriting, nothing unusual in the paper. Not that I expected there would be."

"I don't suppose King's College could have a connection to the King's Boys?"

"Highly improbable. I shall have to focus on finding the sword and the next clue." He sighed and turned his head at the sound of a knock on the door. "Yes?"

Davis opened it and peered in. "A Mr. Prentice Hancock to see you, Lady Emily. I've put him in the crimson drawing room. It seemed the most appropriate place for someone who looks so much like Father Christmas."

Truly, my butler was a man after my own heart.

38
1415

Alys heard the horses before Cecily, who was kneeling next to a tree, praying so fervently nothing could have distracted her. It was only when the nurse pulled her by the shoulder that she crossed herself and rose to her feet, steeling herself. Two un-armed women would be easy prey for ban-dits. Cecily vowed she would never again be so unprepared, although she could not blame herself in the circumstances. Lord Esterby had not allowed her to take anything with her when he flung her out of his castle.

Before fear settled into her, relief replaced it. She saw William's standard and then caught the gleam of his scabbard through the thick trees. As he approached, she gasped when she saw the jagged red scar on his cheek. She dropped back onto her knees and began to weep.

"I knew it to be ugly, but had no inkling it was so bad," William said, jumping down from his horse and crouching beside her.

"I see nothing ugly," Cecily said. "I weep in relief that the wound did not kill you. I had no idea you were hurt."

"All men are hurt in battle, one way or another. It is nothing that should trouble you. Tell me, wife, why you are here in the woods."

She glanced at the men with him and saw Hugh de Morland. "No doubt your friend has already shared my sad story. I swear to you I have done no wrong."

"But Lord Esterby has," William said. "And I suspect his wife is no better."

"You must allow me to defend myself." Cecily could not bring herself to meet his eyes. "I would never behave in a manner that would bring such shame to you."

"You are my wife, Cecily, and I trust you implicitly. There is no need for explanation or defense. I take you at your word and now want only to restore your honor." He motioned to his men and one of the squires dismounted and brought his horse forward. He helped Alys climb atop it, her full skirts making it difficult, but not impossible for her to sit astride the saddle. William, back on his chestnut steed, motioned again, and another squire boosted Cecily up behind him. She sat sideways, her arms tight around her husband's waist.

The women had not covered much distance since their expulsion, and it took very little time for William's party to reach the castle. Once they had passed through the outer and inner gates, William shouted to the men guarding the inner courtyard, identifying himself and commanding them to bring the baron to him.

To Cecily, it seemed as though it took Lord Esterby longer to cover the distance from his hall to the courtyard than it had taken her husband's retinue to make its way through the forest. Adeline was at his side, her shoulders thrown back, a wicked look of glee on her face. It was she, rather than her husband, who spoke first.

"You ought not have come back here, Cecily," she spat. "You are no longer welcome."

"I am here to speak with you, Lord Esterby," William said. "There is no need for a scene."

"It was an attempt to avoid a scene that led me to ask Lady Hargrave to leave," the baron said. "You know I would not have done such a thing had I any other option."

"I will not stand idle when anyone besmirches the good name of my wife," William said, his hand resting on the pommel of his sword. Father Simon, who had been standing behind Adeline, stepped forward.

"Violence will solve nothing, William."

"I have not come for violence, Simon, my old friend," he said. "I have come to collect Cecily's belongings. We neither of us seek further acquaintance with any who would believe lies. Bring her things at once, her books included, and we shall be gone."

"She can't deny the accusations," Adeline said.

"I have no interest in doing so," Cecily replied. She slid down from her husband's horse and walked with slow, measured steps until she stood directly in front of the other woman. "Virtue is a reward unto itself, and it is a reward I know well. I need not sully another's reputation in a vain attempt to save mine, for all who are decent and honest know the truth about me. I am afraid of nothing and of no one. I thank you for the hospitality you and Lord Esterby have given me and bear neither of you a grudge. I pray you find much happiness with each other." Finished, she turned on her heel and quitted the courtyard, not pausing even to exchange a glance with William. She did not stop until she had exited the outer gate of the castle and reached the edge of the woods surrounding it.

Her heart pounding, she wondered what William would say. Instead of allowing him to defend her, she had made a spectacle of herself. She heard someone approaching from behind and squeezed her eyes shut, terrified to see his reaction. If he had even come himself.

He had. He pulled off his gloves and touched her chin with a single finger, lifting it up. Still, she kept her eyes closed. "Open," he commanded. She obeyed. "What a thing it is to learn one has taken a wife as fit to do battle as a knight himself. I could not ask for a better partner. Come, now, we must on to Derbyshire without delay. We've a house to build and an estate to manage. I've much to tell you."

39
1901

Before we descended from the study to the drawing room, Colin and I had a refreshing discussion about how to approach Mr. Hancock. My husband felt we ought not accuse him outright of running the King's Boys, while I felt direct assault the most likely way to get an unguarded reaction from him. In the end, however, I acquiesced to Colin's demands. He presses me on very few occasions, and when he does, uses methods I shall not discuss except to say I do not consider them entirely fair. They all but guarantee him a satisfactory result and leave me incapable of voicing complaint. We would go easy on Mr. Hancock.

"What a delight to find you had called," he said, after refusing my offer of tea. "I'm more sorry than I can say to have missed you. You ought not be wandering around the East End, Lady Emily, even with an escort. It can be rather dangerous."

His words struck me as more ominous than he had likely intended. "I was in the neighborhood on other business and heard mention of your name," I said. "As I told you when we met, I am looking for charitable works I might support in the area."

"It's very good of you," he said. "I do hope we can find a way to work together. There is so much to be done."

"Quite," Colin said. "If you will forgive me, my dear, I do have concerns about your plans. I've heard a galling number of stories about the gangs that run riot in the neighborhood, the King's Boys in particular. I don't like the thought of my wife being harassed by them."

"The King's Boys are no worse than some of the others, and better in ways than most," Mr. Hancock said. "That might be why I've had no luck turning its members away from crime. They're not so recklessly violent, and, hence, tend to spend less time in jail than some of their compatriots."

"How do you entice them to leave their evil ways behind?" I asked.

"I have a certain reputation, you understand," he said. "It is known that I will help anyone willing to do honest work find a position, even if I have to guarantee his — or her — character myself. I can offer a bit of money to ease the transition and do my best to show them an example of a better way of life. I am not a rich man, Lady Emily, but I have done well enough to live comfortably. What man could ask for more?"

"I'm surprised to hear you say the King's Boys aren't so violent as other gangs." Colin crossed to the table upon which stood a crystal decanter filled with his favorite whisky. He poured two glasses and gave one of them to our guest. "I know you'd rather not indulge, my dear." I smiled sweetly and hoped I looked demure. In truth, I wanted to laugh at him playing the part of the typical husband. He returned to his seat and continued. "I've been told more than once that the King's Boys are the most notorious villains in the East End, that their leaders operate anonymously, and that their treatment of their underlings is quite vile. But of course, you have far more experience than I."

"I'm afraid I don't. Closer proximity to them, perhaps, but little else. All I know is that despite years of trying, I've never been able to persuade even one of the King's Boys to pursue an honest life."

"I spoke with someone this morning, not far from your house. He was wearing a green scarf — I believe that represents the King's Boys, does it not?" I asked. Mr. Hancock nodded. "He was called Rodney and seemed not altogether dedicated to the organization. I could be wrong, of course, but it felt to me like he was looking for a way out. He was considerably older than I expected, which is silly as there would have to be adults at the top of the organization. I hadn't seen anyone else his age sporting a green scarf, which led me to approach him. I thought he might be running the show, but it became clear he reports to someone else. Have you met him?"

"Rodney?" Mr. Hancock frowned. "No, I don't believe I have. I can't think of anyone of my acquaintance called that."

So much for drawing Rodney's surname out of him. "Well, you ought to seek him out, Mr. Hancock," I said. "I am certain he's ripe for conversion. I understand that a number of Lizzie Hopman's friends ran with the King's Boys. Did you recognize any of them at her funeral?"

"I can't say I did, Lady Emily." His eyes danced. "You've got quite a spitfire here, don't you, Mr. Hargreaves? I reckon she could have the whole East End cleaned up in a fortnight if she set her mind to it."

"She's unstoppable," Colin said. "Which

is why I'm so grateful that she's found you, Mr. Hancock. Perhaps together we can persuade her that she can offer the backing required for your work while you handle whatever must be done in situ."

"An admirable suggestion, sir, admirable. I had hoped for as much, and, as a result, brought you a little summary of some of my plans. If you would be so kind as to look through this list, Lady Emily, and select whichever strikes your fancy, we could, perhaps, start there. There is an orphanage not far from St. Botolph's that is in dire need of renovation. The poor children don't even have a yard to play in. I could see at once that you have a kind heart and thought this might be a wonderful way for us to begin our partnership, if I may be so bold as to call it that."

I took the folder he held out to me. "How marvelously observant you are. I shall read through this all as quickly as I can and make a decision. Would it be best if I send a cheque along with my response? That way we can get to work with as little delay as possible."

"I am speechless, Lady Emily, at your generosity, but there is no need to send money at once. Let us first set our goals and construct a plan. Take your time considering the options and reach out to me when you are ready. In the meantime, please accept my thanks for your gracious assistance." He thanked Colin for the whisky, complimented me on my housekeeping, and left us with a charming smile.

"He seems less and less like a criminal mastermind," I said. "If he hadn't rejected my offer of a cheque —"

"He seems to me more and more like a criminal mastermind," Colin interrupted. "Too smart to let us think he was after money, careful not to make you feel pressured, full of compliments and kind words."

"I had hoped he might be able to give us information about Rodney, but he showed no sign of knowing the man. But then, if he is, as you suggest, a criminal mastermind, he would be careful to reveal nothing."

"You leap to the conclusion that Rodney is significant to anything. Most likely he's a mid-level thug who doesn't even matter to his mother. She would have given up on him years ago."

I frowned. "I hope you're right. Not about his mother, but that he isn't important to the organization. Mentioning his name might put him at risk. I should have thought of that. It was careless of me not to."

"Would you like some whisky, my dear? I

hated not to offer any to you, but thought it best in the circumstances. I had the impression you wanted Mr. Hancock to see you as a very earnest and very naïve sort of wife."

"I did, indeed," I said. "Was it not what you counseled me to do? But no whisky for me, thank you. I'd prefer port if anything, but need a clear head at the moment. I still worry that we ought to have warned him about the possible threat to whoever is running the King's Boys."

"I don't see how we could have done that without revealing more than we wanted to." He crouched in front of the settee upon which I was sitting and took my hands in his. "If Hancock is involved in the gang, he is dangerous and deceitful. As I've said before, a warning of any sort might alert him to you not being entirely honest about your own role in this mess. And that, my dear, could put you in an intolerable amount of danger."

"But not having done so could prove fatal to him."

"There are times when one must accept that risk as part of the job. It is unpleasant — surprisingly so when the individuals involved are the worst sort of reprobates — yet unavoidable. A decent man, or woman, does not take anyone's life lightly. Sometimes the only comfort one has is knowing that one's actions, in the end, do more good than harm." Still in front of me, he opened my hands, turned them over, and kissed each of their palms.

"I am most grateful for your wise words," I said. "I realize you have far more experience than I."

He raised an eyebrow. "What exactly are you planning to do that spurs you to take advance action to soothe my ego?"

"Nothing at all," I said. "Although I cannot help feeling that we are missing something. Given that all of the clues in your scavenger hunt have to do with Henry V, is there some connection between him and the Battle of Hastings? Did he admire William the Conqueror above all other kings or show signs of fascination with his military tactics? There is, after all, a sword drawn on the note you found at the museum."

"Not that I can think of." He stood up and poured himself another whisky. "I do see what you're getting at, though. If the murders and the letters are related, discovering how might help us prevent more violence. You've ordered Pickering to find out everything he can from the constables who cover the area where the King's Boys are active?"

"Yes. He thought it unlikely they'd have anything to say beyond what we've already read in reports, but it's worth a try. And I assume the wretched Inspector Gale is still convinced it's all a plot to assassinate Bertie, er, the king?"

"Naturally. He's a stubborn buffoon, but that doesn't mean he's wrong," Colin said. "The king's safety must be my primary concern, even if I'm beginning to come around to your idea that this may be more about revenge and gangs than the monarchy."

Now I raised an eyebrow. "And what, pray tell, are *you* planning that spurs you to take advance action to soothe my ego?"

"I've not the slightest idea what you're talking about," he said. "Come, let's go see the boys. I haven't heard a peep from them in hours and I'm rather concerned Henry may have taken the others, Nanny included, prisoner."

Jeremy collected me in the motorcar the following morning, shockingly early as I requested, a sin he was not likely to forgive anytime soon. "I have a reputation, Em," he said, passing me his spare set of goggles. "I can't be seen zipping around town before noon. What will people say?"

"Tell them it's only because you haven't yet gone home from the night before," I suggested.

"Darling, if I'm out all night, it would be due to a romantic encounter, and I would never motor to those. First, because the motorcar is rather conspicuous and I wouldn't dare draw attention to my presence in such a circumstance. Second, the speed at which it travels has a rather deleterious effect on one's appearance, don't you think? And I would never want to disappoint a lady."

"If you're trying to shock me, it won't work," I said. "I asked Colin about your habit of kissing married ladies and he only laughed."

"Good man, Hargreaves," Jeremy said. "Perhaps I've underrated him all these years." We lurched forward before I could reply and once in motion found that it was all I could do to keep my hat on my head, despite having secured it with a scandalous number of pins and tied the whole thing round with a long, filmy scarf. Clearly Jeremy had no intention of letting me question him further about his romantic dalliances, and that was fine by me. I had other things to ponder.

We were headed back to the East End,

where I hoped the motorcar — and my friend's habit of flinging coins to the boys who vied to keep an eye on it — would provide illumination on several matters. I had asked Jeremy to park near the Black Swan, thereby giving us the opportunity to see what we could get out of the boys as well as enabling me to check in on Mary, from whom I'd heard nothing since Lizzie's funeral. I did not want Jeremy to accompany me inside, knowing that he was likely to provoke a fight with Mr. Brown — an outcome I might welcome at another time, but that would prove inconvenient to my accomplishing what I hoped to — so I suggested, in my most magnanimous tone, that he was better suited to questioning the boys than I.

They swarmed around the vehicle before he had finished parking it, and I gave them a cheery wave. The tallest, whom I recognized from our previous visit, shook his head when he saw me.

"She don't mind trouble, does she, sir? Can't keep her in hand, can you?"

"My dear boy, I would never dare try," Jeremy said. I could tell from his tone that he was on the verge of offering a load of highly inappropriate advice on the subject of ladies to the lad, so I hastened to my destination, knowing that nothing good could come from my hearing what he said.

Mr. Brown, the proprietor of the Black Swan since Mr. Casby's death, managed to hide most of his chagrin upon seeing me once again cross his threshold. I had brought a sturdy parasol with me, emulating a lady about whom I had read in the newspapers. She had, on numerous occasions, wielded a similar accessory as a weapon, and I recognized the wisdom of this at once. Not that I expected to come to blows with Mr. Brown, but I could well envision drawing great satisfaction from poking him with a pointed ferrule.

"Aw, blimey, Lady Emily, what have I done now to draw your attention? Can't you let a fellow run a legitimate business?"

"We are both all too well aware that you are doing nothing of the sort," I said. "Where is Mary Skypton? I need to speak with her."

"I suppose you might as well. She's ill and of no use to me. I won't even charge you for her time. You can go up to her room. It's the third door on the left."

I narrowed my eyes but didn't bother to point out that his comment about charging for her time proved just how illegitimate his business was, contenting myself with throwing him a searing glare and giving him a swift jab with my parasol. The action was even more pleasurable than I had anticipated and I decided to write a brief note of thanks to the lady from whom I had borrowed the idea.

Worn carpet that emitted a moldy odor when trod upon covered the stairs to the first floor. The poky corridor at the top was dimly lit by one flickering gaslight. I rapped on Mary's door and turned the handle to open it without waiting for a reply. Her small room was dark, its single window covered with a thick curtain that might once have been velvet. Now it looked as if it had been gnawed on by any number of unpleasant creatures.

"Come to check on your charity case?" came a voice from the narrow bed that filled most of the room. She had a grotty blanket pulled up to her chin.

"What are you playing at?" I asked. "You don't look ill." Enough light made its way in from the corridor for me to see that her face was bright and clear and her eyes were flashing.

"Close the door, will you?" She was whispering. "I don't want him to hear."

I did as she asked but only after opening the curtain to reveal a filthy window and turning on the one small light in the room. "Why are you hiding up here?"

"Don't get excited and think I've decided to reform myself," she said, sitting up and swinging her legs around so they hung off the side of the bed. "I will admit that you have shown me a different sort of life, but I don't want to be no one's servant. I might, however, be able to go out on my own and have a better place than this. Attract a higher class of client, if you catch my meaning."

I preferred not to discuss her clients, higher class or otherwise. "I think you could do far better than that, but I shan't try to convince you at the moment. I came to ask you about the King's Boys. What do you know about them?"

"You think they had something to do with Casby's murder?" she asked. "It don't seem their style. They may fight brutally, but they don't generally kill anyone but their own members, and then only when they've betrayed the gang. Casby paid for protection, naturally, he had no choice, but he had nothing else to do with them."

"Several of Lizzie's friends were members of the King's Boys. Do you know if any of them — Ned Traddles, for example, or Gilbert Barton — got into trouble?"

"I already told you I didn't know Ned. Gil, well, I do remember him a bit. Decent-seeming bloke, quite good-looking. Always wished I could land him as a client. He seems the sort who would know what to do with a —"

"Please don't elaborate," I said. "There was another man, called Rodney, who Lizzie may have —"

"Oh, Rodney, yeah, I know him quite, quite well." She grinned and I could see she was enjoying this. "He's a real operator, that one. Don't take nonsense from anyone and will protect a girl like anything. I've spent many nights —"

"Do you know where I can find him?"

"I wouldn't have thought he's your type, Lady Emily."

I sighed. "Mary, I am perfectly well aware of what your chosen profession requires, so there is no point in your trying to shock me. Where can I find Rodney?"

"In the morgue, I suppose. He died in a fight last night."

40
1419

William had told Cecily that King Henry had given him some of the prettiest acres in England, and even now, four years after she had first laid eyes on the land he had granted her husband, she could not help but gasp at their beauty. Rolling hills covered with thick forests gave way to deep green dales, and the peaks of the Pennines were never out of sight. Their stone manor house, now complete, was situated to take advantage of the sweeping views. Cecily had designed the tapestries hanging in the solar and William had overseen the construction of the immense great hall, with its tall, timbered ceiling and enormous fireplace.

Private rooms surrounded the courtyard, and the gatehouse was more for show than safety. There was little danger of being attacked, not now that England was so stable; war was limited to France. The money William received from the families of the prisoners he had ransomed at Agincourt paid for the house and the beautiful chapel that stood near it and left the family coffers still overflowing. He had already ordered alabaster effigies of himself and his wife, so that they might be buried together, never forgotten by their descendants. Father Simon, horrified by the truth about Adeline's behavior, had come with them to Derbyshire and lived in a small rectory next to the church. Hugh de Morland visited them frequently, the three men the closest of friends.

William was a good landlord, and when the king summoned him to join his latest campaign in France, his tenants lined the road outside the house at Anglemore to bid him farewell. They would all pray for his safe return, but none could match Cecily's fervor. She had come to view him not only as her lord and husband, but as her closest confidant and the other half of her soul.

After he had left, she retreated to the chapel, where she knelt before the altarpiece, fashioned after the diptych he had given her on the day they wed. She was no longer haunted by guilt over her mother's death; she had come to terms with that, spurred on by the birth of her own child, a boy they named Nicholas after the saint in whose church King Henry had given thanks after his victory at Agincourt. The moment Alys had put the tiny infant, so helpless and vulnerable, into her arms, Cecily was consumed with peace and clarity. This little baby, nicknamed Colin, could harm no one, just as she could not have harmed anyone on the day she was born. God had answered her mother's prayers and brought her home, and Cecily ought never have thought she bore the responsibility for any of it.

Two days later, when she was busily picking herbs in the kitchen garden, she was interrupted by one of her servants, a young girl who showed great aptitude for learning. Cecily was teaching her to read, and expected she had come to ask when her next lesson would be. Instead, she brought news.

"An old friend of yours has arrived, my lady," she said. "The Baroness Esterby."

41
1901

I am not certain I am capable of adequately describing the emotions that coursed through me after Mary told me Rodney was dead. First came a blow of shock, hard and cold, but then something more sinister and unsettling began to brew. Had I not, just the day before, drawn Mr. Hancock's attention to him? Could I believe that the timing of his death was mere coincidence?

Of course I could not. Guilt and horror mingled deep in my abdomen and ran through my veins. I drew a long breath and did my best to keep my composure as I asked Mary for more details. She said she supposed it was an ordinary sort of fight, the kind gangs get into all the time, but that she didn't know anything else. I took my leave from her, not even having the presence of mind to again offer her assistance should she desire a different sort of life, and rushed to find Jeremy.

He was still conversing with the boys surrounding his motorcar. I hung back for a
moment, watching them, surprised by the
easy manner in which he handled them,
teasing and goading. When he saw me, he
waved, and the boys scattered, as if they had
been warned to avoid confrontation with
ladies.

"You look a fright, Em," he said. "I guess
Mary wasn't helpful."

"Too helpful, rather," I said and told him
about Rodney. "I think we'd better go to
Scotland Yard. No, perhaps to the morgue.
I'm not sure."

His eyebrows shot up. "It's not like you to
be so indecisive. Look, Em, you can't blame
yourself. Even if Father Christmas did order
him killed —"

"Don't call him that."

"Hancock, whatever. If he's the one behind it, it's still his fault, not yours. But
don't dismiss the possibility that this was
nothing more than an ordinary fight between violent ruffians." He took me by the
hand and helped me into the motorcar. "I'm
taking you home."

We had not driven more than two miles
when I managed to master my emotions and
was once more thinking rationally. I ordered
him to the coroner's mortuary. He started

to balk, but knew better than to argue. Needless to say, the coroner's assistants were less than eager to let us view the body, but, once again, Jeremy's title proved its worth. Ducal command eliminated all of their objections and after a short wait, a thin, nervous-looking man led us into a well-lit room that contained three slab tables, two of which were empty.

On the third, beneath a sheet, lay Rodney Dawkins, as we now knew him to be. Jeremy nodded at the man, who then pulled back the sheet. Bile caught in my throat and I covered my mouth with my hand. His face was all but pulverized. I turned away, nearly regretting my decision to come, but pulled myself together.

"The cause of death?" I asked.

"Multiple internal injuries, madam," the man said. "He was in a fight, you see. Not much need for an inquest, but it's scheduled for tomorrow."

"Was anyone else killed in this fight?"

"No, madam. The police would be better able to give you further details should you require them, as they're the ones who brought the body in."

"When is the funeral?" I asked.

"Three days from now," he said. "His sister is handling the arrangements."

I did not envy her the task. Jeremy took me firmly by the arm and guided me out of the awful place. I was trembling and upset, but glad that I had come. I thought about what Colin had told me, that one of the risks of this sort of work was that people would be killed. How could I not take at least some responsibility for what had happened to this poor man? In the end, I might be working for the greater good, but that did not mean I could accept with ease the heavy cost paid to achieve it.

Jeremy and I were silent on the drive back to Park Lane. Colin was not at home, and my friend insisted on bringing me inside. He tried to ply me with whisky, as he had done on a previous occasion, some years ago, when we had faced the hideous aftermath of another violent death, but I rejected his attempt. Instead, I asked him to telephone Inspector Pickering.

An hour later, the young man was sitting with us. "I understand that you feel responsible, Lady Emily," he said, "but I assure you nothing could be further from the truth, regardless of what you said to Hancock. Dawkins was killed because he chose to live his life in a criminal gang. Two constables heard sounds of a struggle last night around three o'clock in the morning, and came upon what looked to them like a gang fight. It turned out to be an internal argument of sorts, as there were only members of the King's Boys present. Dawkins took the brunt of the beating, but those present insisted that the fight had started as the result of an argument about a girl. The constables thought it looked more like a planned attack, as no one else bore injuries even close to those suffered by Dawkins. He was still alive when they found him, but was not conscious, and died shortly thereafter."

I swallowed hard and ignored the burning sensation in my stomach. "Now that we know his surname, were you able to learn anything further about him?"

"He has the arrest record one would expect to find for someone affiliated with a gang," Inspector Pickering said. "Nothing out of the ordinary, except when viewed through our current lens. He was twice arrested with Gilbert Barton. I've already been to the address he gave — if he ever did live in the place, he's long gone — and no one I questioned admitted even the slightest acquaintance with either of them. Beyond that, I've found no sign of Barton. Perhaps he's moved up high enough in the organization to have gone underground."

"What about Mr. Hancock?" I asked.

"Has he been questioned after Rodney's death?"

"No, Lady Emily, and he won't be." The inspector didn't bother to stop his spectacles from slipping down his nose. "There is nothing that links him to the crime."

"But he —"

"We have nothing on him. Better that we expend our efforts elsewhere."

I did not attempt to change his mind; I was busy trying to decide whether, despite everything, I should warn Mr. Hancock that his life might be in danger. I could no longer doubt that he was the leader of the King's Boys. After having seen the bloodied remains of Rodney Dawkins, I felt no sympathy or concern for Mr. Hancock, but if I let him suffer a similar fate when I might have stopped it, was I any better than he?

Of course I was. However, as I hold myself to what I believe is a high standard of moral behavior, I penned him a quick note, which I gave to the inspector to hand deliver, and instructed the young man to keep a close eye on Mr. Hancock. Unlikely though it was he would put any stock in my warning, I could not ignore the possibility that he could lead us — wittingly or not — to the man responsible for the deaths of Mr. Grummidge, Mr. Casby, and Mr. Crofton.

Through all of this, Jeremy had sat, silent, in a cozy corner of the library, helping himself to Colin's whisky. I admit I had encouraged him to do so. He had not overindulged, however, and my own frame of mind had improved considerably after I had sent Inspector Pickering off to the East End.

"You never told me what you learned from the boys," I said. "I do hope you managed to direct the conversation away from the treatment of ladies, as that's what it sounded like you were discussing when I left."

He flashed a wry smile. "I'm not certain anything I learned is of value at this point. The tall one — he's called Moggy Kelvin — admitted that he works, rather, worked, under Dawkins. A particularly useless revelation in the face of things. I did ask him about Hancock, and he insisted that they all avoid him like the plague because their loyalty is to, as he put it, the king."

"Do you think he was telling the truth?" I asked.

Jeremy shrugged. "Impossible to know, but I can't say he appeared anything less than candid. He was irritated at the mention of Hancock, and didn't seem to be putting it on. Told me that men like Hancock don't know the best way to run a neighbor-hood."

I blew out a long breath. "Still, I can't believe Mr. Hancock isn't the head of the organization. The inspector said the leaders remain anonymous, and Mr. Hancock's public persona, that of someone bent on improving life in the East End, is a simple but effective disguise."

"Moggy did tell me one other thing," Jeremy said. "When any of the King's Boys betrays the gang, the rest of them are marched past the body. To remind them of what will happen should they make the same mistake as their fallen comrade."

"Did he mention this in the context of Dawkins's death?" I asked.

"I believe so, although he didn't refer to Dawkins by name. I'm afraid he was rather looking forward to the wake. That's when they see the body."

I felt sick again. "Was he not betraying the gang by sharing that with you?"

"Far from it, Em. He was bragging about it. He hopes to move up in the organization now that Dawkins is gone."

"But he can't be more than twelve years old."

"That's ancient in his world," Jeremy said. "Although Dawkins was an adult, of an age with Ned Traddles, if I had to guess."

I frowned. "I don't suppose I could per-suade you to take me on another excur-sion?"

"Bloody hell, Em — forgive me — you can't want to go back —"

"No, nothing like that," I said. "I know we're missing something, and I haven't the slightest idea what it is. Remember the second article we found in the Tower pas-sage, the one about the textile mill in West Ham? Perhaps its pertinence to the case will become clear if we go there."

"I suppose there's no harm in it and I can't think of anything better to do."

"You might let me drive part of the way there."

"Don't even think about it, Em. Har-greaves would have my hide."

Holbrooke & Sons seemed in every way a model of safety and efficiency. I was dis-heartened to see so many children working — their nimble limbs and small size making it easy for them to dash under and around the hulking machines that processed raw materials into coarse jute sacks — but I could not say they were being ill-treated insofar as the current labor laws saw it. Laws, I might add, that I found wholly inadequate.

The foreman, Mr. Riggs, gave us a tour of the premises. Large windows let in loads of light, flooding the factory floor with brightness, and the machines looked to be in good working order. The place was far less dingy and cluttered than other factories I had seen, but I still did not believe that children should be working when they could be in school. I did not bother to voice my opinion to Mr. Riggs. I would take it up instead with a few members of Parliament I suspected would be sympathetic to my views.

Instead, I asked him if he was acquainted with Prentice Hancock, explaining that I understood he was known for offering assistance to children from poor families. Mr. Riggs brightened at the question, and said that Mr. Hancock frequently sent wayward youth to Holbrooke & Sons. He offered high praise of the man, and said London would be a better place if more of its residents emulated Mr. Hancock's example. I did not disabuse him of this notion.

I asked to be allowed to speak to some of the children, and Mr. Riggs granted my request with a smile. He brought three boys and two girls to me, each of whom beamed when they told me how much they enjoyed their work. I half suspected Mr. Riggs of having lined them up and coached them in advance on what to say whenever visitors came. Two other girls watched from afar as we talked to their colleagues, their wide eyes hard and almost scared. I wished I could question them away from their supervisor, suspecting they might be more forthcoming than their peers. The only revelation of interest from the individuals to whom we were allowed to speak was that they were paid less than their counterparts at other factories.

"What do they think of being paid a lower wage?" I asked.

"Safety, Lady Emily, does not come cheap," Mr. Riggs said, after dismissing his small employees. "Holbrooke & Sons has to turn a profit and wouldn't be able to do so if we didn't adjust the wages accordingly. Which is not to say the workers bear the full brunt of it. Mr. Holbrooke himself puts half of his share back into the factory, which allows us to pay more than we'd be able to otherwise. It's a fair trade-off for those working on the floor. They appreciate the better conditions and the knowledge that they won't get injured. Everyone is happy."

"Is Mr. Holbrooke open to outside investment?" Jeremy asked. "I'd quite like to support his work."

"He'd be most obliged, your grace," Mr. Riggs said. "He's abroad at the moment. Our raw materials come from India, you see, and he's negotiating for better terms with our suppliers."

"When do you expect him to return?" I asked.

"Next month, Lady Emily. If you'd like, your grace, I can put you in touch with him the moment he sets foot on British soil."

"Yes, that would be good of you, Riggs," Jeremy said in his most condescending drawl. "I'll count on you to take care of it."

The foreman gave a smugly satisfied smile and led us back to the factory office. Photographs of smiling workers covered one of the walls, and a copy of the article from *The Times* hung in a wooden frame. "That is the very piece that drew our attention to your facility," I said, pointing at the article. "I'm sure we're not the first to call on you as a result."

"Mr. Holbrooke hopes that this factory will serve as a model for others."

"Does anyone object to your practices?" I asked. "There are so many people loath to accept change and progress."

"No one who matters," Mr. Riggs said. "At least not to us. We can't convert every- one to our ways and don't waste our time on those who aren't interested. But there isn't much for anyone to object to."

"Quite right," Jeremy said. "I look forward to speaking to you again, Riggs. Don't forget — I'm counting on you." He shook the foreman's hand and ushered me out of the factory. "You didn't believe a word of that, did you?" he asked.

"It was all too perfect to be true," I said. "And Mr. Hancock supplies much of the labor. There is something rotten here."

"Yes, but what?" Jeremy asked. He pulled out his watch and glanced at the time. "The shift will end in forty-five minutes. We could skulk around and try to get more candid answers out of some of the other employees. Or we could call on Mr. Holbrooke, who I don't believe for a minute is in India."

I was studying the façade of the factory, wondering if anything in its construction could link it to Hastings or William the Conqueror, but the idea was too ridiculous to contemplate. "Would it be useful to speak to whatever inspectors in the government cover Holbrooke & Sons?"

"Doubtful," Jeremy said. "I agree there's something not quite right about the place, but it doesn't seem unsafe. Holbrooke is probably exploiting his workers by not offering them better pay, but we'd be hard-pressed to do anything about that. Riggs is right that many people would give up some money in exchange for safety."

"If they're actually getting that in return," I said. "How can they know?"

"I haven't the slightest idea, Em, and we're not going to figure it out by standing around here."

I caught movement out of the corner of my eye, a man carrying a bundle of something and slinking into an alley near the factory. He was followed by three unnervingly plump rats. "I don't think there's anything else for us here now," I said. "But I'm not ready to go home."

42
1419

Cecily hadn't thought about Adeline in years, not since her expulsion from Lord Esterby's castle. She certainly had not expected Adeline to seek out her company, not after she had done her best to tarnish Cecily's reputation and all but accused her of adultery in front of the baron's entire retinue. Yet here she was, standing before her, a stricken look on her face.

"I had nowhere else to go," Adeline said, keeping very still. She had been admitted into the courtyard, no doubt because the guards would not have considered such a bedraggled-looking woman capable of posing any threat to Sir William's family. Cecily said nothing, but took her by the arm and led her into the house.

After ordering a maid to assist Adeline with a bath and a clean gown — she was much thinner than she used to be, all her pleasant curves planed into sharp angles —

Cecily stopped on the stone staircase outside her bedchamber and gathered her thoughts. Her heart was racing, an inexplicable development, as there was no longer anything Adeline could do to hurt her. Was there?

She continued downstairs, going first to the kitchen to direct the cook to prepare a cold dinner for her visitor, and then outside and to the chapel, where she searched in vain for Father Simon. She found him in the rectory, bent over a table and carefully copying out the text of a manuscript she did not recognize.

"She's come, hasn't she?" he asked, without even looking up. "I suspected it was only a question of time."

The siege of Harfleur had paled in terms of brutality to that of Rouen. King Henry's army remembered all too well the disease and hunger that had plagued them during that earlier expedition into France. This time, their enemy was even better prepared, relentlessly pelting the English with crossbow bolts and cannon shot. A trebuchet protected every gate in the sturdy walls. Henry knew he could not break through the defenses, and instead of trying, settled in for a long siege, confident that he and his men could outlast the French. The great wealth of the city was useless to its inhabitants, for gold and silver and treasure of any kind cannot feed the hungry. Nor could it be used to purchase food after the English king, whose men had dragged ships across the land, laid thick chains across the river Seine, isolating the unlucky souls in Rouen.

Still, months would pass before these measures took a toll on the city, and in the meantime, there were attacks to be repelled. William well understood siege tactics, but he preferred a bloody fight to the infinite patience it took to wait for the food in a well-stocked city to run out. He hated the cries of hungry women and children, hated that disease would soon ravage the population. Plague came with the winter, and before Christmas, city officials expelled twelve thousand of the citizens of Rouen from the protection of its walls.

William had watched them make their way through the gates, women clutching small children, the weak and infirm following, unsteady on their feet. He turned away, not wanting to look, despising the French even more for this act. They hoped to take advantage of King Henry's compassion and fairness, but they failed to realize he would be guided by military judgment. He could not give these refugees safe passage through the English army; they would cost him food and supplies that he could not afford to take away from his own men.

The dark clouds that hung heavy in the sky opened, drenching everyone below with a cold rain that continued for day after day, week after week. William hated the sounds of the dying exiles, who had nothing but trenches and dirt to shield them from the elements as they slowly starved to death. Still the nobles inside the city would not bend to King Henry's will.

Respite — brief and not enough — came on Christmas itself, for the king would not fail to observe that holy day. He called for a truce and offered food to the starving. It was insufficient to change the sad course of those still clinging to life in the trenches.

They had been outside Rouen for nearly six months. How much longer would it take for King Henry to capture what was rightly his?

43
1901

Mrs. Grummidge did not look surprised to see us when she greeted us in her snug parlor. As always, her eyes lit up when she saw Jeremy. He graciously accepted her offer of tea, and sat in attendance upon her as if she were the most important courtier in Buckingham Palace. We had not come to socialize, however, and after giving her the news of Rodney Dawkins's death, I implored her to remember everything she could about Gilbert Barton. "He is the last of your group who has remained unaffected by the murders," I said.

"Surely you can't believe he's in danger?" Mrs. Grummidge asked.

I most certainly did not; if anything, I had the direst suspicions of him, but I knew sharing them with Mrs. Grummidge was unlikely to entice her to give me any information she might have about a boy she had once considered a friend. "No, I do not

415

believe him to be in danger," I said. "But we must do everything we can to stop these murders. Do you remember seeing an older gentleman at Lizzie's funeral? He has a white beard and —"

"Looks quite like Father Christmas?" she asked. "Yes, I saw him, but I can't claim him as an acquaintance."

I remembered that he had said the same about her. "Does the name Prentice Hancock mean anything to you?"

She screwed her eyebrows together. "No, I can't say it does."

"That's all right," I said. "We must focus on Mr. Barton. You told me that you never knew where he lived, but have you seen him or heard anything about him recently?"

"No. Mr. Grummidge discouraged me from keeping in touch with the friends of my youth. He didn't think they were fitting companions for a woman of substance, which is what he fancied me to be."

More likely, he wanted to keep her as isolated as possible, so that she would have no means of fleeing from his abusive ways. "Could you tell us more about Mr. Barton? Every detail you can recall may be important. Not just a physical description, but one of his character and his interests as well."

"He was always painfully thin, which is probably what made the chimney sweeps want him for work when he was little, and he never grew very much. He was only a few inches taller than I. Medium brown hair, didn't wear a beard — at least when I knew him — and he has hazel eyes with a rim of gold. That was his most identifying feature, I'd say. Other than his eyes, he looked quite ordinary."

"Can you recall any of his interests?" I asked.

"Let's see . . . he loved meat pies and I'm sorry to say stole them whenever he could, but you could hardly fault him for that, as the poor boy was hungry nearly all the time. And he always went to watch the football at the Memorial Grounds. He supports Thames Ironworks. I can't think of anything else. He never had an easy life, Lady Emily, and had very little time for amusement."

"Was he ever romantically attached to anyone?" Jeremy asked.

"When we were quite young, we used to go for walks together if I could slip away without my parents noticing, but I'm not sure that merits an attachment," she said, blushing. "He was kind and sensitive, at least when he wasn't around the rest of the King's Boys. They were a rough crowd."

"When was the last time you saw him?" I asked.

"I can't even recall," she said. "At least six years ago. Although there was one time, perhaps two months ago now, when I thought I saw him in the street, not far from this very house. I called to him, but he didn't respond, and I realized it was probably just someone similar to him in appearance."

Jeremy shot me a questioning glance. "We've troubled you enough," I said. "Forgive the intrusion and please don't hesitate to reach out if there's anything you need."

"Or if you recall anything about your old friend," Jeremy said. "No detail is too small."

Frustrated, we left the house. "I wonder . . ." I let my voice trail as my brain tried to grasp an elusive thought. "If Gilbert Barton is our man — which seems to me increasingly likely — he murdered Mr. Grummidge because of the way he treated his wife. But how could he have known what was going on behind closed doors?"

"Servants are known to gossip," Jeremy said.

"And they generally can be counted on to have a keen knowledge of everything going on in a house." Scotland Yard had interviewed the Grummidges' staff, but they would have had no cause to ask them specifically about Gilbert Barton. I turned back to the house and in less than a quarter of an hour was settled in the housekeeper's room, speaking to each of the servants in turn, while Jeremy sat with the young widow in her parlor.

Achieving my goal was so simple I nearly laughed. Mr. Grummidge had no valet, but he did employ a man in his mid-twenties who served in that capacity as needed along with fulfilling the combined duties of footman and a butler of sorts. When I asked him about Gilbert Barton, he grinned.

"Gil? Oh, yes. One of my best mates, he is. He's not in trouble, is he?"

"No, no," I said, not being entirely honest. "Were you aware that he and Mrs. Grummidge were friends in their youth?"

"Blimey. Is that right? He never breathed a word of it to me."

"Samuel, it's very important that you answer this question honestly," I said. "Did you ever mention to him Mr. Grummidge's treatment of his wife?" The man's face clouded. "No one would begrudge you for having done so. It would be difficult for any of us to stand by silent in the face of such a situation."

"I should've done more, madam," he said. "I did ask Gil for his advice about it, but what could I do? I was in no position to stop my employer, and I need this job."

"What did Gil suggest?" I asked.

"He said it wasn't my place to interfere, but that if Mrs. Grummidge asked for my help, I should do whatever she wanted. Of course, she never did ask."

"And when did this conversation take place?"

"I reckon three or four weeks ago."

"Where does Gil live?"

"Over in West Ham, not far from the football ground. I don't know exactly where."

"It is crucial that I speak with him," I said. "How can I reach him?"

"I meet him at the pub every Thursday night. That's my evening off. But you could find him tomorrow at Memorial Grounds. He never misses a match."

"He's a Thames Ironworks supporter, I understand."

"Not quite, madam. They're West Ham United now. Changed the name just a few months ago. Same blokes, though. Not sure what the fuss was all about, but then I'm a Villa supporter. Born and bred in Birmingham."

I thanked him for his help, and asked him if he would be willing to help me identify his friend at the grounds before the match. He agreed, so long as Mrs. Grummidge didn't object, and naturally, she didn't. I felt a bit uneasy at being so underhanded with him, but I could not risk missing the opportunity to find Gilbert Barton. Even if the man's motives for murder were pure — so far as motives for murder could be — people cannot be allowed to mete out justice outside of the courts. No civilization could stand for that.

At my direction, Jeremy next drove to Mr. Hancock's house. He would have received my note of warning hours ago, but I wanted to speak to the man face-to-face. He might be able to tell me where I could find Mr. Barton. Overruling Jeremy's protests, I insisted that he remain in the motorcar while I went inside, hoping Mr. Hancock would be more inclined to confide in me if I was alone.

I was shown into the parlor at once, and found Mr. Hancock already there. His eyes no longer looked so kind as they had on our previous meeting, and his smile seemed more sinister than warm. He did not offer me any refreshment as I took the seat across from him. There could be no denying that he no longer considered me a friend.

"Your note was a revelation," he said. "You have not been entirely honest with me, Lady Emily. I do not appreciate deception."

"Nor do I, sir," I said. "This, however, is not the time for recrimination. I have cause to believe that your life is in danger and am here only to warn you."

He laughed. "You are an earnest little thing, aren't you? Do you really believe that some disgruntled reprobate can trouble me with hollow threats?"

"Gilbert Barton may do more than make threats."

He shook his head. "I don't know him."

"Of course you do. Don't you see that there's nothing to be gained by lying to me? I know all about you and the King's Boys. And I know that Mr. Barton is behind three murders."

"Whoever this Barton is, he's nothing to do with me."

"That is categorically untrue," I said. "Please, if you have any idea where I might find him, tell me."

"I know nothing of the man."

Frustration surged in me. "What happens to you is of no consequence to me. I'd hoped you could lead me to Mr. Barton, and, in doing so, help me to save your life.

As you refuse, I can only plead that you heed my words: be vigilant, Mr. Hancock, or you'll be the next dead king."

He laughed again. "You are prone to dramatics, aren't you? I admit you are a clever girl, and I do appreciate your concern for my humble self. But you need not worry your pretty little head about my safety. No one in the East End would dare touch me. I am, after all, the only person here who bothers to try to give anyone a better life. Your erroneous conclusions about my other business activities notwithstanding, I assure you I am in no danger. As for you, however, you will find yourself in a far more uncomfortable position should you continue with your current course of action. There's no love for anyone like you in the East End."

44
1420

Cecily decided without hesitating to take in Adeline, whose wanton ways had at last become impossible for her husband to deny. Adeline was with child, and the baron knew it was not his. Three other friends had refused to offer her sanctuary, condemning her for having sullied the reputation of the Burgeys family. But Cecily, who still recalled with pain the feeling that she had never lived up to the memory of her holy mother, decided that forgiveness was the best way forward. Adeline's child was born six months later, a girl she called Beatrix as a gesture of respect to her hostess. Cecily showered the child with love, and felt, in a way, that the little girl enabled her, at last, to make a final and lasting peace with her mother.

William remained in France with the king. His second son, named for himself, was born nine weeks after his departure. Only

God knew how old the boy would be when his father again set foot on English soil. Cecily was tired of the war, tired of France, and tired of being without William, but there was nothing to be done, other than pray in front of her diptych for his safe return.

Rouen did fall, in time, and once again King Henry was victorious in France, controlling all of Normandy, and, finally, reaching the outskirts of Paris. Now there would be no more fighting, only waiting, as a treaty could be negotiated. The French king — known by all to be mad; William heard it said he thought he was made from glass and would shatter if those around him did not treat him with the utmost care — offered his pretty daughter, Catherine, as bride to Henry. The royal couple married in France at the cathedral in Troyes, the town where the terms of peace were hammered out. When King Charles died, Henry, an Englishman, would succeed him. The crown of France would be his at last.

By autumn, the French were well and truly subdued. King Henry and his retinue, William included, returned to England. Grateful that his sovereign did not press him to accompany him to Windsor, William rode north. With luck and good weather, he might be home in time for Christmas.

45
1901

While I had not expected Mr. Hancock to heed my warning, I had hoped that the plainclothes officers assigned to discreetly watch him would be able to prevent him from coming to harm — and, in the process, catch our murderer. In this, my hopes were dashed. When I met Inspector Pickering the next morning outside the Memorial Grounds, he told me that Mr. Hancock had managed to evade them altogether. They had lost sight of him and had no idea where he was.

This news, coming after our utter failure the previous night to find anyone who claimed an acquaintance with Gilbert Barton in the pub he frequented, left me with a piercing sense of frustration, but I refused to abandon hope. Inspector Pickering and I had no trouble persuading the management at the Memorial Grounds to make an announcement asking Gilbert Barton to come to the front gate before the start of that week's football match. The inspector had mustered a number of constables, stationing one at each entrance to the grounds, and Samuel, Mrs. Grummidge's servant, searched for his friend in the crowd. Alas, he caught no sight of him, and no man claiming to be Barton came forward.

"We could go back to the pub," the inspector said. "He's likely to show up there after the match."

"I think I shall leave that to you and Samuel," I said. "I have another idea." I did not get to act on it, however, as before I could even begin to explain it to my colleague, I felt a firm hand grab me and turned to see my husband, his countenance grave.

"Hancock is dead."

Barton — for I was now convinced beyond doubt, reasonable or otherwise, that he was our murderer — had chosen an unexpected site to recreate the scene of the death of poor Harold Godwinson. Rather than a location evoking Hastings, he left Mr. Hancock's body, dressed in mail and a surcoat emblazoned with the cross of St. George, in the very location where Rodney Dawkins had met his untimely end. As expected, his killer had stuck a long arrow into Mr. Hancock's eye. It was a gruesome sight.

"Is this the end of it, do you think?" Inspector Pickering asked me, grimacing as he turned away from the body. "So far as we know, there are no more costumes waiting to be used."

"We can't be certain of that," Colin said. "Only that there are none left of which we are aware."

"I think he's finished," I said. "He did what he set out to. He killed the people who hurt those he loved, and he sent the message that no one, not even a king, is safe. Surely no one can doubt that Mr. Hancock was the leader of the King's Boys."

In fact, quite a few people still doubted that, and even I had to admit we could not prove it, one way or another. But the choice of location — the site of what could be viewed as a battle between the King's Boys and a perceived (if wrongly accused as a result of my own actions) traitor — was significant. I was confident it would all be explained when I found Gilbert Barton. And find him, I would. After sending Inspector Pickering back to Barton's favorite pub, I enlisted the aid of my husband in my next task.

We took a cab to Holbrooke & Sons in

West Ham. Work stopped by noon on Saturdays, so the factory was quiet, but this did not deter me. While it would be simple to recognize the children I had spoken to with Mr. Riggs's blessing when I had visited, I also remembered the faces of those two girls I had not been able to question alone. Deducing that they likely lived near their place of employment, I wanted to search the area.

"The entire area?" Colin said, his dark eyebrows tilting.

"Not door to door, if that's what you mean," I said. "We will ask around and try to find someone who works there. How hard can it be?"

Fortunately, it was not difficult in the least. I cannot claim this was due to my excellent — if amorphous — strategy, but instead to the fact that a group of children, all of whom worked for Holbrooke & Sons, were playing in the street not half a block from the factory. Several of them remembered me, and I greeted them all warmly before introducing Colin. One, a girl, hung back from the group, and I recognized the look in her eyes. She was one of those I had not met at the factory — one of two whose expressions of cold fear were burned into my memory. My husband noticed me watching her, and with a quick nod gathered the others around him, asking if they wanted to play a game. I pulled her aside while they were distracted.

"Everything is not well at Holbrooke & Sons, is it?" I asked.

"I can't talk about this, madam," she said, her eyes darting about nervously. "Not here."

I nodded, understanding the peril she might face. "Tell me your name and where you live. I'll come to you there in an hour."

Colin's game, which consisted of wielding a rather sorry-looking stick in the manner of a cricket bat, ended as soon as I signaled to him that I had what we needed. A man selling roasted chestnuts passed by, so Colin bought packets for each of the children, who dispersed soon thereafter, delighted with the treat.

At the appointed time, we went to the girl's home. Her family lived in one room on the second floor of a terrace house that they shared with three other families. Sarah looked nervous when she saw us, but her mother welcomed us inside and insisted on giving us tea.

"I've hoped someone would come," she said, as her daughter hung back from us, looking more scared than ever. "That factory isn't so safe as they claim, at least that's what my Sarah tells me. It looks pretty, that's for sure, but fences around the machines and lots of bright light aren't the only things that matter. She tells me they lock them in, they do, and won't let them out until the end of their shift. And that piles of rags and lint are left to accumulate in heaps hidden from sight. One spark near them is all it would take and the whole place would go up in a flash. And if it happened while they was working, they wouldn't be able to get out unless someone unlocked the door. And fire, you know, can come too quickly for that." She sighed. "But there's nowhere better for her to work, is there?"

Horrifying though Sarah's mother's words were — on the spot I resolved to go back to Holbrooke & Sons first thing Monday morning — they did not include anything that connected the factory to Gilbert Barton. Neither she nor her daughter recognized his name, nor that of Prentice Hancock.

"Perhaps this is all useless," I said, as Colin hailed a cab and helped me into it. "But I simply cannot believe that the article about the factory is wholly irrelevant. And what about your mysterious notes and the hunt they've sent you on? We're no closer to

432

discovering the truth about them than we were when the late queen handed you the first one."

"Don't lose faith, my dear. We will figure it all out in due course."

I was not so confident. When we reached home, Inspector Pickering was waiting for us in the library. He leapt to his feet the instant we entered and started apologizing for coming without an invitation, his words tumbling out in an incoherent fashion I can only credit to his awe at finding himself once again in Colin's presence. Hero worship can prove awfully inconvenient for everyone involved. He managed to compose himself — and barrage us with another round of apologies — before, at last, telling us why he had come.

"I haven't found Gilbert Barton, let me say that straightaway, so you don't get your hopes up," he began. "But it occurred to me that it's highly unusual for anyone to be so elusive. There are no records of him anywhere, except pertaining to his arrests."

"A person of his class can easily slip through the cracks," Colin said.

"You are absolutely correct, sir. The poor aren't likely to have their birth or baptism recorded, and a boy like Barton wouldn't have gone to school. When you told me,

Lady Emily, about the Holbrooke & Sons article, I decided to mark on a map the locations of Barton's arrests. They are, after all, the only official records we have of his existence. Aside from two, every one of his run-ins with the law occurred within two blocks of either a factory or a shop where work conditions were particularly vile. And within weeks of him being released from jail, something happened at each of those places that shut them down permanently. He was arrested with Rodney Dawkins twice, if you recall, and those are the only times when it was for a crime that you'd expect from a gang member. They were caught stealing. But every other time, he was hauled in for disturbing the peace or petty vandalism. The King's Boys don't typically engage in either."

"Are you suggesting he was getting arrested on purpose?" I asked.

"I think so, Lady Emily." His cheeks darkened. "But I confess I have not the slightest inkling as to why."

"I assume you have the details as to what led to the closure of the establishments in question?" Colin asked.

"Yes, sir, of course," Inspector Pickering replied. "Arson, each time. The buildings went up in flames when they were vacant.

No one was injured in any of them."

"Holbrooke & Sons," I said. "He's going to set it on fire. There is no shift Saturday afternoon or Sunday. This is his opportunity."

It was barely seven o'clock in the evening, and the sun had long ago slipped below the horizon. As we approached Holbrooke & Sons, I expected to see the sky ablaze above it. Instead, there was only unrelenting darkness. We slunk out of the carriage and made our way to the entrance of the factory, but of course it was locked. Two constables, walking their beat, called out to us, assuming we were bent on some nefarious end.

The inspector presented them with his credentials and Colin spoke to them in a low, measured tone that no one could ignore. I could not hear his words, but when he stopped speaking, they nodded and set off down the street.

"They'll have the fire brigade at the ready, should it become necessary," he said.

And then I saw it — a small, flickering light shimmering through a glass window on the building's first floor. No sooner had I called out and pointed toward it, than a huge blast blew me off my feet, and the building, in an instant, was engulfed in flames. I pulled myself up to my knees, caught my breath, and looked around for Colin. He and the inspector were a few yards away from me, both of them looking as battered as I imagined I did, but neither showing sign of serious injury. We came together, standing on the pavement on the other side of the street, watching the blaze.

Then, the dark figure of a man appeared from behind the building. He was running and waving his arms as he shouted.

"There's someone inside!"

46
1421

Once again, Cecily had watched her husband set off to France to fight for their king, after the army, headed by his brother the Duke of Clarence, suffered a scathing defeat at the hands of French and Scottish forces near Anjou. Clarence had been killed, and King Henry was ready to take his place at the head of his troops once again.

Cecily was heavy with child, a babe who would be born when its father was far across the Channel, but she had become accustomed to such things. Following Christine de Pizan's advice, she had learned to run every part of their estate, and she knew she was capable of managing any difficulty that arose in her husband's absence, down to and including defending it with the weapons she had insisted he teach her to use. Not that she expected to ever be called upon to do so.

She would miss him, as would his sons.

But her work here was as important as his in France. She was securing the foundations of their family. Generations from now, the Hargrave family would still reside on the beautiful land granted to them by the king, land earned by her husband's fierce bravery. They had already expanded the manor house twice, and she was considering new methods of farming she had learned about from travelers who came from the south. A pang in her abdomen caused her to double over. She sank to her knees and called for the midwife. Hours later, she cradled her daughter in her arms.

Meaux, currently besieged by the English army, showed no signs of falling as easily — if one could call any victory by siege easy — as nearby Dreux had. Once again, the bloody flux and shortages of food plagued the army. One of the French leaders, the lord of Offémont, led a group of men into the English camp, hoping to make a surprise attack. God was not on the Frenchman's side that night; Offémont fell from the walls, and the sound of his plate armor crashing against stone alerted the English to the scheme.

Better still, a lowly cook took the mighty Offémont prisoner. The English all rejoiced at their enemy's defeat and humiliation.

It was only after that insult that the brutal man inside the city walls began to see that he would not be able to hold the city indefinitely. He was called the Bastard of Vaurus, and there was not a man among the English who had not heard tales of his cruelty. Now he decided to set the city on fire, preferring destruction to defeat.

King Henry's spies told him of the Bastard's decision, and this spurred the noble leader to attack without delay. The citizens of Meaux did not stand in his way; perhaps they preferred him to their vicious lord. Victory was not immediate, however, and the fighting continued for week after week.

But it did come, eventually, and at an uncommonly high cost. King Henry himself had fallen ill during the siege. No one doubted he would recover with speed, but William, seeing the gray tint on his liege's face, could not help but worry.

47
1901

The man rushed forward and pushed against the factory's door with his shoulder, over and over again until it gave way. Colin had run after him, first trying to stop him and then, after a brief exchange of words, followed him into the burning building. I knew he had to be Gilbert Barton, not only because of our suspicions about him, but because he was so much shorter than my husband. Inspector Pickering started for the building, but I grabbed him by the arm.

"There is no point in putting your life in danger, too," I said, sounding inconceivably calm. Terror consumed me, but it was as if my voice alone had no understanding of what was at stake.

A crowd had gathered around the perimeter of Holbrooke & Sons, keeping what they all hoped was a safe distance from the flames. Snow started to fall, the large white flakes incongruous with the glow of the fire.

Loud pops and the sound of wood splitting assaulted the silence of the night. I crossed my arms tightly and wished I could tear my eyes away from the scene, afraid of what I might see.

"He will come to no harm," Inspector Pickering said.

Fortunately, I did not have to reply, for almost the moment he spoke, Colin stumbled out of the building, holding a child in his arms. It was Sarah, or so I surmised when I saw her mother push her way through the crowd calling for her.

"She's not hurt, just scared," my husband said, gently handing the girl to the woman. Tears streaming down her face, she clutched her daughter to her chest.

"What about you?" I asked, now that Sarah was safe.

"I'm perfectly fine." His face was black with smoke and he coughed as he spoke. "No permanent damage."

A second man staggered out of the building. He collapsed on the ground, clutching at his throat. Colin and I rushed to him, Inspector Pickering close on our heels.

"I would never have done it if I knew someone was inside," he said, his voice weak and raspy.

"Are you Gilbert Barton?" I asked.

"I am." He was struggling to breathe. Burns covered much of his body and his face was hideously disfigured. "It is, I'm afraid, time for me to confess to a multitude of sins."

"Not now," I said. "First, we must get you to hospital."

"I won't make it that far."

The sound of bells announced the arrival of the fire brigade. Colin went straight to them. "The fire was started with a small explosive device located in the back of the first floor. There was one person inside, but she's out now."

I looked back down at Gilbert Barton. He tried to lift his hand, but the effort was too great. I wished I could offer him some sort of comfort, but feared that even the gentlest touch would cause him pain.

"Please listen to me," he whispered. "I must tell someone what I've done."

When Colin and I arrived home, Inspector Pickering in tow, Davis met us at the door, explaining that Jeremy had turned up on the doorstep and insisted on waiting for us in the library. I had guessed as much when I saw the motorcar in front of the house.

"Good Gad!" he exclaimed when he saw us. We reeked of smoke and Colin's clothes

442

were singed. "You all look like something the cat would refuse to drag in." As if on cue, Ailouros, who was curled up in front of the fireplace, hissed. "I'm glad you're back, however, as I've discovered the most extraordinary thing. That Hancock bloke — the one who looks like Father Christmas — had an absolutely massive fortune, acquired, not surprisingly, through illegal means. At least that's what everyone's saying. I'm certain you were right, Em, about him running the King's Boys. The details of his will have been made public — everyone at my club was talking about it — he's left every penny of it to that young lad, Moggy, who took such an interest in my motorcar with the instruction that the boy carry on Hancock's good works."

Colin grunted. "Someone had better take the boy firmly in hand."

"No doubt someone will," Jeremy said. "But what have the lot of you been up to? You're an absolute fright."

We told him about the fire and about Gilbert Barton, who had managed to recount for me the sad tale of his crimes before he died outside the factory he had burned to the ground. "He knew it to be unsafe, for all the reasons little Sarah told us, and wanted it destroyed when no one was there. But the girl went there today, to clean the place up a bit. Our conversation had frightened her, and she decided that if she could at least empty out the heaps of rags and lint that were accumulating out of sight, there would be less of a risk of fire. Barton, of course, had no idea she was there, until he noticed a light moving inside — the same light we saw. He had already lit the fuse of his explosives, and knew he had very little time before the building would be consumed. So, he ran back inside to fetch her out."

"*Nothing in his life became him like the leaving it,*" Colin said. "When I reached him, he had found Sarah, but they were trapped by some of those very rags that she knew to be dangerous. The flames were too hot. He managed to toss the child to me, high enough that she was not harmed, but the only way out for him was to run through them. The burns he received proved fatal."

"Poor bloke," Jeremy said.

"You might feel differently when you hear the rest," Colin said. "He admitted to all four of our murders. He killed Grummidge and Casby in the room you found in the Tower passage, knocking them both unconscious before taking them there."

"Which is why there was river water in

Grummidge's lungs," I said. "Mr. Crofton's murder proved more complicated. Mr. Barton had decided he wanted to poison the man's food, so talked a grocer into hiring him as a deliveryman. With only a skeleton staff in the house before the Croftons arrived, he was able to chat up the kitchen maid who was working and learned that while Mrs. Crofton despises mushrooms, her husband adored them and had them once a week at lunch in a dish the cook specially prepared only for him. Mr. Barton substituted toadstools for the mushrooms in the first order after they came to London. The cook never noticed. More than a week later, Mr. Crofton was dead due to the slow-acting poison."

"Barton had followed him to the man's club daily, ready to act at the first sign that the poison was taking its toll," Colin said. "Crofton had taken ill gradually, but on that final day, collapsed as he was walking a few blocks from his club. Barton acted as if he would help him get medical assistance, but instead took him to the hidden room in the Tower. Once he was dead, he dressed him as Richard and then posed the body in the Savoy Chapel."

"How did he avoid anyone seeing him enter the church with a well-dressed corpse?" Jeremy asked.

"He did it in the middle of the night," I said. "Picked the lock to get inside, a skill he'd learned as a boy."

"When it came to Hancock, Barton lured him to the spot where Dawkins died," Colin continued. "Sent a note. Hancock came without hesitating, not quite able to believe his former henchman would harm him."

"A mistake that cost him his life," Jeremy said.

"He was shot through the heart with a pistol. The arrow through the eye was window dressing. It all happened in the space of seconds." Colin took my hand.

"Mr. Barton staged the scenes carefully, waiting for the right moment when he was confident he wouldn't be caught," I said. "He chose well, because no one ever noticed him."

"People are remarkably unaware of their surroundings," Jeremy said. "I should think a miscreant could drop six or seven bodies at least in front of Bainbridge House before I'd notice a thing. Thank heavens it's all over — and, honestly, that the poor man is dead. I can't argue with his thinking. The powerful ought never take advantage of the weak."

"On that count, I must give credit to my

dear wife's intuition," Colin said. "She suspected Barton's motive long before I did. He was seeking revenge against those who had hurt those closest to him and felt he had no other way to bring the perpetrators to justice."

"Mr. Barton was an orphan, treated horribly by a chimney sweep and then abandoned," I said. "He was eleven years old, had no way to earn a living, and was sleeping under a bridge. Lizzie Hopman saw him one day and brought him some food. She and her dear friend Violet Atherton — whom we know as Mrs. Grummidge — helped him whenever they could. Their other mate, Ned Traddles, introduced him to the King's Boys. For a time, he considered the gang to have saved him. He had money and was treated with respect by the other members. But eventually, as he rose through the ranks, he saw that the group's leader, Prentice Hancock, was using him and his friends in an unforgiveable fashion."

"Even though he was better off than before, he discovered that Hancock was piling up money gained through the exploitation of the boys in the gang," Colin said. "They were the ones taking the risks — and spending time in jail — while their leader pretended to be living an honorable life.

Most of the boys didn't even know who Hancock was. He kept his identity secret from all but those at the top. Admitting Barton to those ranks was a mistake, for when he saw the truth, he confronted Hancock, who then threw him out of the gang and did everything he could to heap misery upon him."

"He's fortunate he didn't suffer the same fate as Rodney Dawkins," Jeremy said.

"Hancock tried," Colin said, "but Barton managed to escape. He's a good fighter. After that, he had to be careful everywhere he went, and did what he could to change his appearance. He knew if anyone from the King's Boys recognized him, he'd be dead."

"But this fire," Jeremy said. "I don't understand why he would choose to do such a thing. Obviously, he couldn't be sure he would harm no one in the process."

"You're quite right," I replied. "He had, however, done the same thing numerous other times, burning down factories or mills he knew to be dangerous to workers. On those occasions, no one was harmed."

"I confess that I still do not see the connection between his arrests and the arsons," Inspector Pickering said. "It was as if he was leaving a trail in the hope someone would catch him."

"Each time he was arrested, he was able to see how long it took for the police to interfere at the location in question," Colin said. "He felt this to be a reliable method of deducing how much time he was likely to have when he went back to set the place on fire, crucial information to have if someone spotted him breaking in and summoned help. He was detained and released only yesterday for disturbing the peace half a block from Holbrooke & Sons."

"I'm not sure it was such a good plan," Jeremy said.

"In the end, it wasn't," I said. "But it worked, time and time again."

"So why the turn from arson to murder?" Jeremy asked.

"Ned Traddles's death gutted him," I said. "The mining job had been an attempt to live an honest life, and when Barton learned that his friend had been killed as the result of careless safety standards, he was furious. Even more so when he saw the sort of life the owner of the mine led. It reminded him all too much of Prentice Hancock and the King's Boys — the very things Ned had sought to leave behind him. And then, when his friend Samuel confided in him about Mrs. Grummidge's treatment at the hand of her husband, he became unhinged with rage. Here was another man, pretending to lead an honorable life, behaving in a diabolical way."

"He had hoped that the manner in which he staged the bodies would send a warning to anyone guilty of exploiting the weak and the poor: even a king can be killed," Colin said. "Unfortunately, it did not have the effect he desired."

"So all the worry and concern over poor Bertie's safety was wholly unfounded?" Jeremy asked.

"Yes, at least so far as it pertained to these particular murders," Colin said. "It did, however, catalyze us to take a closer look at the king's security, and that is a good thing."

"A good thing for everyone except the wretched Inspector Gale," I said. "Forgive me if I criticize your colleague."

"There is no need to apologize," Inspector Pickering said, a grim smile on his face. "I know him too well to admire him. His primary goal is self-aggrandizement. If he happens to stop some criminals along the way, so much the better, but justice has never inspired him."

"The less said about it, the better." Colin frowned. "I'd best be off to Marlborough House. The king, at least, deserves an update. Why don't you come with me, Pickering? You've earned it."

The young inspector blinked rapidly, his cheeks colored, and he opened and closed his mouth without managing to say anything. Colin raised an eyebrow and steered him from the room, leaving me with Jeremy.

"So, tell me, Em, what's the explanation for the mysterious messages your husband found?"

I shook my head. "That, Jeremy, I do not know. It's still an absolute mystery."

48
1422

King Henry did not succumb to his illness — not at first. But after months passed without recovery, he sent for another physician from England. The queen came to him as well, and those in the army who did not know just how ill their sovereign was assumed her visit was intended to ensure a second royal heir. Henry had only one son, a babe not even a year old. But if securing the line of succession was Catherine's intention, she would have known the moment she saw her husband that there would be no other child. No one could deny the seriousness of the king's condition.

Before the summer was over, Henry could no longer sit upright on his horse, and soon after that, he knew the end was near. He called for his advisors, wrote codicils for his will, and arranged a regency for his infant son's imminent reign. And then he called for William Hargrave, the man who had fought so bravely beside him at Agincourt.

William steeled himself as he stood before the king's bed, shocked to see how wasted and gaunt the man's lean frame had become.

"Speak no words of sympathy or despair," the king said. "Our life has always been in the hands of God. We will not balk at His plan. You, Sir William, have shown us your courage and your strength time and time again, and we would ask you to take on a crucial responsibility for us. Prince Henry, my son, is but a small child, and many will want to bring him harm. Who is more vulnerable than an infant king? We can think of no one better capable of protecting him than you. Swear you will keep watch over him, and if it seems he will live longer than you, instruct him to appoint another to take your place."

"Of course I will do as you bid, my lord. But —"

"Do not draw attention to your position. We would have it that no one knows your true place at court, else you, too, will be vulnerable to attack. My boy will have other guards, but we know it is you who will keep him safe. We give you this as a sign of our faith in you." The king passed him a livery badge fashioned from gold in the shape of a fire beacon with rubies inlaid as the flames. "Give it, in turn, to the one who takes your place when the time comes. Fasten it to your surcoat now, good man, and swear an oath that you will do as we ask."

William fell to his knees and uttered the solemn words. Never would he let down his king.

49
1901

The fallout from the fire at Holbrooke & Sons combined with the revelations about Gilbert Barton's murders kept the gossips of London well-sated, but I still felt unsatisfied. Colin and I had yet to unravel the meaning behind the scavenger hunt upon which Queen Victoria had started him. I had continued to postulate theories, none of which stood up to even the slightest scrutiny, and was beginning to wonder if this particular puzzle would never be solved. We were dissecting them all again, were sitting in the library, Colin with his whisky and I with my port.

"A lance, a stone, a chalice, and a sword," he said. "It does put me to mind of the quest for the Holy Grail. The grail being the chalice, of course."

"And there was the sword in a stone. But the lance?" I asked.

"A bleeding lance appears over the grail

table in the Vulgate cycle, and later, when Galahad dies, his friends see his soul lifted into heaven, along with the grail and a lance."

"Then the sword must represent King Arthur's Excalibur," I said.

"Not necessarily," my husband replied. "There are many other swords in the various versions of the grail quest. Galahad, too, removes a sword from a stone, and finds another on a ship. One that only he can grip properly. Then there's the sword broken into three pieces that he fixes —"

I felt a glimmer of excitement building in me. Why had I not thought of it before? "We are on the wrong track entirely," I said. "Distracted by legend. Every message pertains to Henry V. And, if you recall, there is a sword —"

"— hanging among his funeral achievements in Westminster Abbey," Colin finished for me. "Of course. How could I have been so bloody stupid?"

"You might have been a bit distracted, what with trying to solve four murders while keeping the king safe."

He pulled me from my chair and within moments we were en route to the Abbey, where, standing in front of Henry V's tomb, we saw a man, well past his prime, a remarkable gold brooch pinned to his overcoat.

"I knew you would find me at last, Hargreaves," he said, shaking my husband's hand. "You came in such a tear I feared I would not get here before you, but I had less distance to travel. My man rang the moment you left your house."

I wondered if Davis was his man, but, no, that couldn't be. Could it?

"I'm afraid I don't understand your meaning, sir," Colin said.

"You don't need to."

"Who are you?"

"My name is not important. May we speak privately?"

"I keep no secrets from my wife."

The man lifted a monocle to his eye and examined me from head to toe. "Yes. She has proven useful. She followed the first clue, didn't she?"

"I found the note in the Tower," I said.

"Her Majesty never did quite approve of you, but even she had to admit your occasional usefulness." He handed my husband an envelope, again bearing the Hargreaves coat of arms. Colin opened it and read aloud:

My hope does not wish for even one man more. Victory is not seen to be given on

457

the basis of numbers. God is all-powerful. My cause is put into His hands. Here he pressed us down with disease. Being merciful, He will not let us be killed by these enemies. Let pious prayers be offered to Him.

"Another chronicle?" I asked.

Colin nodded. "Holinshed again. The one that inspired Shakespeare's famous speech."

"You are a well-educated man, Hargreaves," the man said, "but that is not why she chose you."

"Chose me?"

"To protect the king. Ever since the death of Henry V, a man has stood as silent and secret guardian of the sovereign. The Hammer of the Gauls knew his infant son, Henry VI, would be in a precarious position and he asked a trusted knight to watch over the boy. When that man grew too old for the task, the king selected another, and passed on the responsibility. And so it has gone over the centuries. Queen Victoria required more of us than any other monarch — there were five, each before me aging out of the job. And now, it is my turn to notify my own successor. Her Majesty chose you, Hargreaves, to look after her son."

Colin shook his head, disbelief on his face,

his voice sharp. "If you believe the king is in need of protecting, why did you not ask me before his mother died?"

"Hargreaves, Hargreaves, there is no need to get upset. I was on the case in the interim. In centuries past, other protectors put their successors through a series of tests. In the Middle Ages, these took the form of tournaments. When the Tudors reigned, a series of physical challenges had to be met. There was a charming phase during the Enlightenment when philosophical puzzles were part of the initiation. There is no need for such things now, particularly when it comes to a man like you, who has proven his worth again and again. But over the past century we have adopted the practice of staging a series of clues, just like those that led you to me today. A scavenger hunt for the chosen, if you will."

"What would you have done if he hadn't decoded them?" I asked.

"I never doubted he would and I am always right about such things." He handed Colin a battered leather-bound book. "In here, you will find suggestions and advice from each of your predecessors. Some are frightfully out of date, of course, but don't skip over any of them. The medieval il- luminations are unparalleled in their beauty.

And you must also have this." He removed the pin from his coat.

Colin took it gently in his palm. "I've never seen its equal." It was solid gold, approximately two inches high, less than half that wide, and fashioned to look like a blazing beacon, with flames of rubies rising from its top.

"What is it?" I asked.

"A medieval livery badge," Colin said. "One of Henry V's, is it not? The fire beacon."

"Quite right," the man said. "That king himself presented it, on his deathbed, to a knight he thought strong and honorable enough to protect his young son, who was less than a year old when he inherited the throne. You need not wear it all the time — to do so would be unfortunately conspicuous these days — but on certain occasions, you will find it useful."

"What if I refuse?"

"My dear man, you will not. I know your sense of duty too well. When King Edward feels it is time, he will come to you and tell you who he chooses to take care of his heir, and you will do as I have done. Unless, of course, you decide staging a tournament would be more appropriate." His lips curled. "You have the book. Beyond that, we do not give each other instructions. We would not be chosen if we required direction." That said, he tipped his hat, smiled brightly at me, and disappeared into the shadows of the abbey.

"I —" Colin stood, his mouth open, and examined the livery badge. "I don't know what to say."

"A modern version of the medieval quest." I sighed. "This means you're all but a knight in shining armor. Just when I think you couldn't be more attractive, you go and prove me wrong."

"I've done nothing of the sort." He slipped the badge into the inside pocket of his coat. "Home, my dear. I've not the slightest idea what to make of all this."

Back in Park Lane, he poured himself a whisky in the library and studied the book he'd been given until Davis knocked on the door. "Sir, most sorry to disturb, but His Majesty —"

"Don't bother to announce me, my good man." Bertie pushed past my butler. "See here, Hargreaves, I knew nothing about any of this. Blasted inconvenient for you to have been distracted by such a lot of nonsense." He turned to me and looked me over, grinning. "Lady Emily, you are more fetching than ever."

"Er, thank you, Your Majesty," I said, bobbing a curtsy.

"I'm not some child and am in need of no special protection, but I will say I'd far prefer to have you overseeing my safety than that nitwit Gale. Tedious man, always on about something or the other. You'll do it for me, won't you, old chap?"

"Of course, Your Majesty," Colin said. "It will be an honor."

An honor he could not possibly have wanted. The cat screeched and the door to the library flew open. Henry dashed through it, Richard and Thomas not far behind.

"Is it true, Papa? Is the king really here?" Henry's face was bright red.

"I certainly am, my good lad," Bertie said. "It is a pleasure to make your acquaintance."

I had to admit that when Bertie was charming, there were few people more pleasant, and he was on his best behavior as he graciously accepted neat bows from each of my sons and then shook their hands.

"If you're the king, why aren't you wearing a crown?" Henry asked.

"They're frightfully heavy, if you must know," the king replied.

"If I were king, I wouldn't care how heavy it was." Henry crossed his arms with a defiant scowl. "I'd wear my crown all the time."

"If you're a good boy and do everything your mama asks of you, I shall take you to the Tower and let you try it on and see for yourself."

Henry's eyes widened and he murmured a reply I could hardly hear. Bertie looked rather pleased.

"Where'd you get that, Papa?" Tom asked, pointing to the golden fire beacon, which Colin had laid on his desk. "It's Sir William's badge, isn't it?"

"Sir William's?" I asked.

"Well, of course, it is," Richard said. "Anyone could see that. It's a perfect match to the one on the effigy."

"Whose effigy?" I asked.

"Sir William Hargrave's, naturally," Tom said and turned to his other brother. "It's my turn to be him next time we play Agincourt, and Richard will be the king, so don't try anything underhanded, Henry."

"I'm named for the king in question," my recalcitrant son said. "It's only fair that I get to be him whenever I want."

"Sir William Hargrave?" I looked from my husband to my sons. "Is he —"

"The ancestor to whom Henry V, as recognition for valiant service at Agincourt, gave the land we now call Anglemore Park,"

Colin said. "According to the book our mysterious friend gave me, he was the first to receive the fire beacon in exchange for royal service."

"Well, then, it's all in the family," Bertie said. "Can't argue with that, can we? Must be off. Much to do. Again, dashed sorry you weren't enlightened about all this sooner. My mother preferred things that way. You'll find I'm quite different."

The boys clamored to follow him out, gasping when they saw the motorcar parked in front of our house.

"Papa," Henry said. "If the king has one, surely, we can, too?"

I had never expected the unruliest of my boys to become a worthy ally.

50
1459

William felt his age more than ever these days, especially in the winter, despite the poultices Cecily concocted for him. Sometimes, when he was about to fall asleep, he entered into a state of half dream, and it felt for all the world that he was back at Agincourt. Now, sitting in his chamber at his house in Devonshire, he fingered the livery badge the old King Henry had given him, only two days before his infant son succeeded to the throne, and remembered the oath he had sworn. He had not expected the job to be as difficult as it proved, having assumed, at first, that the young king would not require his services once he'd reached the age of majority.

He had, however, and William had protected his sovereign from countless dangers, perceived and unperceived, always acting from the background, never letting anyone know what the old king had charged him to do. But now he had grown too aged, and he knew the time had come for him to give another the symbol of his position.

The young knight standing before him, a hint of confusion writ on his noble brow, would handle the task well — the tournament had proven that — and as William explained to him what would be required, the man nodded, but said not a word. William removed the fire beacon badge from his tunic and passed it to his successor.

"When the time comes, you will do as I have today," he said. "And for all the centuries to come, whoever sits on the throne of England will remain safe from harm."

51
1901

"You know, it hasn't worked, this protection business," I said, turning on my side to face my husband. I'd retired before him, but was not yet asleep when he slipped into our bed. "Not even in the beginning. Henry VI was murdered —"

"My dear, that is hardly the point," Colin replied. "All any of us can do is our best to protect the sovereign. No one can absolutely guarantee the safety of any man, no matter what his position."

"We've just lived through four murders that remind us of the deaths of kings," I said. "Surely you can't be required to —"

"It is done, Emily," he said. "If you had hoped that Bertie's, er, King Edward's disdain for me would enable me to wriggle out of a role that no honorable man could refuse —"

"Oh, do stop." I sighed. "I had only hoped that perhaps we could have a little break from adventure. Retire to Anglemore and watch the boys grow, far from any royal demands."

"You would be bored silly in three days flat," he said, and kissed me. "And think — Bertie has always had a high opinion of you. It may be that he will prove more open than his mother was to your, shall we say, interference in matters that require more than a modicum of discretion. Perhaps you, not I, will soon be the favorite agent of the Crown." I confess, the idea perked me up, but before I could reply, my husband silenced me with another kiss. "First, though, you shall have to persuade me that I should step aside and let you vie for his favor. Can you make it worth my while?"

AUTHOR'S NOTE

My fascination with the Middle Ages took hold when I was quite young, probably seven years old, after seeing a reproduction of an illuminated image showing Christine de Pizan writing in her study, a small dog at her feet. Later, while at the University of Notre Dame, I was fortunate enough to study in the Medieval Institute under D'Arcy Jonathan Dacre Boulton and Dolores Warwick Frese. One of my fondest college memories was writing a paper for Dr. Boulton about the Carolingian queens, and it was a delight to get back to medieval sources for this novel. Beyond the writings of Christine de Pizan and Andreas Capellanus's *The Art of Courtly Love,* I relied on *The Paston Letters* (a fantastic collection of correspondence written by three generations of an English family in the fifteenth century), Frances and Joseph Gies's *Marriage and Family in the Middle Ages,* Jennifer

Ward's *Women in Medieval Europe 1200–1500,* and the extensive body of work done by Juliet Barker and Anne Curry about Henry V. In particular, I used Barker's phenomenal books *Agincourt: Henry V and the Battle that Made England* and *Conquest: The English Kingdom of France* to guide my descriptions of Henry's campaigns in France. The lectures I attended at the 2013 conference at Canterbury Cathedral commemorating the 600th anniversary of the death of Henry IV proved insightful and enlightening, especially Dr. Curry's "Father and Son Revisited: Henry IV and Henry Prince of Wales," and Dr. Ian Mortimer's "Henry IV, his Reputation and Legacy." Kevin Goodman's article "The Strange Case of Henry V's Wandering Wound" provided information about the wound and subsequent treatment Henry received at Shrewsbury. My son, Alexander Tyska, has proved himself again and again a historian of impeccable knowledge and was invaluable to me when I was researching this book. As always, with so many wonderful sources, any mistakes are my own.

I have long wanted to give readers a glimpse into the Hargreaves family history. Up to this volume of the series, all we knew was they had an ancestor who distinguished himself at Agincourt, earning the land that became Anglemore Park. I hope readers recognize some of Colin's traits in both William and Cecily.

The appeal of English history and the Tower of London is undeniable. I could only resist it for so long before incorporating it into a novel, and am delighted to be able to have Emily read Mrs. Braddon's *The Infidel.* Moogy, the boy Jeremy befriends in the East End, is inspired by a photograph in Horace Warner's *Spitalfields Nippers.* A collection of photographs he took of London's poorest residents around the turn of the twentieth century, these pictures offer a profoundly moving look at children living in poverty. One of them, of a boy named Moogy Kelvin, haunted me from the moment I saw it, so I decided to put him in the book.

Finally, I can't believe we've reached the end of the Victorian era. In 2003, when I wrote the first Emily book, *And Only to Deceive,* I harbored a hope that it might be the start of a long-running series, but it seemed like hubris to breathe that out loud. Now, all these years later, I owe my success to the marvelous readers who have supported me for a decade and beyond. I am more grateful than you can ever know and hope you'll stick with me now that Emily and Colin are Edwardians. . . .

ABOUT THE AUTHOR

Tasha Alexander, the daughter of two philosophy professors, studied English Literature and Medieval History at the University of Notre Dame. She and her husband, novelist Andrew Grant, live on a ranch in southeastern Wyoming.